I0662823

WHICH WITCHERY IS THAT?

SAM CHEEVER

ELECTRIC PROSE PUBLICATIONS

Don't ever let anyone tell you that getting on the wrong side of a curse is a small thing. Even when you think you've got a handle on them, those suckers have a way of jumping up and chewing on your nose before flinging you into the pits of Hell.

Have you ever heard of a Groundhog Day curse? Yeah, I hadn't either. Until somebody put one on a certain goth teenager, who means a lot to me. I'm determined to find the source of Wanda's curse and fix it. But the timetable for that becomes greatly accelerated when she goes missing, and I get a vision of her begging for help.

Not good. The curse has just gone from inconvenient to deadly.

Unfortunately, the path to saving Wanda is long, twisted, and fraught with challenges. Did I say challenges? Silly me. We only need to overcome an array of murderous sea monsters. A legendarily wicked crone. Corrupt, power-hungry witches and a cadre of deadly demons.

Piece of cake, right?

Sigh... I've only been on the job for a couple of months, and already I need a vacation.

ABOUT ROME

Crafting worlds is crazy good fun. Authors love to make stuff up. Sometimes locations that are created for books seem like real places, even though they're not. That's actually good, because it means the author has done her job well. My fictional town of Rome, Indiana is not based on a real place. I've created a location that lives in my mind—one that fits the stories I wanted to tell. Hopefully you have enjoyed the picturesque town of Rome with all its paranormal challenges. I'm thankful for the opportunity to share this fictional town and its inhabitants with you.

xo

Sam Cheever

STAY IN TOUCH

Sam doesn't give away a lot of books. But she values her readers and, to show it, she's gifting you a copy of a fun book just for signing up for her newsletter!

SIGN UP HERE!
https://samcheever.com/newsletter/

AN ALLY COMES IN SEARCH OF AID

A curse to keep a child in thrall, the magic's
overarching pall, if darkness wins a historian's heart,
though goodness tries to do its part, the human soul
will be at risk, the Lares must her fight persist.

Cursed to Wander Familiar Ground,
Another's Plight Will Keep Her Bound,
An Ally Comes in Search of Aid,
A Bargain Not so Easily Made,
A Soul That's Lost, A Frightened Plea,
The Spell will Help the Blind to See,
A Hidey Hole, A Hidden Life,
The Lares Must See Through the Strife,
Friend or Foe, They Must Decide,
Beneath the Surface Doubt Resides,
Into a World of Terror Deep,
Our Lares Must Her Patience Keep,

Bugs Under Glass, Our Warriors Be,
Like Tasty Morsels, Beneath the Sea,
Beasties Rule the Placid Waters,
Our Heroes Much Like Fishy Fodder,
Into the Mythical Legend's Lair,
The Pursuit of Knowledge Languishing There,
Alas, a Friend Hath Come To Call,
The Coming Journey Unpleasant For All,
An Unworthy Plea From One Most Foul,
The Villain's Complaint a Tainted Howl,
A Surprising Partner in the Fight,
An Awful Verdict, A Stunning Plight,
Into the Demon's Fetid Nest,
A Deadlier Visit Than the Rest,
At Last, the Lares Finds Her Stride,
The Loss of Doubt, A Mother's Pride.

CURSED TO WANDER FAMILIAR GROUND

A slender crescent moon hung high overhead, its silver glow painting the boards beneath my feet. Behind me, my dog explored a massive cobweb in the corner of the belfry, his tail wagging with interest.

I leaned against the wide sill of the open archway overlooking my backyard. Far below me, appearing even more spectral than usual, the ghostly Reverend Dodson moved through the tombstones, looking peaceful and content.

A rhythmic pounding sounded from the house below. Trish and Luke had been working long hours every day for a week trying to get all my beautiful windows reinstalled after the emergence of a demonic vortex shattered them. It had taken almost a month to get the glass, with its unique size and shape, and I was sick of having a dark and gloomy house from being boarded up.

The thought brought on a shudder, as I remembered the vortex. If I never saw another demon, it would be too soon.

A cold nose touched the back of my ankle, Monty's way of letting me know he was there. I looked down and smiled at my black and tan, long-haired dachshund. Like the good reverend, Monty was a happy soul, his doggy enthusiasm a bright spot in even the darkest day. "Did you get that mean old spider?" I asked my little hero.

He grinned back at me, his small body wagging happily. Spider web silk hung from one floppy ear and covered his left eye like a pirate's patch. I reached down and wiped it off. "You might not have caught the spider," I told him. "But you definitely caught its house."

A soft chirp brought my gaze up to the bat in my belfry. The yellow eyes were inexplicably locked on me. "Yes, Your Chirpiness?"

The bat hung there, wings tidily folded and tiny claws clinging to a narrow piece of wood that ran from the peak of the bell tower to the top of the wall. We stared at each other until I gave in and shook my head. "I know you talk. You've spoken to me before. Why are you being so stubborn?"

The last few nights, I'd been climbing the narrow staircase and having my pre-bedtime glass of wine up there with Monty. He enjoyed snuffling around. I enjoyed looking out over the moon-painted yard, and I'd been trying to get the bat to talk to me. She apparently communicated with Wanda, the youngest member of my council, all the time. The belfry was the teen's favorite spot in my house. She and Bathilda, or Batty as I liked to call her, had spent a lot of hours since I'd moved into the church, chatting about things that neither of them shared with me.

There was another reason why I'd been spending the last half hour of my day in the belfry. It was a reason I was reluctant to admit even to myself.

I was looking for something.

It was something that I'd caught out of the corner of my eye several days earlier. But I hadn't seen it again. And I was starting to think the sighting had just been the result of wishful thinking on my part.

I sipped my wine and looked back up at Bathilda. "What's going through the kid's head?" I asked. "I know she tells you. I just want to help." There'd been a new sadness in Wanda's gaze lately. She'd been lacking her usual perpetual confidence, to the point that she seemed unwilling to offer an opinion or even draw attention to herself.

It was worrying me.

The tiny bat spread its wings as if stretching and then refolded them, blinking slowly in my direction.

Nothing.

Curse, curse, dang bat.

With a long-suffering sigh, I turned my attention back to the yard, taking another sip of my wine. Despite my frustration with the magical flying rodent, I was relaxed and happy. Life was falling into a comfortable rhythm. I was starting to get the hang of my new career as a guardian for the town of Rome, Indiana. And the moment in time I was currently living was filled with magic and promise.

Down below, the world had soft edges and a pale haze that made it look enchanted. On the furthest edges of that world, something moved through the shadows, just beyond the moonlight's reach.

My gaze whipped in that direction and held. My breathing turned shallow. The shadows stilled, nothing moving within them. Just when I was ready to give up and go downstairs, I saw it again.

A flash of white, gleaming through the trees.

The soft sound of wings above my head didn't even tempt me to look. I kept my gaze locked on that spot between the trees, far at the back of my property. My pulse picked up. My heart beat hopefully against my ribs. "Come on," I whispered.

In my peripheral vision, I watched Bathilda flutter out into the night, darting and dipping as she munched mosquitoes and, presumably, other flying bugs.

Moments later, when my eyes were starting to

sting from my unrelenting focus on that spot, I saw it again. A gleaming white form, moving through the trees.

I smiled. "There you are, beautiful. Come out and let me feast my eyes on you." As if she'd heard my words, the enormous, elegant creature stepped into the moonlight.

Tears burned my eyes. Tears of relief and happiness. "Hello, there, beauty," I breathed.

The ethereally stunning white horse tossed its head, its thick mane dancing silkily around its elegant head. We stared at each other across the distance for several moments. I was afraid to move or look away for fear she would disappear.

Finally, with another toss of her head and a flash of her bright green gaze, the white horse spun around and galloped into the night.

Trish and Luke were standing in my kitchen drinking large glasses of water when Monty and I came down from the belfry. Trish smiled at my happy little warrior when he ran over to greet her. "Hello, my man. Did you give that nasty bat the business?"

I laughed. "He killed the heck out of a spider web."

"Good boy!" she cooed, laughing when his entire

body wagged. When she straightened, Trish reached out and brushed her hand down my shoulder-length straight black hair, which I'd tipped in silver on a whim when I'd turned forty. "Looks like Monty's not the only one who had a close encounter with a spider web." She brushed her hand over her well-worn jeans to dispel the spider silk.

Never wanting to leave anybody out, Monty bounced over and put his paws on Luke's dusty, jean-clad thighs, sniffing around his pocket. His friend, the wolf-shifter, patted Monty's soft head. "Hey, little buddy," Luke said. "What's so interesting about my pocket?"

Monty's fat feet hit the floor and he barked, his eyes alight.

"Are you looking for this?" Luke asked, smiling. He pulled out a dog cookie and Monty leaped into the air, grinning a doggy grin.

"You guys are spoiling him," I said, trying to look unhappy about it. I couldn't pull it off. Monty carefully took his treat from Luke's big, square fingers and hurried to his favorite spot underneath the kitchen table to savor it.

"Sorry, not sorry," Luke said in his deep, slow drawl. "His goofy excitement is too hard to resist."

Shaking my head, I said. "Do you guys want a beer before you hit the road?"

"I shouldn't," Trish said, at the same time Luke said, "Sure."

I arched a brow at Trish, and she laughed. "Sure. Just one. It's late."

I got them each a beer and refilled my wine glass halfway.

"How are things in the queendom," Luke asked, a teasing light in his golden-brown eyes.

"Huh?" I asked, dropping into a chair at the table.

"Weren't you up there surveying your queendom?"

I laughed. "I'm trying to shame that curse swear bat into talking."

Trish sat down across from me. "You really think it talks?"

"Wanda claims she talks to it. Plus, I've heard a voice in my head a few times that had to have come from her."

"From Wanda?" Luke asked, looking confused.

"No. Bathilda."

He nodded.

"That bat is here for a reason," I told them. "But I have no idea what that reason is."

"No words of wisdom from the flying rodent tonight, huh?" Trish asked.

"Not a peep. A few chirps, but no peeps. All it did was stare at me with those creepy eyes and then fly off to munch bugs."

We sat in silence for a moment, then I broached the question I'd wanted Bathilda to answer. "How much do you guys know about Wanda? I mean, outside of council business?"

Trish spun her beer bottle on the table, looking thoughtful.

Luke threw his empty into the trash. "I've never seen or spoken to her outside of council business."

"Really? But you sometimes arrive with her. I just assumed maybe you picked her up somewhere."

"No," Trish said, frowning. "I've offered to give her a ride a few times, but she just shrugs and changes the subject." She looked up, catching my gaze. "I'm worried about her, Aggy."

"Yeah," I said. "Me too. We need to get that curse off her. In fact, I wanted to talk to you about that. How soon do you think the shop will be ready for business?"

Her eyes went wide. "Business? I don't think..."

"Not candle-selling business. I just need it good enough to have meetings in."

"Oh. Well. Luke and I got the last window replaced in there tonight. The floors are done, and the painting needs just one more coat. We're going to finish the trim work tomorrow. I suppose you could have meetings in there by the end of the week, but it will still stink like paint. Why? What do you have in mind?"

I sipped wine, my foot stroking Monty's silky fur under the table. "I'd like to host coven meetings here. If it's okay with the coven."

Trish didn't even try to hide her surprise. "We'd have to vote on it. But I don't know why anybody would mind. This would be a much better spot than where we've been holding them."

"Where are you holding meetings now?" Luke asked. He was leaning against the counter, arms and ankles crossed. He looked relaxed and comfortable, a sight I hadn't seen much of since he'd become part of my council. Granted, none of us had enjoyed a lot of relaxation time since I'd moved into the church.

My seating had been a wild, dangerous, and unpredictable time. And our last adventure...if I could call it that...had been a hair past terrifying.

"In Wilhelmina's basement," Trish said, grimacing. "It smells like feet and dirty jockstraps down there."

I grimaced. "Jockstraps?"

"She has twin seventeen-year-old boys. They're animals."

"I resent that characterization," said the wolf.

Trish shook her head. "I'll call a meeting for this week and let you know what we decide."

"Thanks," I said. "And thank you for working so hard to finish the shop. I really appreciate it." I frowned, thinking about my dwindling construction budget. I was almost out of money, and my bedroom and bath weren't done. Not to mention, we'd decided I needed to add a second, small bathroom in the shop, so I didn't have customers using mine.

"I know that look," Trish said. "Stop worrying about the money. It's going to work out."

"I appreciate the sentiment," I told her. "But you can't keep donating your labor. It's not fair to you."

"I trust you to make good on it. Later."

"Isn't there some kind of salary attached to this Lares gig?" Luke asked.

I'd wondered the same thing. In fact, I'd put a stickie note on my bathroom mirror telling me to call my dad and ask him. I'd learned when going through my seating that my father was also serving a community as its Lares, a fact that explained a lot about my mostly fatherless teenage years. Ancient history and hurt childhood feelings aside, Andrew Lenore was an experienced Lares. He'd know if there was any kind of payment for the job and, if so, how I got it set up. I was hoping there were enough funds available to at least cover expenses.

The reminder stickie had been on my mirror for a few days. Begging for money and talking to my dad were both uncomfortable tasks, that I'd been putting off.

"We should go," Trish said, pushing to her feet. "I'll be back at eight in the morning to start that trim work."

I hugged her. "You're the best. Thanks so much."

She bent down and kissed Monty on the head and motioned for Luke to follow.

He hung back.

I could tell by the way he was looking at me that he had something to say. "What is it?" I asked, my spidey senses flaring.

"You know that Ferral and I have been taking turns patrolling the church grounds?"

"Yes." Ferral was my advocate, which really meant he was my advisor regarding the machinations of the magical world. Like Luke, he shifted into a canine-type creature. But Ferral's form was a moon hound, where Luke's was a big black wolf.

"I wanted to let you know that I've been picking up a new scent lately."

"Oh? What type of scent?"

"It's crazy, but it smells like a horse, and there's a tang of magic there too." He shook his head. "I know there's not much chance you have a horse trotting around your yard."

I fought to keep my expression neutral.

"But maybe a unicorn or a centaur?" At my look of surprise, he shrugged. "Occasionally, they cross the veil and end up in the Mystical Wood. They generally don't cause any problems. But I wanted you to know, so you wouldn't be caught off guard."

My eyes went wide at the idea that unicorns and centaurs even existed. I didn't say anything, though, because I didn't want Luke to dwell on the subject. "I appreciate that," I told him. "Thanks."

I walked Luke to the front door and waved him and Trish off, excited about Luke's confirmation of the white horse's existence. The beautiful animal had been used as a pawn against us during the attempted Hellmouth invasion a few weeks earlier. When the Hellmouth had shut down, it had supposedly sucked everything demonic back through the vortex as it shrank away.

I'd been afraid the horse had been dragged back with the others, despite the fact that it didn't appear to be demonic.

Monty was already snuggled under the covers when I got to my bedroom, his little head resting on the pillow like a tiny human. As always, the sight made me grin.

After brushing my teeth, I settled into bed beside him and turned off the light, intending to read for a while.

I fell asleep soon after settling in.

And had some really weird dreams.

2

ANOTHER'S PLIGHT WILL KEEP HER BOUND

Monty whimpered softly beside me, his stubby legs flailing beneath the covers. Without opening my eyes, I reached out and placed a hand on his heaving chest. The touch, which usually soothed him, had no effect. He whimpered again, thrashing beneath the covers.

Behind my eyelids a pale gray mist roiled, nebulous shapes shifting behind its obscuring veil.

I tried to open my eyes, but they felt as if they were glued shut. Though I was half asleep, I had an awareness that I was becoming agitated.

A distant scream jerked me fully awake, my eyes finally flying open.

The mist filled my room. It was so thick I couldn't even see my dog, but I could still feel his movements in the gentle quivering of the bed.

I rose to my feet, eyes trained on the shadowy fog

surrounding me. I was walking before I realized I'd moved. With a jolt, I glanced around, looking for the bed. For Monty.

They were gone.

Ahead of me stretched a long hallway roiling with the same shadow-filled fog. I sensed the walls on either side rather than seeing them. The floor beneath me was only real because I felt its rough surface against the soles of my bare feet.

The shadows pressed closer, nearly close enough for me to form them into recognizable shapes. But they never lingered long enough for that.

A rhythmic chanting chorus eased through the mist, its individual sounds lost in the drone of voices. I moved forward, searching for the source of the chanting. Then I was standing in an archway, the haze cold and moist against my skin. Shadowy figures stood in a large circle, arms outstretched and faces obscured by dark robes.

The robed figures were in a low-ceilinged room. Cold air wafted from the room, permeating the air and painting the walls and floor with ice. My feet ached from the cold. Gooseflesh rose along my arms.

The figures stood around a small fire, its flames burning through the fog but not heating it. Their hands reached toward the flickering blaze, which was contained within a large black cauldron. As the robed figures stretched toward the fire, fingers dancing in the creation of a spell, the thick, crimson contents of the cauldron bubbled up, spilling over the sides and hitting the floor with a sizzling sound.

The resulting steam carried a sulfurous stench through the room, finding me where I stood. I wrinkled my nose, coughing as the brimstone stench bit at the back of my throat.

I stilled, afraid my coughing would pull every gaze my way.

But none of the figures' heads turned.

A different robed figure emerged from the fog. Though it wasn't much bigger than a human, the figure seemed to rise up from the flames, the narrow strip of its face I could see beneath the hood was a chalky white, with crimson eyes that glowed red through the mist.

The mouth was a wide, black slash filled with jagged teeth, a pointed tongue snapping out to taste the air as it approached the cauldron.

I made a small sound of disgust, covering my mouth when I realized I'd given myself away.

The ethereally glowing gaze lifted in my direction and widened with an emotion I couldn't identify. Surprise? Pleasure?

I reached for my magic, bracing for the bite of its power against my fingertips.

Nothing happened. The magic didn't answer my summons. Terror slid through me, digging at my gut with knifelike claws.

The robed figure's gaze fixed on me and the distance between us halved.

I blinked, stumbling backward.

The creature extended an arm, the skin like the thinnest paper, lit from within by the dancing light of the fire. It moved as if it had no feet, fairly floating on the air. Its gaze burned with malevolence. "Agnes Bethany Lenore," the monster said, its long tongue snapping out from between way too many teeth when it spoke. "It is good you have come."

I retreated again, the urge to flee so strong it coated the back of my tongue.

The monster blipped again, reappearing mere inches away. Tilting its hooded head, the creature smiled, the sight of its curved, black lips terrifying. "You and I have much to discuss."

I didn't wait around for the thing to tell me what it wanted. I turned tail and ran, a sound like my rapidly beating heart following me through the mist.

I jerked upright, my heart pounding. Monty lifted his head off the pillow and looked at me, the covers shifting as he wagged his tail.

The nightmare clung to me as I shoved the covers off and lowered my feet to the floor. I shuddered at the memory and lowered my head into my hands.

Too soon.

It was too soon after the Hellmouth battle for me to be seeing demons again. I gave a harsh laugh. Who was I kidding? Ten years in the future would be too soon.

I thought about the creature I'd seen. Had it been a demon? Or was my mind just so scarred from my recent experience that I saw the things wherever I went?

Scrubbing at my face, I pulled air into my lungs and slowly released it, slowing my racing heart.

Beyond my bedroom window, the sky was pink, orange, and purple. A sunrise palette. There was a light wind that made the tree branches dance, throwing shadows over my room. I shuddered again, remembering the shifting shapes in the mist from my nightmare.

What had it meant? Was my mind still rehashing the dark magic that had called the vortex into existence?

If so, why now?

Maybe seeing the white horse the night before had thrown me back into thoughts of demons. Or maybe I was just a spaz with an overactive imagination.

I shoved to my feet and shuffled toward the bathroom. Behind me, there was a soft thump as Monty's fat doxie feet hit the carpet. "I'll let you outside in a minute," I told him.

He sat in the doorway, watching every move as I did my morning thing and washed my hands. I'd like to say he was just that devoted to me. That he couldn't get enough of spending time with me. But I'd be lying to myself.

He was just making sure he didn't miss the moment I grabbed his bowl and filled it with food.

"Potty first," I told the little dog as he danced around my feet all the way to the kitchen. "You know the drill."

He hung back as I headed for the mudroom door off the kitchen, clinging to that one last hope that I'd give in and feed him first.

"Come on," I told him, smiling at his hopeful little face. "Two minutes, and then you can eat. I don't want any accidents in the house."

He sighed and trotted toward me, his floppy ears bouncing as he did. Flipping on the patio light, I let him outside and then, on a whim, went out with him. The morning was cool. But I was hot after tossing and turning for a good part of the night, and it felt good. I stood on the smooth patio stones and watched Monty run into the darkness to do his business in his favorite spot.

I stared at the beautiful sunrise, feeling its normalcy soothe the last of my discomfort from the dream.

A low, dark form bounded toward me from the graveyard. Wraith leaped into the air, twisting in mid-leap to paw at a small, dark shape flying past overhead.

Bathilda dipped and fluttered, seemingly unconcerned with the feline pretending to stalk her.

In slow degrees, my body calmed, and my nerves soothed. This was my home. My safe place. My posse. I shoved the nightmare away and pulled a long breath into my lungs, savoring the sweet floral scent of an abundance of flowers, courtesy of my naked gnome gardener.

My world righted.

I turned to the door. "Come on, Monty. Time to eat."

When he didn't come immediately, I turned back. "Come on, buddy."

Nothing. I peered into the darkness. "Monty!"

The night shifted to my right. I saw the movement out of the corner of my eye, and it didn't sink in for a beat that something had changed.

By the time I reached for my magic, she was already standing at the edge of the light, my dog cradled in her arms.

"Hello, Aggy."

I started forward, intending to wrest my dog from a stranger's clutches. But something in the way she held herself made me stop. "Do I know you?" I asked, my gaze sliding from her pretty face to Monty, who seemed surprisingly calm considering he didn't generally trust strangers.

The woman's only reaction to my question was a slight tightening of her lips. "You *do* know me. However, I understand why you don't recognize me. I've..." She frowned. "...changed."

I wasn't sure what to say to that. "Okay."

We stared at each other a moment, and then she sighed, settling Monty back onto the ground. My little hero promptly licked her ankle, which seemed to please rather than annoy her.

"My dog likes you." I tried a smile, but it was early and I was not in the mood for surprises. Or visitors. Or, particularly, surprising visitors.

"I'm sorry to drop in on you like this," the woman said as if reading my mind. "But I wanted to get here before your guests."

"My guests?" Then I realized she had to be talking about Trish and Luke. I opened my mouth to tell her they were my contractors but then realized they were much more than that. They were helping me with my remodeling, but they were also important members of my council and my friends. I added the fact that she'd obviously been watching me to the list of things that were making me uncomfortable. "Why don't you tell me why you're here."

She stood with her hands clasped. Her copper-colored gaze fixed unwaveringly on me. I got the distinct impression she was waiting for me to do something.

I had no idea what. And, since she didn't seem

inclined to leave, I decided the most expedient thing was to hear her out. "Would you like to come inside?"

She flinched. "No."

Her response both intrigued and relieved me. I didn't really want her inside my home.

I motioned toward the iron and glass table on my little patio. "Sit?"

With only a slight hesitation, the woman inclined her head. "Thank you."

"Coffee?"

She shook her head. I took a moment to look her over, trying to see someone I'd known in the past. Appearing to be in her mid to late twenties, she was tall for a woman. Really tall. I noted that she wasn't wearing shoes, but she still appeared to be several inches taller than my own five feet six inches. If I had to guess, she was close to six feet. The woman wore a thin, cotton dress with cap sleeves and a rounded neckline. It fit tightly over large breasts and wide hips and cinched in at her narrow waist. Her bare feet were clean and slender, on the small side for a woman of her height, I thought, and the toenails were painted in pretty pink polish. Her hair was blonde and surrounded her delicate face in a soft cloud of curls. The woman's copper-colored eyes were unique enough that I was sure I'd have remembered them if I'd met her before. But, I didn't see anything familiar in her face or form, which made me wonder how she could have changed that much. "Well, if you don't mind, I'm going to grab a cup. I'm not much use to anyone before I've had my coffee in the morning."

The woman smiled. "I understand."

"Are you sure you wouldn't like some?"

She hesitated and then nodded. "If you're making it anyway. That would be great."

She sat down at the table when I went inside. I glanced outside and saw that her lips were moving, but I couldn't hear what she was saying through the closed window. Monty sat at her feet, his gaze intent on her as she appeared to speak to him. By the time the first cup was finished, Wraith had also joined the woman at the table, doing figure eights around her slender ankles.

I watched her surreptitiously through the kitchen window while the coffee brewed, wondering what magic she had that allowed her to so easily enthrall my fur-babies.

Or maybe it wasn't magic at all. Maybe she had a good soul, and Monty and Wraith recognized it.

Shaking myself out of my thoughts, I gathered up the two mugs of coffee and headed back outside. Setting a steaming mug on the table in front of the woman, I sat down across from her. "Okay, I'm sorry, you have me at a disadvantage," I told her. "Please tell me who you are."

The young woman lifted her gaze from the black

cat wrapping itself around her calves and fixed me with that startling copper gaze. "I'm your ally, Madam Lares." She cocked her head. "I was your travel buddy through the demonic vortex."

I felt my eyes go wide. Travel buddy? That could only be...

My pulse pounded, and I set my mug down before I spilled its contents. Leaning forward, I narrowed my gaze on her, trying again to see the features I'd once known. They just weren't there. Except maybe something in the eyes... "Layla?"

3

AN ALLY COME IN SEARCH OF AID

"In the flesh," Layla said with a bitter smile. "Such as it is."

I stared at her with my mouth open. The woman in front of me was a lost one. A devil who'd been cast out of the demonic realm for her crimes, which were unknown to me. Punishment for those crimes, ironically, appeared to be banishment to the earthly plane, which is reputedly the worst punishment given her kind.

I had no idea why. I kind of liked the earthly plane.

Princess Layla, however, claimed she and her people were different from other demonic folks. They apparently liked earth and had no desire to go back to the demon realm. We had that in common, at least.

Whether it was true or not, there was no doubt

that she'd used her unique situation to help my people and me not once but several times recently, despite great danger to herself. And she'd offered to be my ally during the Hellmouth experience. She definitely got props for that.

"How?" I asked, casting my gaze over her delicate features, even as I remembered the long, triangular head the slits for nostrils and the horrific collection of jagged teeth. The charcoal gray horns sticking out from the sides. The bloom of soft blonde hair...

Ah...that at least hadn't changed.

Layla shrugged in response to my question. "We aren't sure. But our healers have speculated that the entrance to the vortex stripped me of my devil when we went through, leaving behind only my human side."

Wraith leaped into her lap and sprawled there, belly up.

"You had a human side?" I asked, shocked.

She laughed. "Of course. All of Hades' inhabitants have human sides. We aren't proud of them, of course, but we have them."

I bit back a bark of laughter at that. It was beyond amazing that the lost royal princess preferred her heavy goatlike legs, horns, and snakelike nostrils to the attractive form sitting across from me. I was living in opposite world. My life was an episode of the Twilight Zone. I was down the rabbit hole, and the Queen of Hearts had horns.

"Why did this happen?" I asked, still struggling with the reality sitting before me. Part of me didn't trust it.

"The Commander struck me as we left. I tasted the sting of his foul magic as we went through the gate." She frowned. "It was in retaliation for my helping you escape his grip."

"The Commander?" I asked.

"You remember the army marching toward the gate?"

How could I forget? I especially remembered her warning. *The warriors are amassing inside the vortex. Once they come out, it will be over.*

She hadn't been lying. I would never forget the fear slicing through me at the thunderous sound of thousands of boots marching toward the exit, or gate as Layla called it. I'd never forget that snake's eye with the razor-sharp edges snapping threateningly as Layla and I flew toward it through the vortex.

I'd never forget any of it.

"I'm still having nightmares," I admitted.

She nodded. "Believe me when I tell you they are incensed that we stopped them. And stripping me of my devilish nature was only a small part of what I'll endure if they ever get hold of me." She narrowed her gaze. "Which brings me to my current problem."

I sat back and sipped my too-cool coffee, grimacing. I hated cold coffee. "Tell me," I told Layla. "This happened to you because of me. I'll always be grateful for your help. Whatever I can do to help, I'll do."

"I am pleased to hear it," Layla said, her fingers kneading the fur between Wraith's shoulders. She looked me in the eyes, holding my gaze with an unblinking focus that made dread coil in my belly. "Because I would like to request safe harbor in your home."

"Uh..." My mind spun, but I had nothing. "Ah..."

She smiled. "Don't look so appalled, Aggy," the formerly devilish creature teased. "I'll sleep on your couch. I just need some protection until I figure some things out."

My spinning mind finally landed on a question. "What do you need protection from?"

"Things."

I lowered my brows. "Things that go bump in the night?"

"Of course," Layla said, almost cheerfully. "What other kinds of things does one need protection from?"

"I don't know, crooked politicians, flesh-eating bacteria, rampant garlic breath."

She laughed, tugging Wraith up to kiss her soft head. I frowned as the cat purred even louder, rubbing against Layla's delicate chin. If I'd done that, the cat would have probably bitten my nose.

"What is this magic that you yield, devilish

Layla," I muttered under my breath. Aloud, I asked. "How long were you thinking?"

"As long as it takes for me to come up with a solution to my little problem."

"Tell me about your problem." I gave up on sipping my cold coffee and pushed it away. My stomach rumbled, and I realized Monty hadn't been fed. Glancing at him happily curled around Layla's dainty feet, my frown deepened.

"I've already told you. The Commander wants me dead."

"But he's on the demonic plane, isn't he?"

My heart gave a few stress-induced thumps. Please, goddess, don't tell me the demonic army got through the vortex after all.

"He is. But that doesn't mean he can't call others to do his will."

"This commander is sending demons after you?"

"A few have come. But I'm not worried about those. My people can easily dispatch them." She grimaced. "I'm more worried about being taken down by one of my own."

My eyebrows peaked in surprise. "Your own people are turning against you?"

"Not all of them. I know I told you my people were all happy on earth, but that might have been a bit of an exaggeration."

Ha! I knew it. "Some of them resent being here?"

"Yes. The demonic realm holds certain advantages for creatures like us." For just a beat, there was a glint of regret in her eyes. But she quickly squelched it. "I am happier here. But that does not mean everyone is. The Commander is very good at finding a person's weak spots and using them to get what he wants."

"He's promised your people that they can come home if they dispatch you for him."

She nodded.

"But how would they do that? We killed the vortex."

"We beat it back, yes. But it is far from dead, Aggy. It's important for you to remember that."

I felt all the color leech from my face. I shook my head in denial. "No. It can't come back. Not so soon. I'm..." I swallowed hard, realizing it would be best if I didn't finish that sentence. "You're saying this Commander will try to engage the Hellmouth again."

She shook her head. "No. Bringing it forward was a massive campaign. It will take him a while to recover from the loss. But there is another way."

"Another way for a lost one to return to the demonic plane?"

She nodded. "There is a creature that can pass between the veil to other realms."

"What type of creature?"

"A powerful creature, made of light and purity. I have heard this creature is here. In the human realm.

If that is true, and I have every reason to believe that it is, we must make sure it can't be used by the demons."

I thought about that, a sense of dread blossoming in my chest. "Okay. How do you propose we do that?"

"That is the task I need you to help me accomplish. We need to kill the White Mare. It is the only way I will remain safe."

Vertigo ripped my balance out from under me. Nausea bloomed in my belly. "The White Mare?" I thought of the beautiful creature who'd helped Gren and me during the war against the Hellmouth. The stunning animal whose eyes glowed with pure green light. The gorgeous creature who'd found my little haven and had, recently, been visiting me, watching me from afar to determine if it was safe to approach.

A creature of pure magic with a purer soul.

My heart broke a little at the realization that, by helping one friend stay alive, I'd have to endanger another friend who I'd hoped to coax into my life.

There was a tearing sound in my mind that I was pretty sure was the sound of my heart ripping in two.

4

A BARGAIN NOT SO EASILY MADE

"Are you sure this is safe?" I asked the princess. My home was built on consecrated ground, having once been a church. Layla wouldn't have been able to enter it as a lost princess. What I didn't know, was if she still had enough devil to turn her to ash if she came through my door.

"I think so," she responded, looking a tad bit worried. "I no longer have my devilish side, so it should be okay."

I thought about it for a beat and then said, "Hold on a minute." Hurrying inside the house, I grabbed the bottle of holy water I'd begun keeping in my pantry after the Hellmouth episode. Returning to Layla, I dipped my finger into the water. "Give me your palm."

Layla extended her hand, palm up, and I wiped the water across it.

Nothing happened.

No smoke, no flame, no pain-filled shrieking.

"I think you're good," I told her with a smile.

Layla expelled a long breath, visibly relaxing. "Thanks, Aggy."

Inside my kitchen, the former devilish miss looked around with interest, rubbing her fingers along the granite countertops and peeking into the pantry, which I'd left open after returning the holy water. "Pretty," she said, a touch of surprise in her voice.

I didn't respond to the surprise. She'd been royalty in her prior life. I had never been and never would be royalty. She no doubt thought of me as a peasant. "We're going to have to get creative on sleeping arrangements," I told her. "I only have one bedroom."

Shaking her head, she said, "I can sleep on the floor."

"That won't be necessary. I have a couch. Or we could put a blow-up mattress in the shop area, but that's filled with sawdust right now, and Tish gets here early to start pounding and sawing. You'd probably be more comfortable in the sanctuary."

"The sanctuary?"

"My living room. I'm afraid it gets light really early. There are a lot of windows. Hopefully, you're not a late sleeper." I smiled to lighten the mood, but she didn't return the smile.

"I don't sleep much these days. Anything will be fine."

I nodded. "We'll work it out. Are you hungry?" My cell phone rang. Since it was a normal ringtone rather than some strange and annoying ditty having to do with mothers, I knew it wasn't Mavis. A quick glance told me it was the next best thing. I answered. "Hey, Sis. How's it going?"

"Hey," Bev said, her tone quiet and serious. She was probably at work. "You're scheduled to meet with the coven tonight at seven."

"Oh, good. You're coming too, I hope?"

"Yep. Trish, mom, and I will be there, along with the rest of our coven. Our visiting witch doesn't take to non-witches very well. You'll need us to step in if she tries to browbeat you."

"This is the witch from Chicago?"

"Yes. We were lucky she was visiting the area right now. She knows a lot about curses. Willy knows her pretty well, but I've never met her, so I don't know if she'll be willing to help us." She frowned. "Dell lost some of her coven members recently. Tragically. So I'm a little surprised she even agreed to come."

"What happened to her coven?"

"Willy was vague. But, I gather something went wrong on a high-level spell. Several of them died."

I grimaced. "That's horrible."

"Yeah," Bev agreed.

"Wanda should be there, too. That way, if we come up with something, we can try it right away."

"That's not going to work. Our visitor would have a fit."

I frowned, unhappy with the idea of another delay in helping the teen.

Bev sighed. "I know you're anxious, Aggy. But this is the way it has to be done. Members of the Chicago coven can be prickly. We can't rush Dell."

"Is it possible she'll just be able to point us to a spell, and we can cast it ourselves?"

There was a slight hesitation, during which I was pretty sure Bev was thinking I was clueless. I tried not to bristle about that. I already knew I was clueless about witchery.

"Trust me?" Bev asked.

I did. Sighing, I said, "Of course."

"Good. We'll pick you up at six-thirty. Wear your leathers."

My eyes popped wide as my sister hung up. My leathers? Those were supposed to be only for battles. Were we going to war with the witches? My stomach roiled at the thought. But a beat later, I squared my shoulders. If we needed to fight for Wanda's future, I'd happily do it.

"Is everything okay?" Layla asked from behind me.

I swung around and realized I'd walked away as I answered my phone. Habit. I was becoming cocooned in my little world of mayhem and magic and didn't even realize anymore when I brought up my defenses.

I gave Layla a smile. "It's all good. Just some business I need to take care of tonight." I set my phone down on the counter. "I'm starving. How about you?"

Layla dragged her gaze away from my phone. "I am hungry. But you don't need to feed me. I don't want to make myself a burden."

I didn't ask her how she was going to feed herself because I didn't want to be insulting. But she'd kind of put herself into my hands. And, though I wasn't nearly as good a cook as my mom, I did *not* let people in my home go hungry.

"Woof!"

I looked down into the bright brown gaze of my dog. Poor thing probably thought he was going to die of starvation. "Sorry, buddy. Let's get that little belly filled up."

Layla watched in fascination as I pulled out the container of Monty's kibble and poured some into the bowl that Aunty Bev had gotten him the previous Christmas. The inside bottom of the bowl said, "If you're seeing this, my owner didn't feed me enough."

I grinned every time I filled the bowl. It was so Monty.

"You feed the little furry one?"

I scooped a tablespoon of soft food into the bowl

and mixed it into the dry. "He depends on me to feed him." It was a good thing, too. If I left it up to him, he'd just be a belly with feet. His legs were already short enough.

"He cannot hunt for rodents and birds?"

"Well, yeah, he could. He does actually."

She cocked her head at Monty. He cocked his head at her.

"He is long of body but short of leg." She frowned. "I see that he could not catch a larger creature."

Feeling an inexplicable need to defend my dog, I said, "You'd be surprised how fast he is. Besides, dachshunds were bred to fetch rodents from holes in the ground. He loves to dig up moles in the back-yard. It drives the gnome crazy," I admitted with a grin. Though Niele was decidedly not a mole, he kind of lived like one and seemed to have an affinity for the ugly things. I went along with my greenskeeper's firm request not to let Monty hunt them, mostly because I'd always been anti-critter-murder of any kind. I didn't even kill spiders in the house. Though I didn't lose any sleep if Monty ate them.

Layla nodded. "Gnomes believe the mole is their spirit animal."

"You know a lot about gnomes."

She shrugged, reminding me of Wanda, my teenaged magical historian. "I know of all the magical breeds. As royalty, it is my duty to protect my people. That means I need to understand any potential rivals."

That made sense. I moved past her to the fridge and pulled out some eggs, cheese, butter, and bread. "Now you have to tell me why the gnome walks around with his stick and berries out."

"Stick and berries?"

I washed my hands, glancing at her over my shoulder. I lifted my brows. "Ah. Yes. The stick and berries." She grinned. "It is in the gnomenclature."

The gnomenclature, according to Niele, was the guiding document for gnomish people. From his description, I figured it was a cross between a society guide like *Miss Manners* and a Constitution. I was really glad it wasn't the custom for humans to run around with our sticks, berries, or cantaloupes hanging out.

"He's always using saws and clippers," I said, grimacing. "I worry he'll sever the wrong stick."

Layla barked out a laugh. "That does seem like it would be a problem."

Five minutes later, I settled plates of eggs and toast onto the table, and we tucked in. Monty was under the table, one fat paw occasionally tapping my calf in case I'd forgotten he was there.

I hadn't. But I was loathe to let Layla know that, in addition to feeding him twice a day, I also fed the dog from my plate.

She'd think I'd lost my mind.

The front door slammed, and Trish called out. "Hello?"

Layla jumped to her feet, one hand suddenly gripping a knife with a curved blade and etchings along its handle.

Eyeing her with alarm, I called out, "In the kitchen." I shook my head at Layla and motioned for her to sit. "Trish is my contractor, and she's on my council."

Layla didn't sit, but she dropped the hand with the knife to her side.

I gave her a warning look. "No violence," I said. "That's non-negotiable."

She gave me a slight nod but still didn't sit.

Trish breezed into the kitchen and slid to a stop, her vivid green eyes narrowing. "Hello?"

Okay, it was true I'd never been one for excessive socializing, but I was pretty sure the greeting wasn't supposed to end in a question mark. "Trish, you'll never believe who this is."

"Princess Layla?" the pretty fairy responded with a frown.

I stared at her, my mouth slack with shock. "Seriously? Do you have the place bugged or something?"

She grinned. "No. It's her aura. It's very distinctive." She frowned. "But it has changed a little."

"Changed how?" Layla demanded.

"The color is different. It's bluer than before. I'd guess that's from your newly updated humanity."

I continued to stare at the fairy. She was really blowing my mind. "You don't even look surprised."

"I saw her after you came out of the vortex, remember?"

Ah. That made sense. The damage that had stripped Layla's devilish nature had happened in the vortex. I'd been half dead at the time so I hadn't seen the change myself. "Oh. Okay." I smiled at Trish. "You're even earlier than usual today."

"We have that..." She glanced at Layla. "...thing tonight. I was hoping to finish the trim work today. Next week, I'm starting on your half bath."

We'd made an executive decision to finish the shop and the small customer bathroom before we started on my master bedroom suite. Still, the idea of the shop being done was exciting. One task nearly finished, three to go.

"That's good news," I told her enthusiastically.

She winked at me then looked down at the bakery box she was holding. "Oh. I almost forgot. Mavis asked me to bring these. I go right by Tilly's on my way here."

"Tilly's?" I asked, frowning.

"That new bakery Mavis told you about."

"I remember the giant chocolate chip cookies." I closed my eyes, groaning with pleasure. "Those cookies were better than sex..." I stopped, throwing

Layla an embarrassed glance. Yes, she was a princess. And, yes, she was an adult. I thought. But she was young and I didn't want to corrupt her. "Sectional sofas," I finished awkwardly.

Trish snorted. "That's quite a statement coming from you. I know how much you love sectional sofas."

I glowered at her, taking the box away and peering inside. The sweet scent of a dozen muffins in a variety of delectable flavors wafted up to me, making my eyes cross with pleasure. "Yum."

"Dibs on the chocolate cream filled with sprinkles," Trish said.

"Is there lemon?"

"Lemon cream. They have little pieces of candied lemon on the top."

I groaned again, briefly considering hiding the muffins behind the vegetables in the pantry so nobody would find them.

"Muffins?" Layla said, looking over my shoulder at the delicious pastries.

I turned with the box, lifting the lid and holding it out to her. "Would you like one?"

Layla's face bloomed with happiness. She grabbed the chocolate one, and I turned to look at Trish. Her lips were pressed together, but she didn't say anything. "Next time, I'll get two," she muttered under her breath.

I fought a grin, offering the box to her again. "The chocolate chip muffins look delicious."

Grabbing one, she took a napkin from the holder on the table. "I'm going to get to work. See you at lunchtime. Mavis is bringing subs."

I sighed. My life was perfect.

Gong!

My head came up, my eyes fixed on the narrow door that led to the belfry. Monty scratched frantically at the bottom, whining as if his heart was breaking. The bell was ringing. Magic stung the air, bringing the hairs up along my arms.

Gong!

"What is it, Aggy?" Layla asked. "Do you hear something?"

Apparently, she couldn't hear it. "A summons," I told her.

Following Monty's lead, I started toward the door.

Gong!

Aggy! A disembodied voice called out.

I knew that voice.

"Wanda? What's wrong?"

Aggy! Please! You need to help...ahhhhhhhh!

Gong!

The box of muffins slipped from my fingers, and I was running toward the belfry door. I yanked it open and nearly fell over Monty as he jumped in front of me and bolted up the narrow staircase, tail straight out behind him and ears pinned back. He was barking, the sound lost beneath the roaring in my ears and the pounding of my heart. "Wanda?!" I cleared the last couple of steps and lunged onto the belfry floor.

Monty was standing a foot away from the top of the steps, the hair along his back spiked with alarm. A low rumble throbbed in his throat.

I was vaguely aware of footsteps behind me, but I ignored them.

My attention was caught on the vision hanging in the air in front of me like a hologram.

Wanda was unmoving, curled in the fetal position. I could see the ringing bell and the other side of the belfry through her pale, grayish image. The teen's fists were clenched, stretched out in front of her inert body. Her dark-rimmed eyes were wide with terror, unblinking. And as I watched, her lips formed two words I could barely hear.

Help...me.

5

A SOUL THAT'S LOST, A FRIGHTENED PLEA

"I don't know where to look for her!" I yelled into the phone.

A beat of silence met my outburst and then Bev's voice, carefully calm, said, "Tell me exactly what happened."

I described the vision I'd seen in the belfry as panicked tears slipped down my cheeks. "She begged me to help her," I finished, scraping my wet cheeks with my palms. "How can I do that when I don't even know where to start looking?"

"Her mother was a witch, right?"

"I'm not sure. I got the impression she was, from what Wanda said about the night she was cursed. But she never really said."

I paced back and forth across the kitchen. I could feel Layla's gaze on me, but I couldn't look in her direction. I didn't want to see the expression on her face. She'd come to me looking for protection. She was learning that I couldn't even protect my council.

"Okay, we'll start there by going through the Witch's Registry to find her."

"How will we know who to look for," I said, battling the thread of hope Bev's calm suggestion triggered. I couldn't explain it, but I felt as if fate would dash any hope I had in the cruelest way. "We don't even have a last name."

"No. We don't. That will make it tougher for sure. But we know she had a daughter, and Wanda will make this easier. We know her age. We know her first name. And we know she has magical abilities. Historians are rare, Aggy. Coveted. There has to be a record somewhere of Wanda. I promise I'll find it."

"I want to help."

"I know. I'll bring you in as soon as I can. But you can't enter the witch's library. It's off-limits to all non-witches. Trish isn't even allowed inside."

Dang witches and their closed minds. I sighed. "Okay. But if you can't find it, this might get ugly. I'm going to find Wanda, and if your coven gets in my way..."

"Aggy, you need to trust me."

I nodded. "You're right. I do trust you. Take Mavis too," I said. "Two sets of eyes are better than one."

I disconnected and resumed pacing, the weight of Layla's gaze dragging down every step.

"What can I do?" the lost princess finally said, her voice soft.

I stopped and looked her way, feeling guilty for ignoring her and embarrassed that she was seeing me at my worst. "Unless you can help me find out where my historian is, nothing." I forced myself to add, "But thank you for offering."

Layla was silent for a moment. Finally, she said, "I cannot find your young Wanda."

I blinked, surprised that Layla knew the teen's name. "But I might know someone who can."

I placed my hands on the back of a chair and leaned closer. "I'm listening."

Layla's copper gaze widened slightly. She clasped her hands on the table in front of her. "Historians are rare," she began.

I bit back an impatient response and simply nodded.

"Records on them are scarce."

So far, not much help. I scrubbed a hand over my face, fighting for calm.

Layla held up a hand as if to tell me to chillax. I almost smiled when I realized I was thinking in Wanda-speak. "If she were almost any other magical designation, there would be a record of her somewhere in this realm. But in this case..."

"Please," I interrupted. "I need you to get to the point."

Layla sighed. "Right. Earth speak. Fast and in short segments. I've seen your television shows."

Before I could stop myself, I snorted out a laugh. "You got me."

The ghost of a smile curved the corners of her lips. "Historians keep track of other historians."

That made sense. It made more sense than a witch's library having information on a historian. "But Bev thought they'd have a record of Wanda and her mother..."

"They won't," Layla interrupted. "Only another historian would have that information."

I rubbed my temples. "Do you know another historian?"

"I do."

Against all odds, hope flared.

"Getting to her will be...difficult."

Hope dashed against the jagged rocks of Layla's words. It took my roiling belly with it.

I dragged a long, slow breath into my lungs. "But it's possible?"

"Yes." She frowned. "Maybe."

Hope turned to mist and blew away on a stiff, cold wind.

"Whoever it is, it's worth a try."

She bit her lip.

"What?"

"This creature is not the friendliest."

"I don't care. I'll take my pretty stick with me."

Her frown deepened. She was no doubt wondering what I was talking about. But the belfry door slammed open, the handle crashing against the wall behind it.

I spun to find the doorway empty. It didn't stay that way for long.

Bathilda fluttered through and took two fast turns around the kitchen, yellow eyes too wide. Normally sparrow-sized, she'd grown to the size of Ray, my raven.

The bat refused to land, and as I tried to speak to her, she began to chirp, the sound frantic.

"Batty, you need to calm down. You know I don't speak bat. Talk to me in my head like before."

More frantic chirping.

I shook my head, feeling my blood pressure spike from the bat's agitated behavior. "Still don't speak bat."

Bathilda flew into the mudroom, and I heard the scrape of wings against glass, followed by a series of soft thuds.

Layla and I shared a look.

"Is she slamming herself against the window?" Layla asked.

That was what it sounded like. But if she'd wanted outside, she could have done that from the belfry. I walked into the mudroom. "You want out?"

The bat smacked against the glass again, hard enough to crack it. "Hey!" I hurried over and opened the door. But Batty didn't go outside. She fluttered around my head, making me duck. "Stop it!" I snapped.

"I think she wants *you* to go outside," Layla said.

Knowing the bat's connection to Wanda, I gave in, stepping onto my little patio.

And found myself staring at two enormous, horned devils. Magic surged before I thought about what I was doing.

Seeing the energy snapping around my finger-tips. The largest lost one tensed, his big hands lifting, claws exposed. The other one lifted his spear, but then slid his gaze to something behind me. I didn't dare look away.

"Matthew, Glenn, what is it?"

The two big devils bowed their heads. "Princess, we've come to assess your welfare."

The smaller one of the two stepped around his bigger friend. Actually, calling him smaller was misleading. In no universe would he be considered small. He was probably seven feet tall, and I'd guess he weighed over three hundred pounds. I wasn't that great a judge of other people's weight, but the curved, goat-like back legs and bony, horned head had to weigh a lot.

His more easily riled friend looked to be a foot taller even than he was, and was still glaring at me.

"You're at my home," I snarled, still holding onto my power. "Stand down or leave."

A delicate hand landed on my shoulder. "You needn't worry, Aggy. They are two of my most trusted warriors."

Batty fluttered past me and up to the belfry, curse her. She'd warned me about the intruding devils. But apparently, I was on my own for the rest of it.

"I remember them from the Hellmouth incident," I said, keeping my gaze locked on the bigger one. "But you asked me for protection. I don't know who you need protection from. So, you'll have to accept that I might need assurance when two of your people show up."

"Understood." Her hand left my shoulder, and Layla stepped forward. "Stand down, Matthew."

He hesitated a beat longer until his friend, Glenn, I presumed, glared him down.

"How fare you, my princess?" Glenn asked.

"I am well." Layla gave the big creature a smile. "My friend, Aggy has offered me asylum in her home."

Glenn nodded. "We will guard the perimeter."

I jolted at that. "Whoa. My council already guards the perimeter. I have someone who manages the grounds. You can't stay here." My first thought was that Ferral and Luke would be in danger with lost warriors on the property. Not to mention Niele. My second thought was the horse. Were Layla's warriors on the same page with her about exterminating the veil-hopping equine?

Matthew bristled again. "We *will* protect the princess." His voice boomed across the yard, infused with power.

My hand shot out and I warned Layla, "Heads up." My staff slammed into my palm, and I snapped my arm to extend it to its full size. "You don't make the rules here," I growled.

Layla quickly moved between us. "You have my word they will not go near your people, Madam Lares," she said. "They are only here to make sure I am not attacked."

I hesitated, unsure how to keep resisting without admitting to the horse's potential presence. "I'm not comfortable having them here."

Layla's face fell. "I see." She gave me a smile that seemed forced. "I will leave then. Thank you for allowing me to visit and for the food." She spun around. Flanked by her two warriors, Layla started walking away. Her shoulders were square and her head high. She looked every bit the royal princess she was.

I fought uncertainty for a minute, feeling guilty. "Wait."

The trio stopped and turned back. "Yes?" Layla said.

"They can patrol the yard. But they are not to confront any of my people or any of the magical inhabitants of the Mystical Wood. Or any non-magic creatures in the woods or on my property who aren't aggressive." I was counting on the list of restrictions to cover the horse.

Layla inclined her head. "Thank you." She nodded at the two lost ones, and they moved away, instantly melting into the shadows. "They will accompany us when we visit the crone."

"The crone?" I asked, frowning.

"Yes. The crone is the person I mentioned earlier. She is a magical historian, as well as a powerful healer."

I grimaced. "Why is she called the crone?"

Layla's expression was almost too neutral. Her smile was a bland curving of lips. Her eyes sparkled with mischief. "Let us just say, she takes great pride in making herself unpleasant."

Awesome. Just what the current mess needed.

Yo mama mama, I got ya in my sights. Yo mama mama, I got ya dead to rights. Yo ma...

I punched the answer button. "Well, at least this ringtone has a good beat."

Mavis giggled. "I try. Listen, honey, I heard about Wanda. I'm so sorry. We're going to find her, and it's going to be all right."

"I hope so," I told my overly-optimistic mom.

"The coven is willing to meet tonight. But it has to be at your house if that's okay. Wilhelmina's twins have bad colds and, in Willy's own words, *They're too feral for polite company.*"

"That's fine. Is the sanctuary big enough to hold everybody?"

"Oh, yes. There will actually only be five of us, six with Trish. We've lost several members over the last couple of years."

"Is there a story there?" I asked.

"Definitely. But we'll save that for another time. Right now, let's concentrate on getting our sweet girl back."

"What do you need from me?" I asked.

"The ladies will want to do some spells in the belfry to see if we can backtrack the curse and follow it to Wanda's home."

"You can do that?"

"No promises. But it works about half the time. It depends on how strong the curse is and how recently it's been active. When was the last time Wanda was up there?"

"Two nights ago." Worry churned my stomach. "She didn't show up last night." It hadn't concerned me at the time because Bev and Mavis had been working on removing the groundhog day curse from Wanda, and she'd been showing up at all different times. But looking back, I realized that she might have already been in trouble. Maybe that was why she hadn't shown up. "We need to find her, mom. Fast. You should have heard the fear in her voice." My own voice broke on the words, and tears slipped down my cheeks. "I have a really bad feeling about this."

"Don't focus on bad things, Aggy. We need to keep our minds clear so we can work this out logically. That's the only way we'll be able to save her. Understand?"

I did understand. But I wasn't sure understanding would stop me from gnawing my own hand off like a trapped animal. "I'll try."

6

THE SPELL WILL HELP THE BLIND
TO SEE

Layla left a few minutes before the meeting was scheduled to start. She said she'd be right back, and I figured she needed to talk to the devilish duo patrolling my yard.

Mavis had arrived early and was putting food out on the kitchen table. We'd started setting the food up in the sanctuary but had quickly reconsidered when Monty helped himself to cheese and crackers from the too-low coffee table.

I grabbed a roll of ham and Swiss cheese off the platter, stuffing it into my face. Flavors burst over my tongue, and little birdies flew around my head. "Oh my goddess, this is good." I realized I'd forgotten to eat lunch, and my morning meal had long since left me. "Did you put it together?"

Mavis shook her head, trying a small pastry filled with cheese and closing her eyes in pleasure.

"Tilly's offers party catering services. I haven't tried the catering options before, but I'm starting to suspect she has magic. Everything she makes is exceptional."

"That's the new bakery?" I asked. "The place where you got those amazing cookies?"

Mavis nodded. "Which reminds me. I have cookies too." She pointed to a big white box on the counter. "Can you put them on a plate for me?"

"Happy to. I might accidentally break one, though, and have to eat it."

She grinned. "Break one for me too. I've been too busy to eat today."

We were finishing the last bites of our "flawed" cookies when the front door opened and closed. "We're here!" Bev announced loudly.

Monty ran, barking, toward the front of the house. A moment later, the coos and baby talk started. My little man was making new friends.

I smiled.

"Food's in here!" Mavis called out.

Several sets of footfalls headed our way, accompanied by the clicking of claws on the wood floor.

Monty beat the procession of women into the kitchen, eyes bright and tail whipping. In true dachshund fashion, he immediately forgot his new friends when the scent of food wafted over him. Standing on his back legs, he pawed at the table in hopes that one of the women milling about in the kitchen would be overcome with his cuteness and shove food into his face.

He wasn't going to be that lucky. "Down, Monty," I scolded. "Leave it."

The little dog reluctantly complied, retreating to his spot beneath the table and dropping his head onto his paws with an unhappy sigh.

"Aw, poor baby," said a curvy woman with flames of fiery red curls springing from her head and piercing green eyes. Her pale skin was a solar system of freckles, a testament to the fact that she was a true redhead. She stopped in front of me and stuck out her hand. "Wilhelmina Marks. My friends call me Willy. It's a pleasure to meet you, Madam Lares."

I took her hand, finding it soft and a little moist. "Call me Aggy, please. I'm so happy to meet you. How are your sons? Feeling better, I hope?"

She rolled her eyes. "Men are such babies. You'd think they were dying and all their limbs had been cut off. They refuse to do anything for themselves. Preferring to just lay around in bed all day, moaning and groaning. The floor and their beds are a sea of used tissues and dirty dishes. And the room smells like used magic and spoiled teenaged boy." Willy shook her head. "I owe you an enormous debt for helping me escape." Her eyes roamed over the food-laden table. "And for providing food that didn't come from a can."

"Used magic?" I questioned, grinning. "Your boys are witches too?"

She shrugged. "Theoretically. But they're too lazy and entitled to work on their craft. They mostly just fling it around to open and close doors and change the channel on the TV, because goddess forbid they should walk to a door or punch a button on the remote control with their actual fingers."

"They're not that bad, Willy," Bev said, laughing. "They just like to tweak you."

Willy gave me a wink.

Mavis smacked Bev's hand as she reached for her third cheese pastry. "Wait until you taste the food," she told Willy. "You might never go home."

Willy waggled her brows. "All I need is a sleeping bag on the floor, Aggy. You won't even know I'm here."

Everyone except a tall, gray-haired woman with a long face and pinched features laughed. When she saw me looking at her, the woman stepped forward, offering me her hand and a stiff bow of her head "Madam Lares. I'm Dell Rivers. It's a pleasure to make your acquaintance."

"Nice to meet you, Dell."

While we were setting up the food, Mavis had given me a quick rundown on the three coven members I hadn't met. She'd labeled Dell, the witch from Chicago, as the hard sell on any issue. I could see it in the woman's stiff posture... the tightness of her features...and the way her blue eyes glinted with instinctive irritation.

Dell's lips tightened as if she wanted to set me straight on something, but I smiled and turned to the woman I hadn't been introduced to, taking away the older woman's chance to rain on my parade. "Hi," I said to the woman with flashing brown eyes and smooth brown skin. "You must be Pietra."

Pietra, pronounced pie-tra according to Mavis, gave me a cocky smile. "What gave me away," she asked, winking. "My stunning good looks, or the giant 'P' on my necklace?"

I laughed, liking the tiny woman immediately. "What giant P?" I said, grinning back. The chain of her necklace was as big around as my little finger and appeared to be white gold. The "P" pendant had to be two inches long. Hard to miss. "I love it, by the way. I need one that says ML."

Her laugh was husky. It shook her entire body, her brown eyes sparkling with good humor. In spite of her diminutive size—I judged her to be around five feet tall—everything about Pietra was larger than life. Her lush figure only added to that impression.

"Trish will be here shortly," Bev said. "She was at the hardware store picking up more trim material when I called."

I nodded, motioning toward the food. "Let's eat and drink wine while we talk about how to find

Wanda." All humor fled me as I reset myself to the reason we'd gathered there.

I poured wine as everybody tucked into the pretty spread Mavis had laid out. Dell preferred coffee to wine, so Mavis took care of brewing her a cup.

I had just poured myself a glass of wine when the back door opened, and we all turned to find a white-faced Layla standing there.

"Hey," I said to her. "Layla, these are my friends. They're going to help us find Wanda." I looked around the group. "Ladies, this is Layla. She's staying with me for a while."

Mavis's expression showed shock, and I realized I hadn't told her about Layla. My bad. I was surprised Bev hadn't told her, though. Throwing Mavis an apologetic look, I whispered, "I'll explain later."

She didn't acknowledge my promise, too caught up in staring at the lost princess.

"May I speak to you in private?" Layla asked me.

I nodded. "Of course."

Layla returned outside, and I followed her. She didn't stop at the patio but kept walking until we were ten yards from the house.

I sent her a questioning look when she finally stopped. "Sorry, Aggy. I didn't want the others to hear what I'm about to say to you."

"That's okay. What's up?"

"My people have found something you need to know about."

I tensed, trying to keep panic off my face. If they'd managed to get hold of the white horse, we were going to have a problem. "What did they find?"

"Matthew has identified a magical aura hanging over your belfry."

I glanced up and saw no aura. Even when I bled energy into my gaze, the belfry looked perfectly normal to me. "I don't see it."

"You wouldn't, Aggy. My people are good at cloaking their magic from others. But we can't hide it from each other."

I let her words sink deep for a moment. Then asked, "What are you saying?"

"I'm saying that a demon of some kind has recently used magic in your belfry."

I stood on the small landing of the belfry staircase, which was located three steps down from the top, where the stairs turned. I'd locked Monty in my bedroom to keep him out of trouble and I could hear his angry barking from below.

The belfry floor was about ten feet square, but the bell and its support structure ate up most of the space, leaving about a three-foot-wide space all around. There wasn't a lot of room for the five witches to move around. When we'd first arrived, they'd asked me to describe where I'd seen the vision of Wanda. I'd described it as best I could and then stepped back out of the way.

What followed was a lively discussion over how best to prepare the area for their tracking spell. They'd quickly dismissed the usual practice of purifying the area in preparation for the new spell. They needed the lingering residue of the curse to track Wanda.

Dell was negative about their chances of making the spell work.

Willy was trying to be hopeful, but I could tell she didn't really believe they'd be successful.

Pietra was just happy to be there.

Despite the worry tightening my gut, I had to smile at the witch's happy demeanor and positive attitude.

Bev and Mavis were taskmasters, keeping everyone moving forward while trying to squelch some of Dell's negativity. Judging by the looks they kept throwing me, I suspected that was more an attempt to keep me from assuming the fetal position than anything else.

I squared my shoulders and did my best to paste a neutral expression onto my face. I had faith in Bev and Mavis. And if they believed in the others, then I would too.

Layla's warning ate into my enforced confidence, laying it to waste. A demon? In my belfry? *Curse, curse, swear!* Wasn't it bad enough I had a bat in my belfry?

Our first challenge for the spell had been trying to find something of Wanda's they could use in the spell. That gave me a few panicked moments because Wanda had never left anything at the church. As far as I knew, she'd never so much as used the restroom.

Ray showed up and landed on the window sill. Dancing sideways, the goofy raven kept fluttering his wings as his beady black gaze spanned the room and all the faces in it.

"That's Ray," I told the witches. They all looked from him to me like I was madder than the Mad Hatter. I cleared my throat and looked at the raven. "What's up, Ray?"

He danced sideways, his feathers rippling into tidiness, and opened his beak. "Caw!"

Okay. That wasn't very helpful. "We're kind of busy here, Ray."

He lowered his head and pecked at the sill like a chicken.

We all frowned. I sighed, moving in his direction. "Ray, we need to get this going. We're trying to find Wanda."

The big bird clacked his beak and pecked at the

sill again. I watched him, wondering if he'd damaged his tiny bird brain.

That was when I saw it. "Hair!" I exclaimed, startling Ray into the air. He cawed explosively and then landed again, strutting from one end of the sill to the other with an indignant, pigeon-like swagger. "Pee!"

"Sorry," I murmured, flushing with embarrassment. "I didn't mean to startle you."

"Did he say pee?" Pietra asked, then doubled over in a belly laugh when Bev nodded. "Hi-larious!"

I carefully tugged the strands of straight black hair from where they'd gotten caught in a shard of splintered wood, holding them up for the coven to see. "This is hers. This is Wanda's hair."

"You're sure?" Dell said, her lips pursing.

"I'm positive."

Mavis carefully extracted it from my fingers. "This will work nicely. Thanks, honey."

"Don't thank me," I responded with a grin. "Thank Ray."

Mavis snorted. "Not a chance."

Ray's wings flapped, and he cast his beady gaze on Mavis. "Rude!"

Pietra and Willy lost it, doubling over with laughter.

Ignoring them, Mavis dropped the hair into a wide, shallow bowl and settled it on top of the bell.

After several minutes of discussion, the witches got down to business. I stood back and watched, my eyes like saucers at the sight of five powerful witches arrayed around the bell, hands up and fingers moving to create a spell on the air. Five different colored webs formed in front of them, created from five different styles of weave. And five voices, soft and murmuring, chanted words I didn't understand.

The air changed in the belfry. I felt the touch of strange magic, and all the hair along my arms rose up as the magic tasted the air around me. Five different scents infused the belfry.

The sweet scent of roses. The meaty smell of rich earth. The delicate flavor of lavender flowers. The spicy bite of cinnamon. The clean scent of pine. The air was rich with a chaos of aromas that fought against each other rather than merge.

The door at the bottom of the stairs opened and softly closed. I looked down to find Trish hurrying up the steps, an apology on her face. "Sorry," she whispered to me. "My stupid car broke down, and I had to bum a ride from Luke."

I touched her shoulder and nodded toward the witches. "They just got started."

Trish moved into the belfry, surprising me by popping into her warrior form and flying to the bell. She hovered there, the center of a magical wheel with five spokes reaching toward the center.

Trish raised her small staff and energy spun away from it, surrounding her as she flew in a circle to complete the magical sphere.

The witches stopped chanting and lifted their hands above their heads, a moment fraught with tension stretching between them. Then, on a silent command of some kind, they all clapped their hands at the same time and barked out a single word, "*Invenire!*"

Five strands of magic shot toward Trish's energy circle, five spells burst into mist and flowed toward the center, mingling and fusing into a single wash of pale gray that obscured everything beneath its touch.

Five gazes rose to Trish. She nodded and pointed her staff toward the bowl beneath her. "*Invenire!*"

Flames rose from the bowl, tall tongues of fire licking the magic-drenched air. The individual magics expanded, pulsed several times like a beating heart, and then everything seemed to gather up into a single entity, a slender curve of magic that hung motionless beneath the bowl for a beat and then blew outward, dousing us in the scents, colors, and energy of the combined magics.

The world stilled for a moment, seconds taut with expectation and hope, and then something amazing happened.

7

A HIDEY HOLE, A HIDDEN LIFE

The apartment was small, barely larger than my kitchen. It was tidy, but it had the busy feel of a room with too much furniture. Everything appeared well-worn and comfortable. Within the tiny space were the bare bones of a kitchen...a sink, a small refrigerator, and a stove. A twin-sized bed, mounded with blankets, was pushed against the far wall, and there was a closet-sized bathroom that I could see through a doorway across the room.

"A studio apartment," I said to no one in particular.

Through a narrow window over the kitchen sink, I saw the spires of Saint Paul church on the southern edge of town.

Behind the church, a crescent moon hung in the sky. I remembered that moon. It had hung over the belfry the night before. Was that when Wanda had been taken?

Someone gasped, and I sharpened my attention on the vision in front of me. The covers on the small bed shifted, bunched. A dark head rose from the tangle of covers. A pale face shone through the moonlit darkness.

Wanda!

Her eyes were wide with horror as she stared toward something across the room. She scrambled upward, head shaking and mouth moving in silent denial.

Without warning, her gaze slid to me and she screamed.

Aggy! Please! You need to help...ahhhhhhhh!

"Wanda!" I reached out, but the apartment disappeared, Wanda's scream fading into silence. I sagged downward, blinking rapidly as tears burned my eyes. The world returned in a wave of painful clarity that dropped me back into the belfry, surrounded by concerned faces.

Sadness swamped me, and I felt myself slam down onto a hard surface. The reality I'd returned to was still missing one lonely, scared teen.

I looked up into the circle of faces hovering around me. "What..." I swallowed a dry-as-dust lump in my throat, coughing as it choked me. I was lying on the belfry floor, looking up at the coven. "What happened?"

"You were in some kind of trance," Bev said, her face tight with worry. "You said Wanda's name. Did you see her?"

I nodded, pain searing through me at the memory.

"We found where she lives," Mavis said, squeezing my hand.

I looked at our clasped hands, feeling her touch for the first time since coming out of my stupor. I squeezed back, hope warring with fear for Wanda's safety. "She was so scared," I told Mavis, hot tears bathing my cheeks.

"Did you see who took her?" a sharp, cool voice asked.

I looked up into the face of the woman standing behind Mavis. Dell. The older woman's cold, business-like eyes left no room for sentimentality.

Shaking my head, I sniffed and sat up. "No. But I recognized Saint Paul church and the moon from last night. I saw Wanda just before she was taken."

Trish offered me a hand up and I took it, letting her help me stand. She gave my hand a squeeze before dropping it. "Let's go."

E ven bathed in the dying light of dusk, the old Victorian home showed its advanced age. Its lines were softer than they should have been. Its skirts sagged under chipping paint. The yard was overgrown, sporting more weeds than grass, and held enough toys to tell me at least one young family lived there. The bank of pocked brass mailboxes I could see through the locked front door told me that lots of people lived in the large house. From the curb, the two windows on the uppermost floor had looked like the too-wide gaze of a silent movie star, playing to a fascinated crowd.

The old girl had seen better days, but she still served a purpose.

At that moment, her main purpose was to give me insight into what had happened to Wanda. Eyeing the slender beam of pale gray magic leading us to the topmost window in the peak of the structure, I considered the next barrier to that goal. "How do we get inside?" I glanced around at my posse of witches, wondering if any of them knew a spell to unlock the door.

Pietra gave me a wink and sashayed to the bank of call-buttons on the short wall next to the door. She started pushing buttons, getting a response after the fourth one. "Yeah?"

"Hey, doll," Pietra said in an accent that

reminded me of someone born and raised in Jersey. My imagination didn't have to work hard to see her with big hair, wearing form-fitting capris and high heels, while blowing bubbles with her gum. "How's it goin'? I got a large pepperoni pizza here with your name on it."

A bell buzzed, and Pietra grabbed the handle, pulling it open. I bumped knuckles with her as I moved past into the foyer. Pietra made a little explosion sound and flared her fingers after the knuckle bump.

Behind me, Willy said, "Now I want pepperoni pizza."

Pietra's laugh was bubbly. "We'll get some later, doll."

Ignoring the banter behind me, I hurried up the first set of stairs, then the second, and the third, which ended at a single door. The windowless landing was dark, the walls scarred and painted a dark green that only exacerbated the lack of light. A single fixture in the ceiling gave off weak yellow light through a dirty dome that was filled with dead bugs.

I grimaced, thinking about Wanda spending her time there. Bev came up behind me. "Have you knocked?"

I shook my head, fear locking me in place. What if Wanda was in that apartment? What if she was... I swallowed the lump in my throat, swiping damp palms over my jeans.

Bev reached past me and knocked.

We stared at the heavy oak door for a moment. Nothing moved behind it. No sounds filtered into the hallway.

The group on the stairs behind me was silent, their presence somehow creating extra tension in my chest. I started to second-guess bringing the coven with me, but shoved the thought away. If there was any magic residue in the apartment, they'd told me they might be able to read it. Knowing what type of magic was used could lead us to her abductor. It could help us find Wanda.

Bev tried the knob, and it turned. The door opened.

A chorus of horrific screams filled the tiny landing and a flock of creatures shot out of the apartment, knocking me to my butt as they twisted and thrashed around us. The things were shrieking as if their tails were on fire. They darted and hurtled and spun, shooting between us and charging at our heads. Their screams were painful, causing us to cover our ears in self-defense. They were like those fireworks that blasted, winding and shrieking, into the sky and then exploded into shards of light and brilliant color.

Cold slime from the creatures dripped onto my cheek, splashed against my back, and splatted against the wood floor all around us. The slime was like dry ice, burning everything it touched.

I was dimly aware of the coven screaming as they hit the ground, and of lots of activity that bespoke frantic backtracking down the stairs.

The noise was horrible. Beneath the effort I was making to understand what was attacking us, I nursed a fear that one of the other residents in the house...maybe one of the children who belonged to the toys in the yard...would come up to investigate and get hurt.

Out of the corner of my eye, I saw someone stand and hurry up the steps to the landing. Dell threw her long arms into the air and spread her bony fingers, smacking the air as if it were solid. "*Cessare!*"

The shrieking stopped, and the writhing slimers disappeared.

The silence that followed was stark.

Slowly, we rose to our feet and looked around. There was no sign of the things. No slime on the floor. I touched my cheek and didn't feel any goo there. It was as if we'd imagined the whole thing.

I frowned at Dell.

She stuck her nose into the air and marched past Bev and me. "Phantom tricksters. Witchery 101."

Bev and I shared a look and she shook her head. We followed Dell into Wanda's apartment. The apartment was empty, except for the pervasive stench of magic filling the place and a residual malevolence that even I could feel.

I stood just inside the door, looking around as

the witches tested the space, searching for a magic trail or at least a signature they could read. They huddled together across the room from me. They had their heads together, and I couldn't hear what they were saying. There was reluctant excitement in the energy of their movements, but their frequent glances my way did not give me hope for good news. "Okay, just tell me," I said, narrowing my gaze on the group of women. "Who did this? Where's Wanda?"

They stared at me for a minute. Finally, Willy stepped forward. "The crone has her."

The way she said it made me frown. "Okay. Is that bad?"

From their shocked looks, I clearly should have known who the crone was...what she was capable of...whether she was friend or foe. But I didn't. All I knew was the little bit Layla had told me, and it wasn't enough. "Is she likely to hurt her?"

Trish grimaced. "Hurt? Not intentionally, no. But the crone isn't always..."

"Rational," Bev said.

"Kind," Pietra said.

"Coherent," Mavis said.

"Cooperative," Willy said.

"Sane," Dell snapped.

"There's something else," Trish told me, her face tight with worry. "We think there was a demon here last night."

That made my eyes go wide. "No."

Trish winced. "Sorry, Aggy. It's true."

"But who? How?"

Mavis frowned. "Someone has apparently performed a summoning."

Dell shook her head. "Not so fast. You are aware there are earth-bound demons, correct?"

The other witches winced with embarrassment. Pietra nodded. "That's true. It could have been an earthbound."

I thought about what they'd just told me, weighing the seemingly conflicting information. "So your speculation at this point is that Wanda was taken by a demon and given to the crone?"

They shrugged.

"It could have also been a lost one," Mavis said on a frown. "Their magical signatures are remarkably similar."

"Either way, would that be a normal circumstance? Does the crone generally use the demonic to do her bidding?"

"Not usually," Pietra admitted. "I'm actually not a fan of that conclusion. I think the demon might have attacked Wanda, and the crone stepped in."

I felt my eyes widen. Figuring a fellow historian had to be safer for Wanda, no matter how addle-headed the crone might be, I liked that conclusion better. "What evidence do we have to support either possibility...magically speaking?"

"None," Mavis admitted. "Unfortunately, magic doesn't work that way. It doesn't really offer clues."

I nodded. "Well then, we'll just have to do it the hard way."

8

THE LARES MUST SEE THROUGH
THE STRIFE

I carefully pulled the covers of Wanda's bed back, searching the sheets and blankets for something that might give me a clue as to what had happened. Bev searched the bathroom, Mavis took the kitchen, and the other members of the coven searched the rest of the place and the landing outside.

Finding nothing in the bed, I got down on the floor and looked underneath it. Unlike under my bed...guilty flush...it was free of dust bunnies and boxes of sweaters I rarely wore but didn't want to get rid of.

Oops. When had I made it about me?

Wanda's closet held a few tee shirts on hangars, two pairs of black jeans, also on hangars, a black tee-shirt dress I couldn't imagine her wearing, and three pairs of black shoes, which included a pair of high-topped sneakers, a pair of boots with a flat heel, and a cute pair of leather Mary Janes I'd never seen her wear.

I fingered the tunic she'd been wearing the first time Gren and I had met her...in my kitchen. She'd been rummaging through my food looking for stuff to make a PB&J sandwich and had been peeved because she couldn't find the grape jelly. My chest tightened at the memory, my eyes filling with tears.

"Aggy?" a voice called from behind me. "We found something out on the landing."

I turned to find Willy and Pietra, their expressions grim.

My heart started pounding against my ribs, dread curling talons in my belly. "What did you find?"

Pietra extended her hand. Something was coiled in her palm. I reached for it, carefully taking the thick strands of course white hair. I stared at the locks, perplexed. "This could belong to a neighbor," I offered weakly.

Willy shook her head. "Doubtful. Can't you feel the magic in it?"

"And there's something else." Willy said, glancing at Pietra.

I glanced up, seeing their taut expressions. "Tell me."

They hesitated just long enough for Dell to step in. "Blood, Madam Lares." She stopped a few feet away from me, a small vial held between her long, bony fingers. I focused on the callouses I could see on her fingers rather than the reddish-brown specks, like hideous paint chips, in the bottom of the vial. "If it's the girl's blood, we'll be able to tell by performing a spell," Dell told me, holding up a strand of black hair. "We found this in the bathroom. We have her DNA."

DNA... I swallowed hard, my heart skipping random beats as panic clutched me by the throat and shook me hard.

The witch appeared oblivious to the way she'd rocked my world. Totally ignorant of how my knees wobbled so hard I had to drop heavily onto the bed behind me. Completely blind to the pallor of my face as all the blood fled out of it.

Blood. Was it Wanda's blood? Had the demon hurt her when it took her away? Stars burst before my eyes at the thought. I lowered my head to my hands and closed my eyes, riding out the waves of dizziness that followed.

The mattress dipped, and I was pulled against a soft body. Mavis's warm, familiar scent enfolded me as she held me close in a one-armed hug. "We'll find her, honey. And she's going to be okay. There was no reason for them to take her out of this house if they intended to kill her."

Her words sank in and allowed me to breathe again. She was right. I looked into Mavis's face. "They need her for something."

Mavis nodded. "We know the crone's involved. That's where we have to start."

I pulled air into my lungs, holding it for a beat to settle me, and then expelled it on a nod. "Let's head home. I need to call a council meeting."

I clutched the coarse white hair in my fist as we walked into the sanctuary ten minutes later. Gren stood by the windowed alcove. He turned as I walked into the room, his dark brown gaze sliding to my face, warm and questioning.

I let my gaze skim over his tall, muscular form, admiring the glossy thickness of his longish mahogany hair. He'd recently been letting it grow out a bit, and I loved the way it curled at the back of his neck and over his ears. I gave him a smile. "I'm fine. We have a lead on her."

Anyone else might have had trouble deciphering my shorthand. Gren was different. He understood what I was telling him. I was upset, but at least we were making progress.

My protector could read my emotions better than I did and often seemed to know what I was going to do before I did it. We had a connection I'd never had before with anyone. It went beyond romance, though there was definitely the promise of that too.

"Madam Lares," Ferral said in greeting.

I looked into his cold, handsome face. "You heard about Wanda?"

My advocate wore his customary suit, which was currently a deep, dark brown that complimented his shoulder-length dark blond hair and silver eyes. Clenching his square jaw, he nodded. "I did. I've already sent feelers through the magical community. If she's anywhere within a hundred-mile radius of Rome, we'll find her."

"Thanks." Gratitude smoothed over some of the brittleness encasing my heart. "Luke and Niele?" I asked the advocate.

"I'm here, Madam Lares," the gnome's familiar voice said from the doorway. He gave me a commiserating look and I reached out, taking his slightly gritty hand. His nails were short and even, well-tended despite the soil beneath them. "Thanks for coming so quickly. I know you've been busy in Rome."

Our recent battle with the Hellmouth had created some instabilities in my little town. Many of the buildings were in danger of being swallowed by the earth. Some had already started to sag, prompting Rome's police chief, Davis Marshal, to come to me with his concerns. I'd asked Niele to pull together a team to address the issue.

Niele had brought together the gnomish community to stabilize the structures and put everything back to rights. It had been hard, tedious work, requiring long hours and a level of frustration that seemed to tax even Niele's good nature at times.

I gave him a careful once-over, seeing the lines of strain around his small black eyes and the purple circles beneath them. He also looked like he'd lost weight. "Have you eaten today?"

He frowned. "I'm fine, Madam..."

I shook my head. "Let's move the meeting to the kitchen. We could all use a snack and some coffee."

As we headed to the back of the house, the front door opened and closed. For just a beat, I stopped breathing, thinking it might be Wanda. But the steps were too heavy, too quick, to be hers. I tried not to look disappointed when Luke walked into the kitchen. Steeling myself to face his gaze, I forced a stiff smile onto my face. "It looks like everybody's here. We can get started."

"How do we get to the crone?" I asked my council.

"Not easily," Ferral all but snarled back. He didn't support our going in search of the powerful healer.

I sent him a glower. "Helpful comments only, please." I was leaning against the counter with Gren, too wired to sit. Trish, Niele, and Bev sat at the table.

Mavis was tending the big pot of stew she'd made for our late dinner. The buttery scent of biscuits filled the room, and my mouth was watering.

The giant bakery box that had been filled with cupcakes for the evening's dessert was empty. Only a few smears of strawberry frosting were still left in the box. They'd been delicious.

I set my empty coffee cup on the counter behind me, tempted to have another cup but knowing it would keep me up all night if I did. Then again, if we were setting out after the crone right away, that would be a good thing.

"She's across the veil," Ferral said, staring at his now-cool coffee. "There are limited ways to cross."

"What are the options?" I asked, seemingly the only one who didn't know. As usual, I forced back bitterness at always being the dunce in the room. I'd get there. Eventually, I'd know what I was doing.

"There's a gate in the Mystical Wood," Luke offered. He sent Ferral a tense glance. "But it's through the Malignant Forest. I don't recommend we go that way."

Even I didn't need to ask why something called the Malignant Forest was bad. That seemed obvious.

"There are vessels," Trish suggested. "Maybe we can call one to us."

"Vessels?" Bev asked.

Halleluiah! For once, I hadn't been the one to ask the question.

"Magical creatures who can cross the veil," Ferral explained, his expression far less arrogant when addressing my sister than it would have been with me. I narrowed my gaze on him, wondering what I'd done to prick his angry bone.

"Even with a vessel, we'll probably have to pass through the gate," Luke said, frowning. "But it will be much easier."

Behind me, a bird tapped lightly on the window over the sink. I'd inherited a sparrow that seemed to think he needed to get inside my house for some reason. The goofy thing wouldn't stop pecking at the glass, despite my campaign of shouting at it to stop.

"Are they hard to find?" Bev asked, throwing me an amused glance.

"Yes," Ferral said. He met my narrowed gaze with one of his own, then looked away, perfect nose lifted with disdain. "The deeper issue is the crone herself. She won't take well to us trespassing on her land. Bringing a vessel with us just invites trouble."

"How so?" Trish asked.

Peck. Peck. Peck.

Gren frowned. "It's possible she will try to confiscate it, leaving us stranded. The crone doesn't like that outsiders can invade her veil using vessels. If she doesn't want us there, she'll consider it a personal point of pride to take it away from us."

"So, what type of vessel is the right kind for this journey?" I asked, directing the question at Gren. If the advocate wanted to be snippy, I'd just talk to someone who wasn't.

Peck. Peck. Peck.

He shrugged. "Something large and fast that can run away."

Peck. Peck. Peck.

"Something that can take to the air," Ferral added, refusing to be ignored.

Peck. Peck. Peck.

"I've heard of a badger vessel in the Wood," Luke offered. "Small but mean. Even the crone would think twice about tangling with it."

Peck. Peck. Peck.

"What is that silly bird doing?" Mavis asked. She stepped around me and made shooing motions. "Get lost!"

The sound of rapidly fluttering wings came through the glass, and I frowned. That sounded like a bigger bird than a sparrow.

"We actually have a vessel at our beck and call," Trish said, a mysterious smile on her face.

Bev's eyes went wide. "If you tell me it's that flying rodent, I'm going to put bat guano in your stew."

Trish laughed.

I turned around, just as the pecking started again, catching the culprit in the act. "Ray?"

"Yep," Trish said, surprising all of us. "The raven

is a strong vessel. I'm surprised you all didn't know that."

"Pee!" Ray shouted from the other side of the glass.

"You're not kidding, buddy," I murmured. "Who knew?"

"Okay, that settles that," Ferral said. "Now, let's discuss our plan of attack once we're standing in front of Cayleigh Castle."

I stared at him for a minute and then sighed. I'd have to be the dope again. "What's Cayleigh Castle?"

Disdain dripped...yes, it did...it literally dripped off him. "Madam Lares, how can you expect to do this job if you don't do your homework? The crone is one of the most legendary magical creatures of all time. She's a vital part of the magical ecosystem. You cannot continue to be so clueless..."

I held up a hand to stop him. "I have two words for you, advocate. Seating. Hellmouth."

We stared at each other for a long moment, everyone else in the room watching in fascination.

Ferral slid his gaze away first, a win for me, and then he said, "How long are you going to continue whining about doing your job?"

I was going to punch him in the throat. My fists were formed, and I was taking a step forward when Gren clasped a warm hand around my wrist. "Steady," he murmured softly.

He turned to the advocate. "The Lares is an

extremely busy woman who is in charge of an entire town and all of its people, magical and non-magical. If you are not capable of keeping her up-to-date on things she needs to know to do her job, then please tell us now and we'll find someone who is."

The two men locked gazes, both bristling with palpable anger. Ferral's square jaw was so tight, I was pretty sure he was going to fracture a canine. If he'd been in his moon hound form, his hackles would no doubt have risen along his back.

Gren's grip on my wrist was gentle, his body relaxed, despite the hard glint in his eyes. He looked like a man who knew he was right.

Ferral looked like a man who wanted to lash out at someone. Usually that someone was me, but I was betting he was thinking about whether that would be a good idea. Finally, to my surprise, Ferral inclined his head. "You are correct, Lungren Maker. The Lares is woefully unschooled in nearly every-thing she needs to know. I will set up a daily training schedule with Madam so we can remedy that."

"Gack!" All the blood fled from my face and I made a small choking noise. That had gone so horribly wrong in such a short time. "I really don't think..." Both Gren and Ferral turned to look at me. The weight of their combined gazes bowed my shoulders. I stood there like a whipped puppy, my hands twining nervously before me. "I don't think that's a bad idea at all," I finally said, forcing what was probably a ghastly smile.

Across the room, Bev coughed into her hand, no doubt hiding a laugh. I glared at her, and she coughed again.

Ugh! Just what I needed. *Daily* one-on-one time with the advocate.

My life was over.

"Pee!" Ray screeched through the window glass.

As usual, the bird was spot on.

9

FRIEND OR FOE, THEY MUST DECIDE

We set off before sunrise the next morning. I should probably say, we started to set off before sunrise. We actually stood on my lawn glaring at each other for quite a while first.

"I don't like it," Ferral growled out. He glowered at the two lost soldiers facing him. "I don't trust them."

Layla stood in front of her guards, glaring right back at the advocate. "Have you forgotten our alliance, dog?" she asked, nearly spitting the words.

Ferral snarled, his chest rumbling on a growl. He was seconds away from changing to his moon hound form.

"Stop it!" I bellowed, injecting my voice with power so that it reverberated across the yard and into the trees of the Mystical Wood. All parties turned to me, their scowls still firmly affixed. I held up a hand, looking at Ferral. "She's right," I told him. "Layla and I have an alliance. She risked her life, her..." I sent the princess a look of understanding. "...identity, to bring me out of the vortex alive. And that wasn't the first time she'd risked herself to protect me." I still shuddered at the memory of her fighting off a powerful shadow demon to keep it from killing me. She'd nearly died from that battle. Yet, she'd still shown up to help at the Hellmouth. "I owe her my life, twice over. And we all owe her people for helping to push the Hellmouth back."

Ferral's glare deepened.

Layla gave him a smug grin.

I turned to the princess. "And Ferral's right to be concerned about adding to our party at the last minute."

Layla's grin turned upside down. Her eyes narrowed on me. "You don't really..."

I held up my hand again. "I meant what I said. I value our alliance. I'm just bringing up a point. It's been brought to my attention that the crone doesn't like intruders on her land. So, before we include you in our party, I need to ask. What is your relationship with the crone? Is there any reason to suspect she might be peeved if you showed up on her doorstep?"

Layla's gaze slid sideways before she shrugged, her expression determinedly neutral. "I have no relationship with the crone. If she has an objection to my people or me, I'm not aware of it."

I held her gaze for a long moment, fully aware that her response had been carefully vague. "I need you to tell me if we're going to have a problem. I don't want to be blindsided."

"I assure you that my people and I will cause no problems on the crone's land."

Yeah, more careful vagueness. But I was inclined to want them along. I was traveling into the unknown, and my goal was deadly important. So, after another moment of mutual eye-locks with the devilish princess, I inclined my head. "Okay. I'd be grateful for your assistance, Princess Layla. Our alliance is intact."

My advocate, who'd schooled me on the political speech regarding a magical alliance following the Hellmouth debacle, grimaced when I used it against his judgment.

She inclined her head. "Our alliance is intact."

The soft rustle of wings brought my head up as Ray flew out of the woods. He landed on my shoulder and clacked his beak. "Rude!"

I gently pushed a wing out of my face. "Let me guess, the pixies tried to pull your feathers out again?"

He danced sideways, ruffling his feathers with irritation. "Rude."

I turned to find Layla staring at Ray with an intensity the silly bird shouldn't incite. "Is something wrong?" I asked her.

She blinked, seeming to pull herself out of deep thought, and then shook her head. "No. I was just thinking that you have surrounded yourself with an interesting mix of creatures."

"Heh," I laughed. "More like they surrounded themselves with me." I frowned. "Wait, that didn't come out right."

"Are we going to stand here all day?" Ferral groused. "The sun is rising."

He was right. The top arch of the sun was visible just above the trees of the Mystical Wood, surrounded by an aura of gorgeous golds, reds, and purples. Time was wasting.

I looked around at my small group, warmth blossoming in my chest at the comforting sight. Bev and Mavis stood together at the back of the group. Niele stood next to them, alarmingly moss-less. I only hoped Bev had his moss shorts in the backpack she was carrying. I really didn't want to stare at his stick and berries for the entire trip. Then I remembered I'd have to burrow into the earth to stare at them and felt slightly better.

Gren stood at my back, his presence reassuring. Luke and Trish were staying behind to guard Rome, with some help from the coven of witches and, presumably, the bat.

I smiled at my friends. "Let's get this show on the road."

Niele saluted me with both hands at once and

leaped into the air. He performed a perfect dive into the ground. The earth melted away from his finger-tips, and he disappeared beneath the thick grass and rich black soil as if he was part of it.

Ray took to the air with a strident caw, leaving behind a single black feather that drifted onto my head.

Barking at the raven, Monty's tail wagged as he watched Ray disappear into the trees.

We took off toward the Mystical Wood, Layla's guards taking flank. Gren walked beside me, and Bev and Mavis took up the rear.

A silver light exploded into the soft darkness, and Ferral stood in front of us as an enormous, silver-gray hound. He prowled forward, giant paws pressing the ground flat where Niele's passage had mounded it like an enormous mole trail.

Layla walked on my opposite side from Gren.

Smiling at his enthusiasm, I watched my dog bounce along after Ferral. I'd really debated bringing Monty. My head had told me to leave him at home with Trish and Luke. He'd be safer there since I had no idea what we were about to come up against. But my heart...my instincts...told me to bring him along. Whatever lay ahead, my instincts were screaming that Monty was an important part of the journey.

My heart hadn't needed much convincing.

We neared the edge of the dense, magical woods

and I found myself tensing. I watched Matthew and Glenn step through the trees and disappear from sight. Staring at the slight mounding ahead of us, I knew that Niele had breached the wood too.

At the edge of the woods, Monty stopped and turned back, tail wagging and eyes bright with excitement. He waited for me to approach, his tail drooping when I hesitated.

Magic crackled around us. Power bit my skin like a thousand tiny spiders. The place where I'd found many delightful moments practicing with my staff and running with Monty suddenly felt hostile, unwelcoming.

I knew it was my imagination. It had to be. There was no reason for the Mystical Wood to repel me. I was projecting my own fear of the unknown onto it.

I took a deep breath and, clutching my staff hard enough to turn my knuckles white, stepped into the trees.

The vision smacked me hard in the face, dropping me to my knees.

Ahead of me stretched a long hallway roiling with the same shadow-filled fog as before. The walls were hidden behind the mist. The floor was only real because I felt its rough surface against the soles of my bare feet.

The shadows danced around me, an indefinable threat drawn forward by the rhythmic chanting I could hear in the distance. I followed the droning sound until I was standing beneath an archway, the mist cold and moist against my skin. The chanters stood in a large circle, arms outstretched and faces obscured by dark robes.

The low-ceilinged room was even colder than before, painting the walls and floor with ice. My feet ached from the cold. Gooseflesh rose up along my arms.

The figures stood around a small fire, its flames burning through the fog but not dispelling it. Hands reached toward the flames inside the cauldron just as I remembered, its contents spilling over the sides and hitting the floor with a sizzle.

The steam carried a sulfurous stench that stung my nose and bit at the back of my throat.

Something moved behind the cauldron. Something dark and terrible and...horrifyingly familiar.

The creature seemed to rise up from the flames, the narrow strip of its face a sickly white, with crimson eyes that glowed red through the mist. The wide mouth was a black slash filled with jagged teeth, a pointed tongue snapping out to taste the air as it approached the cauldron.

I felt its foul regard like a thousand tiny cuts against my skin.

Reaching for my magic, I braced for the bite of its energy on my fingertips, but it didn't answer my summons. Terror slid through me, digging at my gut with knifelike claws.

The foul creature's gaze held mine as it moved across the room, burning with malevolence. "Agnes Bethany

Lenore," the monster said. Its long tongue snapped out from between a forest of jagged teeth when it spoke. "Come to me. I await you in the darkness."

I stepped backward, the urge to flee so strong I vibrated with it.

The monster is suddenly standing inches away, those fiery eyes glowing with evil intent. "I grow tired of waiting."

I turned away and started to run, the sound of my rapidly beating heart following me through the mist.

Hands gripped my arms, holding me down. Voices tangled around me, some angry, some sounding frightened. My body felt foreign, unnaturally stiff and uncooperative. I fought against the restraining hands, as well as my own resistant flesh. A long, keening sound emerged from my lips, and I couldn't seem to stop it.

My heart was pounding so hard it ached, and I couldn't draw a breath.

I felt like I was dying.

Somebody was whining, and I didn't think it was me.

A single voice broke through the chaos and found my ears. "Open your eyes, Aggy!" Gren screamed.

The words were incomprehensible gibberish. They flew past me like mosquitoes, bothersome and fleeting.

"Breathe!" Gren yelled, his breath hot against my face.

But I *couldn't* breathe. I was screaming too hard to draw air.

Oh...

Clamping down on the terror, I stopped screaming and sucked in a desperate breath.

My eyes flew open, and I found myself staring up at a worried circle of faces. I was panting too hard to speak, and my chest still felt as if I was having a heart attack.

"Thank the goddess," Mavis said. "Honey, you scared the beans out of us."

Monty licked my cheek and then snuggled his little head beneath my chin. He was trembling, his soft body pressed as close as he could get.

Bev compressed her lips and stared down at me, eyes like saucers in her too-pale face. She gave my shoulder a squeeze but was too upset to speak.

I looked at Gren, who I realized was holding both of my hands in his. "What happened?" I gasped.

His dark chocolate gaze sharpened. "We were hoping you could tell us."

"I...there was a hostile feeling in the magic and then..." I frowned, trying to remember. Bits and pieces started to reveal themselves in my mind. "I think I had a dream." My frown deepened. "But, that's not right because I was awake."

"A vision?" Ferral asked, his tone uncharacteristically kind.

"Yes," I said. "That must be what it was. It was just like the last time."

"The last time?" Bev asked. "This has happened before, and you didn't tell us?"

"No. Not really. Well, technically yes. But it was a dream the last time." Or, at least, I'd thought it was a dream.

Maybe it hadn't been.

"Tell us," Gren said gently.

"There's a cold mist, too thick to see much except shadows. At the end of the hallway was a wide archway, and the room beyond the archway was filled with robed figures." I frowned. "They were around a cauldron with flames shooting out of it."

Mavis and Bev shared a look, and I flinched.

"I know, it sounds crazy."

"It doesn't sound any crazier than a Hellmouth in a senior home," Layla said, grinning.

I snorted. "Point. Anyway, there was something beyond the circle of robed people," I told them.

"What kind of something?" Mavis asked.

I looked at her, seeing a new tautness in her features. Worry lines deepened between her brows.

I hesitated, glancing at Layla. I didn't want to point the finger at her people, but...

"What?" she asked, apparently reading something in my hesitation. Her slender blonde brows lifted. "You saw a demon?"

I chewed on my bottom lip for a beat and then nodded. "It seemed demonic." Devils and demons all came from the demonic plane. Some demons had horns and tails. Some devils had horns... I wasn't sure about the tails. Some looked just like people. "Whatever the thing was, it spoke to me before, and it talked to me just now." I stared at my hands. I'd been nervously twining my fingers and hadn't even noticed. "It seems to think we have something to discuss."

"You didn't recognize the creature?" Gren asked. "Maybe something from the Hellmouth?"

I shook my head. "I didn't recognize any of it. The place, the people, the...thing in the shadows."

Layla's brows lifted. "It wasn't a shadow demon, was it?"

I couldn't blame her for looking alarmed. A shadow demon had made mincemeat out of her and her guards the last time we'd encountered one. "No. I don't think so."

She relaxed fractionally.

I shoved to my feet, wiping my butt off and looking around for my staff. It appeared in front of me, and I looked up into Ferral's face. His expression was dire. "Thanks," I said, taking my weapon from him. The advocate held my gaze for a beat, just long enough to tell me he had thoughts, and then nodded and stepped back.

I took a deep breath and nodded toward the line of mounded earth ahead. "Let's get going. Daylight's burning."

10

BENEATH THE SURFACE DOUBT
RESIDES

Despite my statement, daylight didn't burn inside the Mystical Wood. Simmered, maybe. Did a slow boil. But the sheer number of massive trees, especially as we went deeper into the seemingly endless forest, kept the sun mostly at bay.

Here and there, a random spear of light filtered through the trees, speckling the ground with a hopeful kaleidoscope of pale gold. There wasn't enough light to burn off the damp coolness that made me shiver or dispel the sour stench of mildewed things.

For the first few hours, the constant darting around of glittering pixies entertained us. Their athletic, airborne dance and happy rainbow colors created a riveting performance along the way, like a tiny Broadway production designed specifically for us.

Natural creatures skittered away from our approach. At times they stopped just beyond the reach of the protective undergrowth to watch us move on by, dark eyes gleaming with speculation.

I was charmed by the array of life teeming inside the Mystical Wood. Both magical and natural. The occasional swishing of greenery hugging the tree trunks like frilly bedroom slippers made me wonder what else the woods hid.

What was the magnificent lady protecting? What didn't she want us to see?

The gloom slowly overtook the light. We were well into our first day of travel when the woods changed from a place of life and intrigue to a nebulous creature with foul breath and an icy touch. An entity whose welcoming smile never appeared, offering only a harsh twist of lips and a distrustful gaze with an icy glint.

We'd entered the Malignant Forest.

Conversation between the members of our small group all but stopped, and every step forward felt like a slow march toward Hell. The feeling was so pervasive, I started to imagine I could smell the smoke blossoming up from the unspeakable depths of the fiery pits.

In true horror trope style, the ground beneath our feet went from firm to mushy. Every footfall seemed to sink slowly into the dirt and, for the space of a single gasp, bond with the mushy surface for a beat before the ground released it.

The process of moving forward became slow, agonizing, and exhausting.

"They call it the bogs," Gren informed me during one of our frequent stops to rest our feet and legs. "The experience has been likened to endless sprints through deep sand."

I'd removed my boots and was busily rubbing my feet, trying to ease a pervasive ache in the soles. "That's exactly what it feels like. Any idea how long it lasts?"

He looked off into the distance, his expression unreadable. "The stories are mixed. I've heard some say they go on for days. Others insisted the bogs dissipated in a matter of hours. I don't know if that's a function of where you cross or if there's something else at play."

"Magical trickery?"

He nodded.

I sighed and started rubbing my calves, which felt like they were on the razor edge of cramping up on me. "I'm worried about Niele."

Gren glanced my way. "You still haven't heard from him?"

"No." I'd done a mental check-in with the gnome once every hour since we'd started off. He'd responded readily for the first several hours. But shortly before we hit the bogs, I'd lost him. He'd sounded tired in our last communication, before he went radio silent. I was starting to worry the bogs had taken him down. "How deep do they go?"

"The bogs?" Gren asked. When I nodded, he said, "Nobody's ever found the bottom."

I grimaced. "Can you imagine digging through this?"

Mavis, who was sitting under a nearby tree with her eyes closed, said, "It would be like swimming through sand."

Monty bounced around the trees, happily stalking any bug or small animal that dared to cross his path. He hadn't seemed to have a problem navigating the bog. Apparently, he was too small to sink.

We sat in silence for a bit, thinking about what Niele might be experiencing. "I need him to come up top with us. It's too dangerous for him to be down there."

"He is more comfortable traveling beneath the ground," Gren reminded me. "His perceptions are sharpest there."

"See, that's what I don't understand," I said. "Perceptions of what? A bunch of dirt and tree roots?"

Gren chuckled. "Spoken like a woman who lives above the ground." He looked thoughtful for a beat as if trying to come up with the best way to explain. Then he said, "Niele would have to explain it to you himself. I haven't experienced traveling underground. I don't even travel *on* the ground most times." He grinned.

I bumped his shoulder with my own. "I'm aware. My favorite way to fly is Air Gren. First-class accommodations all the way."

"Beverage service included?" Bev asked with a grin.

I winked at my sister, who was lying atop a large, flat rock doing leg stretches.

"Air Gren isn't that kind of airline," I told her. "It's more air and...well...Gren...than snacks and beverages."

"Don't forget the in-flight movie," Gren said, his eyes alight with humor.

"Oh," Bev said, her own eyes lighting. "Do tell."

"It was *Breathless* the last time I flew," I told her. "But I'm requesting *Dirty Dancing* for the next flight."

Bev waggled her brows.

"You know *Breathless* was a crime film, right?" Layla asked, surprising me with her knowledge of human culture.

Gren shrugged. "Don't be a snot," he told the princess. "You know the title is perfect."

Layla laughed softly.

"We should begin again," Doctor Gloom barked from a spot ten yards away, where he was crouched, seemingly examining the ground. Ferral straightened to the accompaniment of a chorus of groans from the peanut gallery. "It appears the ground is firmer close to the trees. I suggest our progress would be easier if we stayed off the path."

I grabbed my socks and shoes. *Niele? I need you to check in right away. I'm starting to get worried.*

Silence met my request. I tied my shoestrings and stood, looking out over the heavy foliage skirting the path on either side. The deeper we'd gone into the wood, the harder it had been to see the telltale mound showing the gnome's path.

I had a sudden thought. "Layla, can you communicate with your guards?"

She fell in beside me as we started off again. Her slender frame was comfortably ensconced in a pair of my yoga pants, a tee-shirt with dancing dachshunds on it, and an old pair of my sneakers. I still couldn't believe the shoes fit. The other clothing didn't have much structure to it. The pants and shirt were stretchy and slightly looser on her than they were on me, but not enough to look weird.

"I can," she responded, pulling me out of my thoughts. "Why?" The princess walked alongside the path as I did my best to wade through the foliage close to the trees. Some of the green stuff made my ankles itch, and I regretted wearing the capris-length yoga pants instead of my long ones.

"Have you made contact with them lately?"

"About an hour ago."

"And they were okay?"

She studied me for a long moment, a smile playing around her lips. "Why, Madam Lares, are you worried about my devils?"

I feigned offense. "Of course I am," I told her. "You don't really believe I want them to be hurt, do you?"

She released the smile she'd been holding back. "Maybe just a little?"

I laughed. "No. I've grown kind of fond of old Matt. He's just my kind of cranky." I threw Ferral a glance, lifting my brows, and she laughed.

"You do seem to attract the crotchety ones."

"I heard that," Ferral barked out from the front of the line.

We laughed. "He has a dog's hearing," I told Layla.

"I heard that too."

She shook her head. "But, seriously, why do you ask?"

Sighing, I said, "I've been trying to reach Niele for the last hour." Or more. I'd lost track of time since we'd entered the bogs. I felt as if we'd been fighting the sucking stuff for days. But the sun was just setting, so we hadn't even been in the woods for a full day yet. "I'm worried something's happened to him."

Layla went silent. I assumed she was thinking about my statement. But, a moment later, she sent me a worried glance, and I realized she'd been communicating with her guards. "Matthew and Glenn have not felt the quivering of the earth beneath their feet for some time."

I took that to mean they couldn't feel the vibrations Niele caused as he dug through the soil. Panic twisted like a tornado in my chest. "How far ahead of us are they?"

"A mile. Maybe two." Layla's guards were our advance scouts.

I lifted my head, calling out to Ferral. "Niele's in trouble. We need to find him."

Can you go airborne? I asked Gren. *See if you can spot where the gnome mound stops.*

Too many trees, he responded. *I'd have to go above them. My wings are too wide to fly beneath the trees.*

I thought about my options. Lifting my gaze, I searched for the raven. Ray had been flying ahead of us, perching high on the occasional tree to greet us with a strident call before taking off again. I realized I hadn't seen him for a while either. "Ray!" I called out, the sound of my shout swallowed by the sheer density of the forest. I whistled.

Monty cocked his head at me, his tail swiping across the dirt.

"The raven's not a dog," Layla said, looking amused.

"I know. But sometimes he responds to a whistle."

The princess frowned. "There's something…"

Ferral approached, interrupting her. His expression was dire. "I'll change. As my hound, I can scent the gnome."

I nodded. "Good. Keep me apprised."

Ferral shifted in a flash of silver light and took off running, nose to the ground.

I looked at the witches. "Can you do a spell to find Niele?"

They shared a glance.

"No," Bev said. "But we can search for hostile magic."

Layla nodded. "You'll find it. I've been feeling strange magic on the air for a while. It seems dark."

"If we can locate where Niele was lost, we can possibly tap into the magic to figure out what happened," Mavis added.

"Okay," I said. "Let's go then."

The sun had almost entirely disappeared and we hadn't heard from Niele or Ray. Ferral had checked in once with bad news. He'd followed Niele's scent trail for several miles, but had lost it as suddenly as if someone had sliced it off with a blade.

He'd doubled back, looking for a spot where the gnome might have diverged in his route, but found nothing. At a loss for what to do next, the advocate described his location and agreed to wait for us to come to him so we could regroup.

Layla reached out to her men and called them back.

"It's too dark to see anything on the ground," I complained to Gren.

Bev, Mavis, and Layla were walking up ahead. Monty trotted in front of me, his nose to the ground as if he were following Ferral's lead. Despite weariness and concern for Niele, I smiled at my little dog. He might weigh less than twenty-five pounds, but his intentions were wolf-sized.

Where are you? I asked Ferral. *We passed the triple-trunked tree a while ago.*

A large form stepped out of the trees, surprising a gasp out of me.

Right in front of you, the advocate said, censure in his voice. With a dip of his head, the big dog turned around and trotted back through the trees. Monty took off running after him, quickly disappearing into the darkness. What little sun there had been disappeared completely in the densely wooded section Ferral guided us through. Finally, I gave up on seeing anything without help. Tugging my backpack off, I dug inside for the oversized flashlight I'd brought along. I could hear the others doing the same thing behind me.

As I fumbled with the button to turn the flashlight on, light flared brightly through the trees ahead, followed by a "whoosh" of air and a yelp.

Gren took off running.

"Monty!" I slammed my thumb into the button, and illumination flared into the darkness in a wide arc that painted the black trunks and dense canopy of leaves and branches overhead in an eerie light.

I scanned it over the ground in front of me and saw open ground. No Monty. No Ferral.

I took off running. "Monty, come!"

Ferral? I screamed in my mind. *What just happened?*

Static, like broken voices on a cell phone with limited range, flitted through my mind and then went silent.

I ducked under a low-hanging branch, catching my sneaker on a tangle of roots that snaked along the ground like veins. I steadied myself on a tree that had dense, sharp bark, jerking away with a hiss when it slashed the skin of my palms.

The flashlight flew from my grip and hit the ground several feet away, spinning in a circle of weak illumination. The shifting light created a disorienting sensation that gave everything in the small clearing a preternatural aspect.

There was no sign of Gren, Ferral, or my dog.

"Curse, curse, swear!" I yelled in frustration. Shoving away from the tree, I scooped up the flashlight.

Layla pushed through into the small clearing right behind me. "What happened?" Her eyes looked enormous in the refractive illumination from her flashlight. "I heard you yell."

"Did you see that flash? Hear the whoosh of air?" I asked.

Layla frowned. The artificial illumination from the flashlight exaggerated the shadows in her face and made her look like a comic book villain. "I didn't hear anything."

Bev and Mavis came into the clearing. "We didn't hear it either," Mavis assured me.

"There was this big flash of light, and then air rushed past me. It was like when a vacuum seal is broken, you know?"

Mavis and Bev nodded.

I scoured the ground with the light. "There's Niele's mound," I said.

"Why would he have turned off the path?" Bev asked. She pointed to the barrier of trees. "The roots would be impossible here. There had to be a reason why he changed direction."

"Maybe just to get away from the bogs," Gren offered as he joined us in the clearing. "I searched all around this area. There's no sign of the advocate or your little hero."

Remembering what Ferral had said, I followed Niele's mound with my light, scanning it to a spot about five feet in front of me. There, it just stopped.

The dirt was smooth, unbroken. "He didn't burst from the ground," I said, half to myself.

Layla crouched down beside me, smoothing a hand over the hard earth. "Maybe he went deeper?"

That was a possibility. "But why would he do that?"

"To avoid the worst of the tree roots?" Mavis suggested.

"But, what just happened to Ferral and Monty?" I asked. We all scanned our lights around the perimeter, then over the entire clearing. There was no sign of them. "Maybe they left the clearing," I said. "Let's keep walking."

As I took a step toward the far side of the clearing, a strident "Caw!" pierced the night, startling me. I looked up to find a large black bird diving toward my head. Throwing up my arms, I covered my face and stumbled backward.

The air sizzled. Light flared around me, painful in its brightness, and I threw out my arms as magic bit at my flesh.

I had just enough time to see my companions' wide eyes and hear them start to scream my name before the world turned silver and then darkened to pitch black.

11

INTO A WORLD OF TERROR DEEP

The raven slammed into my chest. The impact sent me staggering backward, arms flailing for something to stop my fall.

Wings flapped against my face, forcing me to close my eyes as I hit the ground, taking a painful jolt to my sacroiliac. I yelped in pain, shoving at the feathers still slapping me around the head and shoulders.

"Pee!" yelled Ray.

I gave him a shove, and he flew up and away from me, only to land on my shoulder a beat later.

"Ahhh," I moaned, breathing through the pain. "I think you broke my tailbone."

Ray danced sideways on my shoulder, lifting his wings and smacking me on the cheek again. "Rude!"

"You're rude," I told him, feeling silly for arguing

with a bird. Looking around, I suddenly realized the world wasn't dark anymore. I was also surrounded by rock and sitting on hard, sandy ground. High above me, a clear blue sky formed the backdrop for a brutally hot and painfully bright ball of golden light. "Where am I?"

"Woof! Woof!"

Ray lifted off my shoulder with an outraged caw and flew to a spot on the rock wall high above me.

Ignoring the bird, I grinned at the small, black and tan projectile galloping my way. Monty hit me in the chest, tongue already out and slathering my face. "Hey, buddy. I thought I'd lost you."

Ferral walked around a jutting wall of rock and stared down at me. His pretty silver eyes narrowed as he shot the cuffs of his pristine white shirt. "What are you doing down there?"

I gave him a quelling look that didn't subdue him one little bit. "You might have warned me."

"That would have been hard to do since I was here and you were there."

I moved Monty off my lap so I could stand.

"Where exactly are we?" I asked, gawking around. Did I smell the ocean?

Ferral's dense blond brows lowered. "I'm guessing it's where Niele ended up, as well as where our quarry is currently squatting."

"Our quarry? You mean the crone?"

He nodded.

There was a flash of light behind me, followed by another complaint from Ray. The raven, who'd apparently gone to get the rest of our crew, shot past me and back up to his rocky perch. Bev and Mavis stumbled in, followed quickly by Layla. The three women ran smack into the rock wall, and a comedy of body bumping and outraged yelps ensued.

When they managed to untangle themselves, they glanced dazedly at Ferral and me.

Gren walked out next, his hands shoved into the pockets of his jeans and his expression amused. He dropped a shiny black feather onto the sand, spurring an outraged caw from the raven above our heads.

"Where *were* you?" I asked my erstwhile protector.

"Looking for you," he responded vaguely.

I gave the three ladies a little finger wave. "I'm glad the band's back together."

"What is this place?" Mavis asked, her gaze sliding toward the bright sun overhead. "Are we in Wonderland?"

"Or Oz?" Bev added helpfully.

"Maybe a bit of both," Ferral agreed. "Some of us might need a brain, and I could definitely see the crone lopping off our heads." He tugged on the lapels of his suit coat and sighed. "Well then. I guess we must forge onward. Come along. This is our yellow brick road." He spun on his heel and walked out of sight beyond the jutting rock.

We looked at each other and I shrugged. "Onward ho," I told them, following the advocate through what appeared to be a maze carved into a small mountain.

Several hours and many false starts and dead ends later, we somehow managed to emerge from the maze, only to find ourselves standing on a beach.

The shoreline stretched as far as the eye could see in both directions and was a mile deep in places, the sand as white and pristine as a fairytale. The azure blue water was glassy and unnaturally quiet. No frothy waves beat upon the sand. No constant rumble of agitated water filled the air.

Overall, it had the feeling of being a mirage. But, when I stuck my toe into the water, I found it real enough. And blissfully warm.

The only bird I could see in any direction was the black raven that had, of course, beaten us out of the maze since he could fly above it. At the moment, he was flying low over the water as if he thought he was a seagull.

"What's he doing?" I asked no one in particular.

Gren shrugged. "He's *your* familiar." An enormous set of charcoal gray wings snapped out to either side of my protector. They were gorgeous, shimmering in the sunlight with an iridescent gleam, and I realized it was the first time I'd really looked at them. The only other time I'd seen Gren's wings during daylight, I'd been under attack by a demon and hadn't really had the luxury of examining them. They were stunning.

"I'll head up and see what I can from above."

We all watched as he leaped into the sky and, with three pulses of his powerful wings, was thirty feet in the air and moving over the glassy ocean. Gren traveled a quarter of a mile off shore and began to circle like a giant vulture stalking a juicy corpse. I grimaced at the thought, wondering when I'd become so morbid.

I needed to stop hanging out with demons and monsters.

Gren suddenly speared his body downward and, to our mutual shock if the chorus of gasps were any indication, plunged into the ocean with nary a splash.

"What is he doing?" I murmured to myself.

Mavis and Bev came up beside me. "Um, Aggy?" my sister asked.

I shook my head. "No clue."

We waited in silence for several moments. I was starting to worry Gren wasn't coming back when the water suddenly geysered upward, and he burst into the sky.

Silvery droplets sprayed away from his wings as he spread them and headed in our direction. Gren landed gracefully, his movements lithe and agile as he walked out of the landing. His gaze locked onto mine as he approached, reminding me of a predatory animal stalking the female he'd chosen for a mate.

The thought made me shudder with delight, and I had to scold myself to get a grip.

"The crone lives beneath the ocean," he told us as he stopped in front of the group. "In a castle built of magic."

"A castle?" Mavis asked, clearly surprised.

Gren nodded. "Cayleigh Castle is really quite spectacular. I believe it was fashioned with Atlantis in mind."

"Did you see the aged one?" Ferral asked my protector.

Gren shook his head. "I thought it best to come fetch you before I went in search of her." He glanced toward the sky. "It is getting late. We'll either need to enter the castle before full dark or wait until morning."

I followed his glance and saw that the sun was low on the horizon. "Why?" I asked. "We have waterproof flashlights." In my new line of work, I had to be prepared for anything.

Gren shook his head. "It's not illumination I'm worried about. The light within the dome would be enough to guide us. It's the sea monsters."

There was a collective gulp through our group.

"Sea monsters?" Layla asked, her eyes wide.

"Of course, they aren't real," Ferral said. "Sea monsters don't exist. But they might as well be real. The crone's magic is ancient and powerful."

"So, you're saying these things are like giant, terrifying guard dogs?" I asked him.

"Essentially. Think Cerberus, the three-headed dog guarding the gates of the underworld," he said.

"If they don't exist, does that mean they're mostly just for show?" Mavis asked.

"Unfortunately, no," my protector answered. "The crone's magic makes them very deadly."

"Wait," Bev said. "If the crone drew Niele here, which has to be what happened, that means she wanted us here, right? Maybe she won't sic the monsters on us."

Gren shook his head. "We are intruders on her land. The crone doesn't welcome anyone without forcing them to prove themselves worthy of her. In her mind, battling her monsters beneath the sea is the perfect way for us to prove our worthiness."

Ah, so that was how it was going to be. The crone intended to test my mettle as the newcomer in the magical world. Just ducky.

"None of this matters," Ferral said, drawing our attention back to him. "Because we are not going to bump up against the monsters." He glanced toward the impossibly large, unrealistically bright sun. "As long as we reach the castle before nightfall, we're safe. We have two hours at a minimum to achieve our goal. We will not be faced with the leviathans."

"Well then," Layla said. "We'd best get going."

"What about Matthew and Glenn," I asked her.

The princess pointed toward the opening to the maze, where the two lost guards were just emerging. Ray shot out of the maze over their heads, his cries piercing in the silence of the strange place. "They will be accompanying us."

"I'm not sure that's a good idea," Gren said. "Historically, the crone has not been fond of the lost ones."

So much for Layla being honest with me about the crone's feelings regarding the lost ones. I sent a frown her way.

Layla's pretty features turned stubborn. "As I said before, I have no awareness of any bad feelings toward my people. The guards come with us."

Gren looked to me for support.

I hated to disappoint him, but I was going to, despite her lying to me. "Layla's right. If we're going into this particular lion's den, it sounds as if we're going to need all the allies we can muster."

"Yes," Layla agreed, staring out over the too-smooth ocean with a worried expression. "We are going to need *much* help."

Why did her words, and the look on her face, make my blood suddenly go cold?

We argued again over the best way to make our way to the crone's underwater castle. Despite Ferral's words, it wasn't as simple as just avoiding nightfall. A magic-user who was as powerful as the crone wouldn't simply allow a bunch of people to march into her domain.

After all, there was a reason she'd put her castle at the bottom of the ocean. She likely wasn't a fan of having neighbors stop by asking for a cup of seaweed. Gren admitted there were complicating factors in getting to the dome surrounding the castle.

The leviathans weren't the crone's only safeguards. According to Gren, there was a platoon of enormous sharks. Deadly undercurrents. And the castle's own defensive system, which included a type of catapulting system that threw lightning bolts.

Piece of cake.

"We can't approach it directly," Gren said. "Our best chance is to come at it from underneath."

"Where's Niele when we need him?" I mumbled. That gave me a thought. I lifted my gaze, sliding it around the area while trying to call him. *Niele? Are you here?*

Nothing. If the crone drew him to her, he was probably already in the castle. I shook my head. "We can't approach from underneath the castle," I told him. "We don't have Niele."

"There might be another way," Ferral said, his gaze on a line of rocks about thirty feet off shore.

"What are you thinking?" Layla asked.

"Wait here," he told the group. In a flash of silver light, he became his moon hound and padded across the sand.

Monty trotted after him.

I shared a look with Bev and Mavis, rolling my eyes at his uncooperative ways.

"What do you suppose the dog's up to?" Layla asked.

Shrugging, I said, "We rarely know. He'll tell us when he's ready, I guess."

We watched the huge gray dog trot up to the water's edge and then into the water. I yelled at Monty to stay where he was. His tail drooped as he watched Ferral doggy-paddle away.

Five minutes later, the advocate pulled himself up onto the ridge and shook the water out of his fur.

Monty stood at the edge of the water and barked at his canine buddy.

Ferral walked along the ridge for a moment, nose down and sniffing.

"What is he looking for?" Bev muttered. Since it was a rhetorical question, nobody responded.

Then suddenly, the hound was just...gone.

We took off running toward the waterline. But,

Ferral suddenly reappeared out of thin air. He stood on the rock wall, his elegant gray muzzle pointed in our direction and his silver gaze coolly observing us as we panicked.

With a flash of silver light, he returned to his human form. "I've found a way to get past most of the defenses. You'll need to wade to this wall. We can get into the castle from here."

12

OUR LARES MUST HER PATIENCE
KEEP

I stood in the center of what looked like one of those viewing centers for fish in an aquarium. The ocean spread out around me as if displayed behind pristine glass.

Except there was no glass.

I tentatively stuck out a hand and touched the invisible wall between me and some really intimidating fish.

My fingers went right through the "wall" and came back wet.

I swallowed hard, eyeing a particularly hungry-looking shark heading our way. "There's nothing to stop the fish from coming inside this thing," I told Ferral.

He shook his head. "Watch."

The shark came on, heading right for me. Its small eyes were cold, black, and dead. When it got to within five feet, that enormous maw opened wide, showing a lethal array of sharp, triangular teeth.

Someone behind me squeaked. My heart pounded against my ribs, but my feet wouldn't move. One second the shark was swimming lazily in our direction, and the next, it attacked, shooting forward to snap its jaws over unsuspecting flesh.

I screamed. Ducked. And watched in horror as a fist-sized bright yellow fish was lost between those massive jaws.

The shark swam on past, as insubstantial as a wish, and continued on out the other side of the passageway.

"Goddess guild a gourd," I whispered.

Ferral chuckled meanly. I threw him a glare.

"Come along," he said to the group. "We're wasting time."

We took off again, walking quickly as the busy ocean world around us went on about its business. We were one short in our little group. Ray had refused to follow us into the passage, so we'd left him to entertain himself until we returned.

Monty soon found a fun pastime, lunging at the tiny fish swimming around our magical passageway and trying to snatch them out of the water.

Fortunately, he was too slow to catch anything. But I lived in fear that he'd accidentally fall completely through the passage walls. "What happens if we go through these walls?" I asked the advocate.

He shrugged. "I don't think you can come back inside once you completely leave." He eyed me. "My advice is not to try it."

"Good advice," I told him, gently tugging on Monty's leash to bring him closer to my feet.

The castle lay straight ahead, its jade walls and copper roof sparkling in the last of the day's light. A seaweed forest rose up around it, swaying in the currents, with coral skirts that lent a pop of color to the already stunning environment.

The central area of the structure had a domical copper roof and the wings curved away from it like tentacles. The castle had been built to look like a monstrous octopus, and the constant movement of the water made it look as if it were moving.

Schools of rainbow-hued fish dashed and darted around us, their vibrant scales glinting under the rays of golden light piercing the ocean's depths. It was an unnatural light, since we were deep enough that I doubted true sunlight could reach us. But it was beautiful, whether real or not.

Deeper water lurked at the far edges of the scene, the black water creating shadows that no doubt hid many things I didn't want to encounter. The thought made me walk a little faster, my gaze continually darting over the beautiful but foreign scene spread around me.

Walking on the sparkling white sand was harder than it should have been, reminding me of the bogs we'd fought our way through in the forest. My calves burned and, as I sped up, my breathing became labored. I thought, at first, that it was just me. That I was out of shape. But then I realized everyone was having the same experience.

I glanced at Gren. "Low oxygen," he explained.

I frowned. *Curse, swear!* Like I needed something new to worry about.

After walking an hour or more, we were only halfway to the castle. I couldn't shake the feeling that the beautiful octopus was moving away from us as we moved closer.

Adding to the distance issue, I was pretty sure the light from above was fading. I glanced up every few seconds, eyeing the dimming glow with concern.

Gren leaned close as if he was going to whisper sweet nothings into my ear. "The sun is nearly set," he said. "Prepare to do battle."

Okay, not exactly what I'd been expecting him to say. But accurate. A moment later, the shadowy pools of darkness around us shivered, rolled, and spit three of the most monstrous creations I'd ever seen into the growing darkness.

"Leviathan," Layla murmured behind me, her voice wobbling with fear.

"Leviathan," Ferral agreed.

Curse, curse, swear, curse, swear, swear curse!

Stunned silence infected our little group for a few beats as we watched the massive creatures gather themselves and swim in our direction.

The silence throbbed with fear. My own heart had gone locomotive on me, trying to beat its way out of the cage of my ribs. I glanced down at Monty, wishing I'd left him at home. He could have had a long, happy life with Trish and Luke, loved and safe.

Tears burned my eyes, and I wanted to fold into a puddle on the floor. Maybe if we hid behind the softly waving forest of seaweed, those things would just pass us by, unseen.

My eyes widened. "How well do those things see?" I asked Ferral.

He shrugged. "I don't really know that much about them. But they live in the dark. It's why they don't come out during daylight."

A metaphorical lightbulb flared to life in my head. "Quick, everybody. Flashlights."

I didn't have to tell them twice. Everyone started digging in their backpacks for the flashlights we'd brought.

Layla clutched her light and threw a look toward Matthew and Glenn. Without a word, they gave her a shallow bow and flung themselves through the invisible barrier. They swam fast. Faster than their bulky bodies would suggest was possible.

I looked at Layla.

"They'll buy us some time," she said, her voice void of emotion.

I shook my head, my eyes following the two lost ones as they launched into battle with the massive sea creatures. They looked like guppies taking on a pod of killer whales. There was no way they'd come out of it alive. But if the worst happened, they would have gone to their deaths without hesitation in the protection of their princess.

There was a lesson for me in that. I needed to ovary the heck up.

Right on cue, my own little hero threw himself at the invisible membrane separating us from the ocean. I barely managed to pull the leash taut before he barreled through the barrier, barking and growling, his hackles up. Monty's head, shoulders, and half his chest were in the water before I stopped him, hauling him back into the passage.

One of the sea creatures glided effortlessly toward us through the murky water. The thing had a turtle-like shell on its back and plates protecting its long, narrow head. Its snakelike tail had spikes that sliced the water on either side as it swam. The beak-like snout came to a point so sharp it looked as if it could puncture the castle walls or impale living flesh.

The size of a blue whale, the leviathan covered the distance so quickly that two strokes of its paddle-like front legs transported it the distance of several city blocks. It was almost on us before we managed to react.

"Lights on!" I screamed, fumbling my flashlight in my panic as I watched certain death cut ruthlessly through the water, aiming for us.

One by one, we lifted our lights and shone them directly into the monster's small, slitted eyes. With a roar that sent shock waves through the ocean around us, the thing jerked its head up and slammed the water with its paddles, skimming just over the top of our passageway as it went on by.

The world shook on its axis, rolling chaotically beneath our feet. With nothing to brace against, we fell to the ground under the violent thrashing. As soon as we hit bottom, we shot back to our feet and started running toward the castle.

The two lost ones thrashing around in the murky water with the leviathans would likely not survive, but I wouldn't allow their sacrifice to be for nothing.

We actually made some headway before the second monster broke away from Layla's men, leaving Matthew hanging limply in the water, unmoving.

"Goddess, reward him in his next life," I murmured, digging in to run faster. My chest heaved, every breath like a knife piercing my over-taxed lungs. But adrenaline gave my feet wings, and the sight of what was coming for us made me forget I needed to breathe.

The eel-like creature was the purest black and had glowing yellow eyes. Lightning flared from its whip-like tail. The monster's maw was as wide as its head, its jaws lined in jagged rows of needlelike teeth that were so long they stuck out of its mouth even when it was closed.

I watched in horror as the water around the leviathan sizzled with white-hot energy, realizing it could kill us from afar simply by electrifying the water around us.

I prayed the magical membrane that enclosed the passageway could withstand electricity. If it couldn't, we were farked.

The creature glided toward us, its streamlined body cutting effortlessly through the murk. The sun had gone completely away overhead, leaving the water around us cold and black. The menacing darkness masked both known and unknown dangers.

I shuddered as the blackness surrounded us, the invisible barrier making me feel as if I stood unprotected in its midst. We ran as if our lives depended on it. Because they did. Glancing over my shoulder every few seconds, I couldn't seem to look away as the glowing yellow eyes cutting the darkness headed straight for us.

It came on. Twenty yards. Ten yards. Five yards. Mere feet...

"Lights!" I screamed. Down by my feet, Monty snarled and snapped, fighting my grip in an attempt to get to the monster. My knuckles were white around the leash, bloodless around the flashlight.

Light flashed into the darkness. The monster shot toward us, unaffected. Its fierce yellow gaze took the light and absorbed it, creating shadows that obscured the water around it.

But a residual glow fanned out from the monstrous eel and illuminated the secondary threat we hadn't even seen.

The monster we'd chased off with our flashlights opened its maw and slammed into the passageway, ripping it from its magical moorings and sending us careening into the unending blackness of the ocean.

Screams of fear and helplessness ping-ponged through the wildly whipping structure. Monty yelped, and I wrapped myself around him, tucking into a fetal position as the erratic movements threw me from side to side, lifting me off the ground and smashing me back down. The world beyond the passage was topsy turvy. Terrifying images of teeth, glowing eyes, and claws, along with sizzling arcs of electricity, flashed past so quickly that my mind barely registered them.

We slammed into the sand and rolled, bodies smashing against screaming bodies, our voices raw and our bodies torn and bruised.

A pair of hard, warm arms tugged Monty and me into a buffering embrace. Gren wrapped himself protectively around us, his familiar scent and warm breath creating a cocoon that allowed me to stop shrieking and finally use my brain.

A moment later, the passage stopped spinning and rolling and settled onto the ocean floor. A golden glow pierced the murkiness, and I peeked beneath Gren's arm and saw a deep green forest of waving seaweed obscuring us from the rest of the ocean.

"Cut the light!" I shouted.

Somebody scrambled for the offending flash-light, and we lay there in silence, cataloging our injuries and waiting for the other shoe to drop. I tapped Gren's arms. "I'm okay. You can release us now."

He hesitated. I listened to the rapid pounding of his heart. "I don't want to," he finally said.

I couldn't help it. I had to laugh. Gently shoving at his arms, I said. "Please?"

With a long-suffering sigh, my protector slowly released his grip on us. Monty squirmed away, tail wagging and eyes bright. I swear to the goddess, the canine's ability to recoup from trauma was amazing beyond words.

I glanced around the sprawled forms of my group, trying to see the damage. All but one of us was moving. Squinting at the unmoving form, I panicked. "Mom!"

Bev seemed to jerk back to awareness. She

turned toward the immobile Mavis and gasped. "Goddess, no!"

I crawled over to Mavis, dropping down next to her and lowering my head to feel her breath against my face. "She's breathing," I told my sister, who, even in the low light, appeared gray and colorless.

She gently slapped Mavis's face. "Mom? Wake up."

Nothing. I felt along Mavis's arms and legs. Bev ran her hands over Mavis's face and head, coming away with blood on her fingers.

"She has a head wound," Bev told us, her voice slightly hysterical. "She needs medical help."

"Unfortunately, she *is* our medical help," I responded. I stilled as my fingers encountered a warm wetness along Mavis's side. "There's something else," I said, reaching toward Bev. "Give me your flash."

She hesitated. "Won't the light bring those things down here?"

"I'll be quick."

Gren handed us something soft that smelled of him. "Hold this over it to contain the light."

Bev took the shirt and positioned it over the flashlight like a canopy. I flipped on the light and felt my world go sideways.

I must have made a sound because Layla leaned in, trying to see. "What is it?"

I eyed the triangular yellow object embedded in

Mavis's flesh, fear battling horror as I fought to breathe. "It looks like a tooth. One of those..." I swallowed hard. "One of those things got her."

Bev deflated, Gren's shirt sagging to obscure my view of the wound. "We need to get it out of her." She reached for the tooth, and I grabbed her arm, stopping her.

"No. Wait. We can't take it out."

"Why not?" Her voice was clogged with tears, her movements angry and erratic. "It's doing something to her. She won't wake up."

I shared her fear, but I knew something that scared me even more than having that thing sticking into Mavis. "I'm worried that if we pull it out, she'll bleed to death." My voice broke on the last word. Mavis's death wasn't something I wanted to even consider.

A tense silence throbbed between us as Bev considered what I'd said.

"I'm afraid there's something else," Gren said, his deep voice startling in the quiet.

I turned to look at him. I couldn't see his features, but I could read the tightness in his shoulders. "What?" I asked, my voice thick with despair.

"It appears the advocate is missing."

13

BUGS UNDER GLASS, OUR
WARRIORS BE

"I have to do something!" I said much too loudly.

Gren had pulled me away from the others to discuss our options. At that moment, I was ready to just leave the bubble we were currently trapped in and swim to the castle, which, by some miracle, was situated above us on a massive sandbar. We'd fallen into the murky depths of that black water I'd felt such apprehension about earlier.

Dark shapes, some large enough to make my heart palpitate in an alarming way, moved past us through the inky liquid. The constant swaying of the seaweed beds gave the impression of perpetual movement and offered a prime hiding spot for all manner of predatory creatures.

In other words, I'd landed smack dab into my worst nightmare.

"You're not in Rome, Madam Lares," he

reminded me. "I'm not sure your magic even works here."

I thought about the staff I'd stuffed into my pack. "I'm willing to give it a try. We just need to make a plan and get going on it. Mavis needs help."

He held up his hands. "I know you're worried about the witch."

"You mean my mom?" I asked angrily.

He lifted his hands, palms out. "Of course. My apologies. I sometimes forget your connection."

I bit back the superhuman rage riding me at our untenable situation, closing my eyes to reach for calm. Gren was trying to help. Having me snapping and barking at him like Monty wasn't doing anything to solve our problems. "I don't know how you can forget," I finally said to him. "It's not like we have any stress in our lives."

He stared at me a moment as if unsure whether I was scolding or joking, then finally laughed. The sound warmed some of the ice that had accumulated in my belly. "No, lovely Aggy. No stress at all."

Scrubbing my palms over my face, I filled my lungs and emptied them in a long, slow exhalation. "Okay. Options. How are we going to get to the castle and get Mavis some help with those things out there and the crone's defensive systems?"

He glanced toward the three women down the passage from us. "Even if we could make it with her in tow, it's not safe to carry her through the water.

She's unconscious and bleeding. The predators you see moving around out there would be on her in a heartbeat."

I shuddered at the thought. "Can we bind her wound?"

He shook his head. "Not effectively enough." His gaze skimmed the seaweed around us. "If we stay quiet and inside this passage, we are actually relatively safe until morning."

"What if Mavis doesn't have until morning?" I asked, icy fingers of fear digging into my middle.

"I understand your fear, Aggy. What I'm proposing is that I swim to the castle and get help. You will all be safe here until I return."

I thought about that suggestion, not liking it. Despite the blustery terror infusing me, I knew Gren would be safer if I went with him. I shook my head. "We need to embrace the buddy system. We'll be safer if I go with you."

"Absolutely not!" He moved closer, his tall body tense with emotion. "I won't allow you to endanger yourself unnecessarily."

"It's not your decision to make," I fired back.

"Aggy?"

Bev's voice, though quiet, cut through our back-and-forth like a blade. We both turned to look at her.

I couldn't see her features in the darkness, but I saw the nervous twining of her fingers and her stooped shoulders and heard the quiver in her voice that spoke volumes about her fear. "Mom's cold and shivering. I think she's losing too much blood." Her voice broke on the words, and she clamped her lips together as if she was afraid the words would come out as sobs.

I walked over and embraced my sister, feeling her unease in the tightness of her muscles. "It's going to be fine," I told her. "We're going to get help."

"Where?" Bev asked, tears thick in her voice. She lifted her hands and looked around. "We're in the middle of a goddess-bedamned magical ocean surrounded by predators. How are we going to get help?"

I clasped her cold hands in mine, giving them a reassuring squeeze. "I'm going to give her what healing I can, and then Gren and I are going to swim to the castle. You'll be safe here in the bubble as long as you keep a low profile. We'll bring help back as soon as we can. You have my promise."

Her shoulders squared, and her chin came up. It wasn't as if she believed my happy talk, more like she realized how weak and whiny she sounded and was offended by it. She nodded. "Okay. I'll get busy creating a cloaking spell for the bubble."

"Perfect." I squeezed her arm and moved past her to where Layla bent over Mavis, her hand resting on my surrogate mom's chest. Light flared gently from beneath her palm.

The lost princess looked up as I approached. "I

don't have healing energy, per se, but this realm seems to strengthen what little I have." She removed her hand. "I eased her breathing, but she's going to need real healing soon."

I dropped to my knees and placed both of my palms on Mavis, covering the wound on her head and the one in her side. Closing my eyes, I reached for the core of my magic, tugging it forward with a thought to heal rather than destroy.

I'd only ever used my energy to try to heal a couple of times and hadn't been very successful with it, but I'd never had so much on the line before.

The urgent sound of arguing, spoken in harsh whispers, filtered toward me as I began to ease my magic into Mavis. I forced my mind away from the fighting, trusting Bev and Gren to manage their own issues.

Mavis jumped as my energy entered her body, arching her back and shuddering under its impact.

Gritting my teeth, I realized Layla was right. My magic was stronger in the crone's realm. I needed to work harder to soften it. I gently fed tiny bits of magic into Mavis for several moments, my eyes closed and my muscles rigid with the effort of keeping the flow of energy at the right level to heal and not harm.

Beneath the strain, something wonderous was happening. I envisioned the torn tissue reknitting itself, and felt the moment when the wound rejected the foreign object embedded in it. Slowly, the blood began to slow and clot.

When I felt I'd done all I could, I eased the magic back. As soon as I pulled it free of Mavis's body, exhaustion hit, and I sagged downward.

Warm, strong hands caught me before I hit the ground, easing me gently to the sand. I felt Gren's warmth a second before his lips touched mine. "Sleep, beautiful Aggy. Rest. Trust your friends to carry your load."

I was so tired. My body was limp and unresponsive. My brain was sloggy, fighting to close down for a bit. So, I missed the message hidden in his words. As he'd no doubt known I would.

Just before I fell into a deep, restorative sleep, just the tiniest spark of panic flared to life in my brain. It jolted my senses. I struggled to open my eyes...to question...to argue...but the thread of panic wasn't enough to overcome the weariness.

And it was lost as a coma-like sleep overtook me.

L icking. Snorfling. More licking. When the warm tongue bathing my face threatened to insert itself up my left nostril, I jolted fully awake. "Okay, buddy," I told Monty, gently shoving him away. "You can stop now."

His tail whipped from side to side in happy

exuberance as I pushed to my elbows, looking around. For a moment, I forgot where we were and why I needed to get off the ground and do something.

Fast.

I shot upright, my gaze sliding along the bubble, which seemed to be lit a bit better than when I'd gone to sleep. Mavis slept beside me, her chest rising and falling in a good rhythm. I couldn't see her color, but she didn't seem to be in any pain, and her muscles were relaxed.

Rolling to my knees, I felt her forehead and checked her pulse. No fever. Her pulse seemed strong.

I relaxed, sitting back on my heels with a sigh. At least we'd settled one problem for the moment. Then my head shot up, and I found Layla a distance away, standing very still and staring out at the shadowed black water. She looked pensive.

"Where are they?" I hadn't meant for my voice to come out angry, but it did. At that moment, I realized I *was* angry. Very angry. I clung to the anger because the alternative was worse. Bone-chilling terror. Bev and Gren might have been eaten by any number of predators that swam around and around the castle as if they existed in an enormous moat. "They left without me, didn't they?"

Layla didn't look away from the midnight-hued canvas in front of her. I supposed it could be soothing to look into the dark. If only death wasn't a constantly swimming promise beyond the non-existent walls of our prison.

Or was it a refuge?

It was both, I decided.

"Yes," she said simply.

"How long?"

She finally turned my way, her eyes dark pools as black as the water around us. "How long for what?"

"How long ago did they leave?"

"A couple of hours, I think." She shrugged, turning back to the water. "I have no way to gauge the time."

It was then that I realized she was sad. She'd sent her people to their deaths. "I'm sorry about Matthew and Glenn."

Layla didn't flinch. She didn't respond at all. That was how I knew she was breaking slowly apart inside.

"They saved our lives," I told her.

She cleared her throat and said, "They served their princess well."

Monty licked the back of my ankle. I reached down and plucked him off the ground, burying my face in his fur. He smelled sweet as always, with a touch of salt and sand he'd picked up from our current adventure.

Pain twisted my belly as I remembered someone else we'd lost. "Did you see Ferral...leave?" I couldn't bring myself to admit he'd been taken, or washed out of the bubble as it spun away, unmoored by the magic that had been anchoring it.

I preferred to believe he'd had a plan and set it into motion. In desperation, I tried calling him. *Ferral?* I waited. There was no response. It had been too much to hope for.

"I did not see it," Layla responded. She turned to me. "He was a good man. A warrior. He also served his mistress well."

I nodded, thinking how much the lost princess had changed since her mojo had been ripped away from her. She'd lost more than her devilish physique that day. She'd lost her identity, her confidence, her...well...spirit. She was quiet. Reserved. Sad.

I blinked. The sadness was the hardest thing to accept. The Layla I'd known had been brassy and confident. She'd been no victim but a powerful creature who'd taken great pride in kicking Ferral's "furry butt." I smiled at the memory. "After we get through this, you and I need to talk," I said. If there was a way to help her, I intended to do it.

She shrugged, lost in her observation of the water.

Monty was staring out at the moving shadows. He'd been quiet, alert rather than alarmed. When he softly growled, I glanced outside the air bubble to see what had caused him to react.

I saw nothing beyond the perpetually swaying seaweed.

Layla and I stood quietly for several beats. I hadn't been expecting her to respond to my suggestion of a future discussion, but even if I had, I wouldn't have expected what she finally said.

"I can't swim."

I turned to her, surprise clear in my expression. "Oh." She was feeling guilty for not offering to make the trip up to the castle. No wonder she was brooding.

"I'm not much good to anybody here," I admitted. "I'm totally out of my element. That's why I'm mad they left me behind. Swimming and begging the crone for help are two things I could have done."

She nodded.

Monty growled again.

We stood in companionable silence for a few minutes. I relaxed, feeling as if admitting my failure and giving her the gift of understanding had closed an open wound I'd been carrying around since taking off on our search for the crone.

Layla's calm expression made me hope I'd helped her too.

In the end, it was probably our relaxed state that saved us when the leviathan struck.

14

LIKE TASTY MORSELS, BENEATH THE SEA

It came out of nowhere, moving so quickly it was a blur. Monty snarled, flinging himself toward the massive predator, and I barely got a hand on his collar to stop him before the enormous alligator creature snatched hold of the bubble and sent it spinning. The attack put us into a dizzying rotation that sent us to our knees, panicked and befuddled.

Shapes flashed past.

The razor-toothed predator snapped at us. Schools of fish darted away as the gigantic gator rolled us through the black water, flinging us from one end of our bubble prison to the other.

I barely held onto Monty, wrapping myself around him as best I could, and only managed to reach Mavis through sheer force of will.

The bubble shuddered violently as it slammed into something.

We thumped back to the ground in a battered heap, trying to climb to our feet before the monster grabbed us again.

Too late.

A massive, toothy maw wrapped around our former refuge and shook it like a dog shakes a small mammal to break its neck.

We cushioned Mavis with our bodies, Layla on one side and me on the other, in an attempt to limit the abuse her already injured body took in the attack.

Squished between us, Monty growled and snapped in the direction of the monster, clearly mad he couldn't get to it.

The bubble thudded against what looked like a shelf of jagged black rock and spasmed from the impact, violently juddering along its length.

A second sea monster shot out of the black water, and I screamed. "Another one!"

Layla grabbed hold of my backpack as we went off again, rolling, shuddering, slamming into anything that got in the way.

When we finally stopped moving, she shoved a hand in front of my face. "Use it!"

Seeing my staff, I realized why she'd grabbed my pack. I didn't argue. Didn't think. Except to silently berate myself for not having thought of it sooner.

I took the staff and snapped my arm to extend the weapon to its full length. Yanking every bit of magic from my core, I fed it into the staff and blasted it toward the monster trying to eat us.

The alligator monster shot away on a tidal wave of water, its stubby legs flailing and its two heads thrashing in an attempt to flip over onto its belly again.

Not two monsters as I'd first thought. Just one monster that was cranially advantaged.

I climbed, panting, to my feet and glanced at my prison mates. "Everybody okay?"

Monty was pressed against my calves, shivering with excitement and fear. Mavis's eyes were open, and she was looking around, clearly confused. "What's going on?" she asked in a dry, broken voice. "Why do I feel like somebody's beaten me all over with a meat mallet?"

I barked out a laugh. "That's closer than you think to the truth."

Layla was staring into the water behind me. "Aggy..."

I knelt beside my mom. "Long story short, we're stuck in a magical bubble at the bottom of a mystical ocean underneath the crone's octopus castle, and three bad-tempered, mythological leviathan are trying to eat us."

Mavis stared at me for a minute and then sighed. "Honey, it's never boring around you, is it?"

I barely got off a shrug before Layla screamed, "Aggy!"

I spun around, the hand with my staff coming up before my eyes even registered what I was seeing. Three massive shapes cut toward us through the black water. Three monsters looking ready to take a bite out of the next thing that got in their way.

That would be us.

All of the leviathans were attacking at once.

We were toast.

"Mom, if you have any ideas, magically speaking," I yelled. "Now would be a great time to try them out."

I sent everything I had into my staff, not bothering to gather the energy into a controlled stream, and fired it at the three monsters in a wash of power that pierced the murky water separating us. The magic slammed into them, shoving them back, as Mavis threw out her hands and coated the water between us and the monsters in an opaline wash.

I turned to find her standing beside me, her shoulders squared and fire in her eyes. Only a tiny tremor in her hand as she shoved hair off her face told me she was struggling.

"Is that a barrier?" Layla asked.

We watched the leviathans slam into the spell, their weight and power making it wobble with every strike.

Mavis nodded. "It won't last long under that onslaught. We need a Plan B."

As the last word fell from her lips, the barrier gave.

I sighed. "Plan B coming up." I reached down and grabbed Monty, glanced up at the soft glow of light illuminating the castle above us, and then turned to Layla and Mavis. "Link arms with me and take a deep breath."

"What...?"

Mavis never got the chance to finish that question.

Three massive forms slammed into our magic prison, teeth clamping around it to keep us from flying away, and a massive, be-spined tail pierced the bubble to finish the job.

"Breathe!" I yelled as the magic barrier protecting us gave way. We were flung out of the ragged structure into the icy grip of a roiling ocean, unprotected against anything that might wander by. Not to mention the three mindless hunters that were currently shaking the broken bubble like dogs with a squeak toy.

Monty struggled in my arms and, for a moment, it was all I could do to hold onto him. Beside me, Layla's eyes were wide, filled with terror. Mavis's fingers were moving in some kind of spell. Goddess bless her. She was a good partner to have in a crisis.

I formed a word in my mind and yanked energy from my core to give it power. "Enclose!" I screamed, icy water streaming into my throat as the power took hold. The magic wrapped around us, squeezing tight enough to make panic burn through my veins, and then expanded to push the water away as it swelled around us.

Layla dropped to her knees, coughing and choking on water. She retched violently, her movements shaking our little protective vesicle. Whining piteously, Monty fought to get free. I finally settled him to the floor of the floating blister.

Mavis was still spinning a spell on the air when I glanced her way. "I hope you're cooking up something good," I said, panting so hard my chest hurt.

She flicked a glance toward the castle. "If it works, it will be stupendous."

I looked out over the black water. A gilded edge rimmed the surface high above us. Dawn was coming. But would it get to us in time?

"They're coming back!" Layla yelled. She stood up, fists clenching and unclenching. A shadow slid over her face, temporarily morphing it. For just a beat, it resembled her devilish face, long and triangular, with black horns sticking straight out from her head and too many teeth for her narrow jaw to contain.

But the image faded as quickly as it had come, and I realized I'd imagined it.

I looked where she was looking. Two glowing

eyes sliced toward us through the murk. There was no doubt in my mind where the monster was headed. "How much longer does that spell need to cook?" I asked Mavis.

"Almost there," she responded, her voice sounding strained.

A long, dark shape swam past, bumping almost casually against our little bubble. *A shark!* We careened away, untethered and much less sturdy than the larger vesicle had been.

Another shark bumped us, throwing us against the sides.

Somehow, Mavis kept her spell brewing as she fought to stay upright. I wrapped my arms around her from behind and braced my legs for the next bump, keeping her upright while she worked.

They hit us again.

And again.

Then the leviathan were on us, and the world became a chaos of terror, toothy roars, and brain-rattling movement. Locked together like a human triangle, with Monty cowering between us, we held firm.

The rim of light painting the surface thickened, slowly inching downward. If only we could hold out long enough for it to reach us.

I tried to see the monsters that were attacking us, but they were a blur of constant thrashing and lunging. I couldn't tell if one of them was the glowy-eyed leviathan. If it was, we were in deep trouble because another one was on its way.

Twin orbs of light moved steadily closer across the murky distance.

"Got it!" Mavis screamed. "Hold on, this is going to be a wild ride."

My mouth opened to ask what she meant, but she pulled her hands apart, stretching the web of the spell, and whirled in a circle to wrap it around all four of us.

"When I yell, hit the ground," Mavis said, her expression tense. She lowered a hand, cupping the air in front of her torso, and then lifted it above her head as if she held the most precious item in her cupped hand. "*Sequor!*" She flung her hand toward the castle in the distance, and a shimmering line of pale green energy shot from it, firing toward the structure like a shooting star. As the line lengthened, it grew thicker, more vibrant, and began to pulse.

"Down!" Mavis shouted.

We hit the floor, wrapped tightly around each other, and the bubble jerked with a violence that would have put us on the ground if we weren't already there. I thought we'd been grabbed by one of the leviathans, but the air blister jolted again and took off so fast I was pretty sure I left my innards behind.

"Ahhhhh!!!!" we all screamed in unison, clutching each other as if our lives depended on it.

A beat later, Mavis lifted her head and grinned. "It's working!"

I risked a peek outside the bubble and saw the castle ahead, significantly closer than it had been before. "It is!" We squealed and hugged and grinned, too relieved for words.

Even Layla laughed, the sound rich and happy. Monty bounced around us with a doggy grin, tail wagging maniacally.

Sudden darkness descended. Too sudden to be the result of a cloud sliding over the nascent sun above.

I looked up to find the underside of a giant octopus dropping from above, its tentacles stretched wide as it prepared to envelop us in a killing embrace.

The magic would never survive that much pressure.

"Mavis?" I asked, half question, half scream.

Mavis looked up too, the smile sliding from her face. "Goddess in a girdle!" she screamed.

A massive tentacle wrapped around our little bubble, and our ascent toward the castle jerked to a stop. Monty yelped as he slammed against the side of the vesicle. But, he came up fighting, snarling and snapping at the bubble where the tentacle gripped us.

"No!" I yelled as we started to veer away from the magic track Mavis had set. "Curse, curse, swear!"

Layla drew herself up stiffly. Her expression turned murderous as another tentacle wrapped around the bubble. Her brows lowered. Her jaw clenched. Her pretty face transformed with rage. "That's it. I've had enough!!" Her hand shot out and there were three-inch-long claws where her fingers had been before. She punched through the bubble as if it was made of butter, and grabbed hold of a tentacle. With a growl even Ferral would respect, the princess wrenched the appendage, ripping it away in a bloody clump.

The monster screamed and thrashed above us, violently tossing the bubble as it flailed. Layla braced herself against the movement and punched through the other side, ripping the second tentacle off and flinging it into the murk.

Writhing in pain, the octopus gave up the fight. It drifted away into the black water, leaving a cloud of dark blood in the water where it had been. Our bubble jerked twice and then shot back to the track Mavis had made, continuing its ascent toward the castle.

Layla wiped her, once again perfectly normal, hands off on her pants and glanced up at us. She blinked when she saw us staring wide-eyed at her. "What? I'm sick of being a victim. It was time to assert myself." She reached down and plucked a hunk of tentacle off the floor. "Sushi?"

We dissolved into helpless laughter. My eyes

streaming with tears, I pulled Layla into a hug. "It's nice to have you back, princess."

She grinned. "It's nice to be back."

"Er, what was the deal with those claws?" Mavis asked, her brows lifted.

Layla frowned. "I've been having twinges lately. Something's changing."

For her sake, I hope it was something good.

Another roar sent ripples of water past our bubble, reminding us that the leviathans weren't quite done with us.

I sighed, looking at the trickles of water coming in through the holes Layla had made. To my shock, the bubble walls had snapped mostly closed when she'd withdrawn her arm, but we didn't want to sustain any more damage. We needed to get out of the water. I glanced upward, happy to see that the sun had penetrated the ocean by several feet.

Unfortunately, the leviathan would get to us long before the sun did. Small victories aside, we were still in a barrel of trouble.

A dense jet of silvery energy shot through the murk toward the monsters. At first, I thought it was the eel thing. But if it was, he was shooting at his own guys.

The two-headed alligator thing erupted in a spray of chunks and teeth, its enraged roar burned away in the explosion.

"What in the name of the goddess's pet poodle is that?" Layla asked.

I grinned. Clearly, she'd been hanging around us too long.

Another jolt of energy cut through the black water and sheared off several of the giant octopus's tentacles, finishing the job Layla had started.

"Looks like it will be sushi for everyone," Mavis said.

We laughed.

The other monsters turned tail and swam away from us. The thing I'd thought was another glowy-eyed monster turned its lights on us. The sun glinted off its surface, and I realized what we were looking at. "That's not a sea monster. It's some type of submarine thing," I said.

I spotted a familiar face in one of its windows. "Gren!" I said, moving closer to the wall of our floating bubble.

Mavis moved up next to me. "Please tell me your sister's in there too."

I didn't see Bev's face behind the windows. "Maybe she stayed in the castle." Even as I spoke the excuse, I could hear how weak it sounded. "She's fine, Mom. If Gren made it, then she did. He would not have left her behind."

Mavis nodded, but I could see the doubt in her eyes. The bubble was silent as we lifted toward the castle, each of us caught in our own thoughts and worries.

One of my worries was that we'd reach the castle, only to splat like bugs against its formidable walls, unable to get inside. But, I needn't have worried. A few minutes later, two large doors rolled open with a thunderous noise, revealing an oversized garage filled with water. The bubble eased past the doors and kept going until we bumped softly against the far wall. The submarine thing came in behind us.

The large doors rolled closed with much clanging and banging. Once the room was sealed, a huge drain in the center of the space opened, and water quickly filtered out of it.

Our little travel pod dissipated under my softly spoken command.

I'd barely had a chance to take a deep breath and get my bearings before Gren was there, his face filled with worry. "Are you all right?"

I sighed. "All right? Not even close. It got really hairy out there. But, we're alive."

He pulled me into a hug. "I was losing my mind. The crone took her time ordering your rescue. I nearly jumped back into the water myself."

Seeing new victims, Monty went into party boy mode. He ran from person to person, greeting everyone with a wriggling back end and a cold nose to the ankle.

Gren smiled at his antics. "At least one of you appears to have retained his good humor."

I shook my head, a smile twitching on my lips.

"Where's Bev?" Mavis demanded. "I want to see her."

Gren tore his gaze from mine, settling it on Mavis. "There's a problem with that."

15

BEASTIES RULE THE PLACID WATERS

Mavis sucked in a gasp, her face turning the color of new cream. She grabbed Gren's wrist, her knuckles whitening under her grip. "Tell. Me. She's. Okay."

He covered her hand with his. His expression softened, warmed. "She's fine, Mavis."

My mom expelled air in a rush, smacking him hard on the arm. "You scared the beans right out of me!"

I suddenly found it easier to breathe myself.

He shook his head. "I apologize. That wasn't my intent. I only meant to say that Beverly is not here at the moment."

"Where is she?" I asked, frustration tightening my chest. "She made it here okay, right?" The force of my question was meant to compel a positive response from him. I might have even added a tinge of magic to it.

"She did. We made it to the castle with only minimal problems."

Something in his eyes told me that he and I did not have the same description of "minimal." "We'll come back to that later," I told him, my brows lifted. "Right now, we need to discuss what you've been doing since you arrived. Have you met the crone? How is she? Do I have to worry that she'll try to kill us all?"

"I rarely kill my guests on the first day," said a dry, crackly voice behind me. I spun around and felt my eyes go wide. The speaker cocked her head, a crooked smile spanning her narrow face. "Though, murder is preferable to pesky intrusions as a general rule."

I caught myself flapping like a landed fish and forced my lips closed. For a long moment, all I could do was stare. Then I remembered what Gren had said. "You nearly got us killed out there! Why didn't you rescue us sooner?"

She made a dismissive motion with her hand. "I'd have left you longer, but then I realized you had a baby with you."

I blinked in surprise. "Baby?"

"There's the little man now," the crone cooed. "Such a handsome boy."

Monty put his fat paws on her knees and licked

the air near her face as she bent down to pet him. "He's very sweet, isn't he?"

I shared a disbelieving look with Gren. He shook his head, disgusted.

Watching as she fussed over my dog, I took in the whole picture of the notorious crone.

She was nothing like I'd expected.

Next to the word "crone" in the magical dictionary was a picture of an old woman. A creature who looked as if she'd walked through the fiery pits on the way to a zombie apocalypse and survived with her limbs still attached and not much else.

But even the dictionary people would have been at a loss to describe the woman standing before me.

She was about my height, around five-six, though her shoulders were stooped and her back was slightly rounded with age. She had on well-worn jeans with the knees torn out and green sneakers with dachshunds galivanting across them. Her thin face was smooth, except for deeply etched laugh lines and an array of wrinkles around her mouth that made it look like an anus when she pursed her lips in thought as she was currently doing.

Her hair was pure white, combed off a mostly unlined forehead, and bursting from her scalp in copious waves that stood straight up for a few inches before falling to just above her flat buttocks. She wore a t-shirt on her slight frame that said, "Go Ahead, Underestimate Me. That Will Be Fun."

The crone's eyes were a beautiful ocean blue, touched with green and silver specks that made them always seem to dance with humor.

But it was the glow she wore like a cape that was the most startling thing. She had the brightest, most powerful aura I'd ever seen. Which, let's be honest, wasn't saying much since I'd only been aware of magic for a few months. But Mavis's reaction was enough to make me certain the crone's aura was spectacular.

Biting back my irritation, I offered our hostess my hand. "My name is Aggy. I'm the Lares of Rome, Indiana. It's an honor to meet you. Can I call you Cayleigh?"

"You may not." The crone made a point of shoving her veiny hands into the pockets of her jeans, ignoring my offering. "Lares. I've heard much about your antics from your gnome."

I frowned slightly at the word. I hated to think the life and death struggles my council and I had undertaken over the last months could be reduced to such a frivolous word as *antics*. "Is Niele all right? We were worried when he disappeared."

"He's perfectly fine. His arrival has been providential. I've been needing a gnome. I'm putting him to good use."

"Oh?" I asked, freshly irritated. "I'd like to speak to him."

"There will be time for that. Later."

I opened my mouth to argue, but the crone widened her eyes, something dark slipping through them. She nodded. "Yes. I'd heard about your possessiveness. You should put that away while you're here." She smiled a bit meanly.

"You seem to know a lot about me. Should I be worried?" I'd meant it to be a little joke. But it just came out sounding angry.

She shook her head, dismissing my question. "One of the most important things you'll learn as a leader in the magical world, Agnes, is you must always ask the right questions the first time. Because you might not get another chance to ask them."

I fought to keep irritation off my face at her use of my full name. Nobody but my dad called me Agnes, and I hated when he did it too. "Okay," I said, not sure exactly what she wanted from me.

"For example," the crone went on as if my response hadn't been needed. Apparently, it hadn't. "What you really meant to ask was if I thought you'd done the right things since your seating. Whether I believed you were cut out to be the guardian of such an important place. If I respected your work and your people enough to help you find your young historian now."

I shook my head, her words bringing my hackles up. "Your opinion of me..."

"Stop right there!" she said, her voice booming around the enormous garage space.

Every single living thing in that room stopped moving, going completely still.

His expression tight, Gren stood with one hand outstretched as if he'd intended to grab the crone to stop her. I had a feeling that would have been a fatal mistake.

I fought against my locked muscles but couldn't manage even the tiniest blink.

The crone leaned in, bathing my face with breath that smelled slightly of lemon and fish. Her breakfast, no doubt. "There is one thing in life I cannot abide," she all but growled into my face. "Do not ever be dishonest with me, young Lares. Or, more importantly, with yourself. My opinion of you is everything, girl. It is the most important thing. Do. Not. Ever. Forget. It."

She relaxed slightly, leaning back out of my space. The world around us unlocked, and we all took a collective breath in relief. The crone flipped a hand as if we'd been discussing the benefits of using power words versus written spells. "If you keep that in mind, Agnes Bethany Lenore, you and I will get along just fine."

Gah!

She glared at Layla. "Even if you did bring demonkind into my home."

I slid Layla a quick look but she avoided my gaze.

"Now..." The crone motioned to someone near the vehicle that had brought Gren to us. "Let's get you inside and fed. We have much to discuss."

I stood in a room that was ridiculously fancy for an underwater castle. I'd expected nautical themes, ship's wheels, and lots of shells. But it was worse. Everything was gilded and velvet, in colors of garish reds and purples as if the space belonged to a king or queen from Ancient Europe.

None of it was my taste. And, more surprisingly, it wasn't what I'd expect from the crone, who had dachshunds on her shoes and wore torn jeans. Then again, the healer's strongest asset seemed to be her ability to surprise and shock.

The best part of the room, however, was the wall-sized window overlooking the busy and colorful ocean life around the castle. Fish in vibrant blues, yellows, and oranges darted around brightly-colored coral and an array of seaweeds in vivid shades of green. Everything formed a beautiful contrast to the spectacular white of the sand, which sparkled like diamonds in the sunlight that somehow managed to reach the ocean floor around us.

Juxtaposed to the harmless beauty of the scene, the occasional, shadowy shape of a massive shark moved slowly past, its black eyes cold and merciless as it casually pillaged a school of fish and then moved on to continue its deadly assault on the next happy-go-lucky group.

It was the perfect metaphor for the castle's owner. The crone was a lethal shark wearing cute sneakers and a funny shirt. If one wasn't careful, it would be easy to forget she was a cold-blooded predator.

Someone had taken Monty away when they'd showed me to my room, insisting he needed freshening up as well as food to fill his belly. Given my dog's hatred of baths and obsession with food, I figured he was experiencing both his Heaven and Hell wherever they'd taken him.

Ignoring the spicy scent of the food on the large silver tray behind me, I stared out the window, wondering what had happened to Ferral and the two lost ones who'd given their lives to protect their princess.

It was my first opportunity to grieve, and I was discovering that the grief ran much deeper than I'd expected.

Ferral and I hadn't been friends. Far from it. But his caustic personality and bossy ways had grown on me. Weirdly. And I discovered I would miss him. Particularly his advice about the magical world. His loss would leave a big hole in my heart, knowledge, and training.

There was a soft knock on the door. It opened a beat later and a welcome face popped through. "Do you have a minute?" my sister asked.

Tears burned my eyes when I saw her, and I opened my arms as moisture slid hotly down my cheeks. "I was so worried," I choked out through a suddenly tight throat.

Bev strode over and wrapped me in a hug. "I'm sorry to go behind your back. But I knew mom was safer with you there. The angel kept me safe."

Pulling back, I blinked in surprise. "Angel?"

Bev laughed. "You didn't know?"

Had I known? Probably. On a subconscious level. I realized I'd wanted Gren to tell me. That had seemed important. I shook my head, dismissing the unhelpful thoughts. What Gren was didn't matter. What mattered was that he'd become a vital part of my council. And my life.

I smacked Bev on the arm, glaring at her.

"Ouch!" my sister rubbed her arm. "That hurt."

"Too bad. Don't you ever do that again," I scolded.

She gave me an unrepentant wink. "I probably will. I have no regrets. Everybody's safe. Mom and Layla would have been killed if you hadn't been there."

My scowl slid away. "I wouldn't write the princess off so quickly," I said, thinking about how she'd punched through my bubble and ripped limbs off the huge octopus. I grinned. It had been a thing of beauty.

Also, it had been kind of gross and gory.

"Where were you when we got here?" I asked Bev.

She looked uncomfortable. "The crone asked me to help with something."

Her discomfort fed mine. "Help with what, exactly?"

"Think of it as relationship building," she hedged.

"Bev..."

"Don't worry about it," she said, flipping a dismissive hand. "On the bright side, we recovered Layla's men."

I felt my eyes go wide. "Alive?"

She grimaced. "Mostly?"

"How can they be mostly alive? They're either alive or not."

"They might need to regrow a limb or two, but they're still breathing. Layla and the crone are with them now. The crone's healing magic is amazing."

"Really?" The tension binding my chest loosened. "That's great." I chewed my lip.

"What?"

"Huh?"

"What's bouncing around in that tiny brain of yours."

"I'll have you know my brain is not tiny."

"Neither is your butt."

I smacked her again. Laughing, she rubbed at her sore arm. "You're excessively violent today."

I tried to look stern but couldn't help grinning. Our sisterly banter felt good. It felt real in a place that was anything but. "Is Niele really okay? Have you seen him?"

"He's fine. I spoke to him briefly when we first got here. She's got him working beneath the ocean floor." She frowned as if trying to remember. "Something to do with realigning the castle's moorings." She shook her head. "Niele was excited about the job."

"Good." I chewed my lip some more.

"Spit it out," Bev said.

"Do you know what happened to Ferral. Did they..." I swallowed hard. "Did they find his...body?"

"Not that I'm aware of," she said, her tone gentle. "I'm sorry, Aggy."

When my eyes burned with fresh tears that I tried to blink away, she gave me another hug. "We'll find him, sis. You have my word."

I nodded, sniffling. A change of subject was in order. "Tell me about Casa Crone."

She plopped down onto my bed. "Goddess! Where do I start?" Tugging the silver cover off the food on the tray, Bev plucked a small piece of fried dough off the plate and popped it into her mouth. She grimaced. "For starters," she said before swallowing. "The food's terrible. Everything tastes like fish." Her expression reminded me that my sister was definitely a beef and chicken girl. "I'd kill for a big, juicy burger and fries."

My mouth watered at the thought. "What else?" I asked, plopping down next to her.

"Well, the library is amazing."

My eyes went wide. "She has a magical library?"

Bev nodded, grabbing a chunk of some kind of meat...or fish. It was fried like the dough, so it couldn't be all bad. Right? I took a hunk of something too, sticking it into my mouth and grimacing. "Ugh!" I spit the bite into my hand and dumped it onto the tray, covering it with a napkin. "That's nasty. What kind of seasoning did they use?"

"I wouldn't be surprised to find out they season everything with ground up fish scales," Bev responded, wincing. "Anyway, yes, the library has a ton of magical reference books. Some of them are thousands of years old. To be honest, if I could get food delivered, I'd sit in there and study those books for years." The dreamy look on her face told me she wasn't lying.

"Have you had a chance to read any of them yet?"

"I've skimmed a few. But the crone has kept me pretty busy since I got here. I've barely had time to pee." Her eyes lit up. "Speaking of, have you checked out the toilet?"

"Why would I do that?" My brows shot upward. "You are aware of my lifelong porcelain phobia, right?"

"Then you're in luck. There's no porcelain involved." She grabbed my hand and yanked me to my feet, dragging me across the room to an open doorway I hadn't explored yet. When we reached the door, she threw out a hand, Vanna White style. "I present the newest in oceanic toilets for your potty pleasure."

I narrowed my eyes. The "toilet" was half of an enormous clamshell, pointy edges up, sitting on a platform made of coral. "Um..." I tilted my head to see if it looked any better from another angle. Nope. "If I sat on that, I'd fall in."

"Not to mention you'd slice pieces out of your thighs," Bev said gleefully. "No. You're not supposed to sit on it. You're just supposed to hover."

"Hover?" I'd been getting into better shape recently, but I wasn't sure my middle-aged thighs were up to extended hovering. Especially not first thing in the morning.

Bev giggled happily. She could. She'd always had better thighs than me. "It's not an issue unless you're jumping on the Number Two train. If you know what I mean."

Heat flared in my cheeks. "Keep your mind out of my Number Two train."

She giggled again. "Seriously though, if you think you're too feeble to squat, there's always this handy dandy little apparatus." She marched over and tugged what looked like a sea sponge on a string off the floor.

I didn't want to know. "Goddess help me."

"My recommendation is that you eat your fiber while you're here. Things will get ugly if the Number Two train is slow to the station."

I dropped my face into my hands. "Curse, swear, curse, curse."

"Ooh, a four-swear. I really got to you with that one."

I sighed. "We need to finish our business and get out of here before anybody needs to use that." I pointed to the clamshell.

"Agreed. However, this is one of the very few times in my life when I have to admit guy anatomy has its advantages."

"Only on the Number One train," I murmured, a smile tugging on my lips.

16

OUR HEROES MUCH LIKE FISHY FODDER

We ran the crone to ground in her throne room. Given that it was the size of a high school gymnasium but held only a single piece of furniture—a massive gold and bejeweled throne chair—there was no other name for it.

The castle resembled nothing so much as a beehive. It consisted of a series of maze-like hallways interspersed at odd intervals with rooms in all shapes and sizes, which appeared built to accommodate the hallways rather than the other way around.

The kitchen was in the very center of the space. An odd occurrence that I deduced made food delivery easier but was just plain weird. More interesting, unless we'd somehow missed it during our hours-long hunt for the crone, there didn't seem to be a dining area.

"Everyone must eat alone off of trays," I mused.

"Probably so they'll feel more comfortable spitting the food into their napkins," Bev surmised.

The people who lived in the strange castle were an industrious group. They continually hurried past us without even glancing our way, seemingly intent on their work and too much in a hurry to stop and speak. Dressed in black slacks and crisp white button-up shirts, the worker bees offered us brief nods as they hurried past, but nobody spoke or asked us if we needed help getting somewhere.

"We need a concierge," Bev said after we'd been searching for a while.

Finally, after we'd passed the same woman several times in the halls, she apparently took pity on us. "Can I help you ladies find someone?"

I opened my mouth to tell her we were looking for the crone and then had second thoughts. Was "crone" a pejorative term in the castle? Would they take offense?

Luckily, Bev saved me. "We're looking for the mistress. She wasn't in her rooms."

We'd stopped by the crone's "rooms" before beginning our long journey through the castle, finding them empty. Bev had also shown me the library, which was conveniently located just a hop, skip, and a jump from my room. My assessment of the library matched Bev's, and I would happily have settled in on one of the incredibly comfortable couches with any one of a dozen magical texts if I hadn't been worried sick about Wanda.

"Ah," said the woman, smiling fondly. "She does get around. I believe she's in the multi-purpose room right now," she said, glancing at her watch. "But I'd hurry if I were you. She's scheduled for leviathan watch in three minutes."

We'd thanked the woman and followed her directions toward the room with the throne. The crone had indeed been sitting in the oversized chair, contemplating the insides of her eyelids.

We stood quietly just inside the door, waiting for her to wake up from her nap.

"Well?" the crone's sharp voice rang out. "Did you have a purpose in coming? Or have you been struck completely dumb by the majesty of my person?"

Bev rolled her lips to keep from smiling. "You are quite majestic."

The crone opened one eye and narrowed it on my sister. "Impertinence. I should strap you down and feed you sushi."

Bev gave a whole-body shudder. "My sincerest apologies. Should I grovel?"

The other eye snapped open, sparkling with good humor. "No, daughter, you should not. Groveling gives me gas. But a solid dose of sucking up is good for the constitution," she responded as she glanced at her watch. She bounced out of the chair and hurried across the enormous, seemingly wasted room, motioning for us to follow. "Come along. Those monsters aren't going to watch themselves."

"That was a lovely room," Bev said as we headed back into the endless hallways.

The crone threw her a look. "Are you being sincere?"

Bev hesitated only a beat. "Yes?"

"Is that a question?"

"Maybe?"

"You do not know whether it is a question or if you're being sincere?"

"No?"

The crone cackled happily. "You are a delight, daughter."

I lifted a brow at Bev, wanting to ask her if Mavis was aware of the change in Bev's maternity.

Bev grinned. "The mistress and I have discovered we share the same twisted sense of humor," she explained.

"I prefer unique to twisted," the crone said in a scolding tone.

"Like your toilets," I offered with a grin.

The crone stiffened. Bev's eyes went wide. She gave a warning shake of her head.

The crone turned to me. "You do not like the facilities?" Something cold and threatening passed through the depths of her gaze.

I fought a shudder.

"I...um...er...They're unique?" I ask-answered since it had worked for Bev.

The crone glared at me for a beat and then barked out a laugh, nudging Bev with her elbow. "Got her."

"You certainly did," Bev said. She waited until the old witch turned away to rub her arm.

"Here we are." The crone turned into an open door and disappeared.

I blinked, "How did we get here?" I whispered.

Bev grabbed my wrist, tugging me into the room. "It's best not to question," she responded under her breath.

"But we were just in a never-ending hallway with no doors. This place is like falling down the rabbit hole."

Bev shook her head. "Later."

Sighing, I said. "Okay. But if she screams 'Off with their heads!' I'm making for the exits without looking back."

"I'll be right behind you."

Gren was in front of a bank of computers that would have been right at home in a spaceship. He was standing with his hands clasped behind his back, staring at a wall of glass that overlooked a scene much like the one in my room.

The biggest difference was that, instead of pretty and harmless schools of vibrantly-hued fish darting to and fro, he and the others were staring at something that had probably lived when dinosaurs walked the earth. Or, in this case, swam it.

I jolted to a stop near the door, my memories of the too-close interactions with killer behemoths all too fresh in my mind. The fire-eyed leviathan that had attacked us the night before floated in front of the glass, its glowing eyes seemingly locked on me.

I knew it was just a trick of the light. The creature wouldn't single me out from the rest, but my over-active imagination painted a very convincing picture that my nerves seemed determined to frame.

Gren turned around as if he could sense my fear. He frowned. I must have looked terrified. Stretching out a hand, my protector gave me a smile. "Madam Lares. You're just in time to see."

I frowned. "See what?"

The crone turned to me, scowling. "Well, come on, girl. Don't linger by the door. This is fascinating stuff."

Girl? I bristled, feeling as if she were trying to belittle me. Then I remembered how old the crone was and realized, compared to her, my forty-five years made me a toddler.

The creature beyond the glass suddenly shot forward, its great maw opening to bite at the glass. The enormous viewing window rattled in its frame at the concussive force of the monster's strike, and I spun on my heel and headed back out into the hallway, trying not to embarrass myself by running.

In the hall, the happy sound of nails clicking against the floor brought my head around. *Monty?*

Unfortunately, it wasn't my dog.

Two low-slung creatures with long, silky hair trotted around the corner, eyes bright and tails wagging. One of the two dachshunds was black and tan like Monty. The other was a piebald, with a mostly white body and a black, brown, and white face. Both had long, silky fur that told me they were well taken care of.

The two dogs bounced up to me and danced around my feet, giving my shoes a thorough sniff as their tails wagged in an enthusiastic greeting.

The woman who'd given Bev and me directions to find the crone scurried up behind the little dogs, looking panicked. "There you are, you little rascals," she said in an exasperated voice. "Naughty babies."

The two dogs turned around and greeted her as if she were their favorite person in the world, completely oblivious to her scolding.

The woman looked up and caught me smiling. She flushed. "I was bringing them to the mistress. She always likes to spend time with them after they've had their breakfast."

I nodded. "They're gorgeous."

She beamed as if I'd just told her one of her children was beautiful. "Thank you. We try to keep them groomed. But the little rascals have too much energy for their own good."

I laughed, trying to pet the wriggling dogs and getting poked in both ears and one nostril with wet tongues for my trouble. "I understand. I have a dachshund too."

"Ah, yes. I met your little man. He's a sweetheart. The girls are pampering him now. He should be along shortly."

"Good." I grinned as the two females did zoomies around me, growling playfully. "I miss him."

The woman winked. "He's eating us out of hearth and castle. The boy was apparently empty from stem to stern."

"He always thinks he's empty," I said, chuckling.

The door to the computer room opened, and Gren came out. The two little dogs ducked past him and flew into the room. A beat later, a chorus of adoring exclamations greeted them.

Gren looked at me. "Are you okay?"

I nodded. "A little dachshund therapy works wonders."

Gren glanced at the woman who'd brought the dogs. Her face flushed, and she gave him a shy smile, her eyes wide with awe. "Hello," he said, his voice kind.

The woman turned a deeper shade of red and turned on her heel, scampering away in a fine imitation of her four-footed charges.

He frowned after her. "Did I offend her in some way?"

I laughed. "No. You definitely didn't offend her." I looked at the door. "What's going on in there?"

"The crone says her herd of behemoths is getting too big. Normally they self-limit by eating each other. But she says they've begun working together instead. She's been monitoring their behavior, pitting them against each other individually to try to figure out if there's magical interference at work."

"Ah." Giving him a narrow-eyed gaze, I asked. "Does that have anything to do with Bev's little project?"

He shook his head. "I don't know. The witch..." He caught himself when I bristled. "I apologize. Your sister did not tell me what she and the crone were up to."

"We need to talk to the crone about Wanda. We're wasting time, and I don't know how much of it Wanda has left."

"I agree. But I'm sure by now you've figured out the crone will not be rushed. I was hoping to try to get her full attention after this." He nodded toward the closed door to indicate the monster watching session.

"Fine. I'm going to spend some time in the library. Meet me there after the monster watch?"

"Of course."

17

INTO THE MYTHICAL LEGEND'S LAIR

N ewly delivered back to me, with a full belly and a shiny coat, Monty snuffled around the library looking for bugs or crumbs while I worked my way through a pile of books that I hoped might shed some light on our problem.

The current tome I was perusing, *Time and Space Magic with a Demonic Influence*, seemed promising. But the writing was in an archaic form that made reading it a slow slog. Every paragraph was like a fresh set of riddles.

Once my mind started to understand the strange way of speaking, a picture began to form in my mind, and I wondered if Wanda's sudden disappearance might not be a bad twist of the original Groundhog Day curse, rather than a fresh attack.

Once a time-amending malediction has been

appended to a soul with uncertain affections and a scarcity of confidence in one's magical prowess, the blight must needs persistently alter its formation in an attempt to retain the required levels of power over its quarry.

I rubbed my forehead and reread the sentence for the third time, digging beneath the tendency to overstate everything in an attempt to suss out the bare bones of its meaning.

I finally came up with: The curse adjusts itself over time to stay relevant.

Nodding to myself with satisfaction, I felt as if I'd had a breakthrough.

The next sentence ripped that gratification brutally away.

However, given an opportunity seasoned with potential for true magical augmentation, the malediction will always procure the simplest form available. There is, after all, no reward in endowing where endowment isn't merited. Magical malfeasance is an indulgence best left unexplored.

"What in the name of the goddess's pet iguana does that even mean?" I dropped my head into my hands, rubbing my aching temples with my thumbs.

"I'd ask how it's going, but I'm guessing by the groaning and temple rubbing that it's not good?" Gren asked as he came into the room.

I sighed, sitting back in the leather chair. "These texts all talk about demonic curses having to do with time." I swung an arm to indicate a dozen magical texts, all open to information that seemed like it might be helpful once we figured out what we were dealing with.

The "what" was both the problem and the solution.

"I swear they're all written with the goal of driving the reader crazy," I lamented.

Gren nodded, glancing over the chaos of information. "Why demonic?" His carefully neutral expression told me he thought my brain had locked into "demonic everything" mode since the vortex incident.

"Because all these visions I've been having have included what appears to be a demonic figure." I thought about the hooded figure with the blazing eyes and chalky pallor. "Or at least someone who's been possessed by a demon. Wanda's description of the creature who hexed her seems to support that," I told him just a tiny bit defensively. "I figured that was a good place to start."

"And," added my sister as she strode into the room. "Mom and I and the coven have gone through every book on time and location magic we can find in the witches' library and haven't found a single spell that works on Wanda's hex."

Gren nodded. "Leading you to believe it's something other than pure witch magic," he said. "That makes sense."

She stopped next to me, looking over the mess of books. "Have you found anything useful?"

I stopped rubbing my temples and looked up at her. "Yeah. I've found that demonic magical texts give me a splitting headache."

She grinned. "Let me help." Bev's long fingers danced on the air above the book, creating a pale green web of a spell that looked like advanced calculus to my eyes. She finished the weave with a twirl of one index finger in the center and then touched the book with the spell, dispersing it into the yellowed pages.

I watched in awe as the words on the page lost their curly aspect. Half of the text disappeared, leaving behind shorter words that were put together with a more modern slant. A grin found my face.

"Magic texts for dummies," she said, chuckling.

I smacked her on the leg but didn't put anything behind it. I was too happy to discover that I could actually read the texts without straining my brain. "This is great. Now, why don't you help me plow through them."

Her grin disappeared. "Ugh!"

Monty suddenly reappeared from somewhere with spider web silk draped over his head and an enthusiastic wag in his butt. A moment later, I heard the telltale click of nails that told me the crone and her cute entourage were coming.

"Ah," I said, scratching his head. "That's why you

suddenly showed back up. You heard the girls coming. You dog you."

Monty gave a little "woof" of excitement and took off out of the room. He returned a minute later, trotting happily between the two little girl dachshunds, bouncing and yipping an invitation to play. The girls were only too happy to comply. Zooming away across the library, they glanced back to make sure Monty followed as they dove between the shelves filled with books.

Mavis and the crone followed the dogs into the room. Mavis was holding a steaming cup of something I prayed was for me. The crone was wearing a shirt with a dachshund on it that said, "A woman cannot live on wine alone. She also needs a dachshund."

I grinned. She wasn't wrong.

"How'd the monster mash go?" I asked, shoving the book I'd been reading away to make room for the tea Mavis handed me.

The crone frowned. "I can't get them to fight. It's frustrating."

"Are you really worried they'll gang up on you?" I asked.

She fixed me with a thoughtful look but didn't respond. Apparently, she considered my question rhetorical. Finally, she said. "Tell me why you're here."

The brusque question gave me a jolt. It sounded

like a rebuke. Which, if I was honest with myself, I should have expected. We did barge in on her. In a manner of speaking. "I need your help."

She gave me a cold stare. "Go on."

"My historian, a young girl, has gone missing."

The air in the room seemed to thicken, energy snapping like static electricity around us. The little hairs on my nape lifted and a chill slid through me.

"Are you accusing me of taking her?" the crone growled.

"What? No!" I held up a hand. "Wanda was under some kind of repetitive time spell. I believe there was a demonic aspect to it."

As the ancient witch continued to stare coldly at me, I remembered the magic signature the coven had found at Wanda's. And the white hair that looked just like the crone's own, long white locks. "But you already knew that, didn't you? You were there. At Wanda's place."

The density of the air increased, making it hard to draw a breath. Behind me, the dogs' playful scampering stopped.

I coughed, my breathing taking on a wheezing aspect in the magic-drenched air. "Were you trying to help my historian?" I asked, deciding to take the bull by the horns. "Or hurt her?"

Electricity snapped around me, biting my skin like fire ants. The others scratched their exposed flesh as the magic stung them too.

A ball of static energy rolled through the air. The static bomb exploded into light when it hit the nearest shelf of books, sizzling harmlessly over them. I waited for something else to happen but realized the ball of static was simply a sign of the crone's irritation with me.

The ancient witch's aspect changed. She was no longer a quirky, dachshund-loving oddball with oversized aquatic pets and bad toilets. The shadows had wrapped around her, clinging like an extra aura. The glooms highlighted the high slash of her cheeks and the fierce light behind her eyes. Even the dachshund on her tee-shirt suddenly appeared menacing.

Tap, tap, tap, tap.

We glanced down to find the two little females staring up at their mistress, their wagging tails tapping nervously against the table leg.

The crone observed them for a moment and then smiled, the air clearing as she reached down and scratched each little girl beneath a silky chin. "Sorry, ladies. I'll chillax. I promise."

The dogs bounced up with happy yips, dancing around her feet.

She seemed surprised to find us staring at her when she glanced up a beat later. "What? Oh, sorry. Did I vamp out again?" She tsked enthusiastically, poking her head with a finger. "I've got a bit of sea madness. It comes and goes."

Awesome, I thought.

"So. What were we talking about?"

"Wanda," I told her. "My missing historian. "

"Ah. Yes, cute child. I enjoyed talking to her very much."

We all stared at the witch, blinking in surprise—not that she'd seen Wanda, we already knew that—but that she would freely admit it.

"You went to her little apartment?" Bev asked, clarifying what the crone was admitting to.

The ancient witch frowned. "Yes. Where else would I talk to her? The child never leaves that place unless the magic pulls her out."

Although I'd suspected as much, hearing the crone say the words was like a knife shoved right into my heart. "That magic is what we're trying to defeat," I told her. "I had a vision that Wanda was in danger."

She shook her head, dropping into a chair at the table. "You've started in the middle. You must begin at the beginning. Tell me what we're up against so I can give you an intelligent response."

So, I did.

I told her about the first time we'd met Wanda. About the way she'd helped during my seating and the subsequent attack of the demons. I explained how she seemed to know magical history, which led us to understand that she was a historian. I went over the vision I'd had...how Wanda had pled with me to help her. I finished with the tracking spell and our visit to Wanda's room, where we found evidence that the crone had visited.

When I'd finished, the crone sat quietly for a long moment, her chin resting in one hand. Then she said. "You believe demons are involved?"

"From Wanda's description, I believe the creature that hexed her was from the demonic realm," I agreed.

"Yet, you don't seem to realize that you've allied yourself with just such creatures. Did Princess Layla not have suggestions as to who might have hexed the girl?"

"No." Even as I responded, I knew I was being naïve. The likelihood that Layla knew the culprit was higher than the possibility she didn't. "She hasn't admitted to knowing who it is, anyway."

The crone nodded. "I believe the princess is as honorable as her kind can be. But she's broken. You must always keep in mind, Lares, that Layla may no longer look like a devil, but she still carries a devil's soul within that human form."

She wasn't telling me anything I didn't already know. But her words spurred a desire within me to defend Layla. "She's saved my life twice at huge risk to herself," I said.

"Three times," Mavis pointed out. "She saved us from that octopus thing out there." Mavis pointed toward the wall, and I understood she was referring to the ocean.

"Ah," said the crone. "And she was not also saving herself."

It wasn't a question. It was a poke in the ribs.

"I trust her," I told the old woman. "With my life."

"Yes." She nodded as if I'd asked her a question. "But, do you also trust her with Wanda's life?"

Silence beat between us for a moment.

Gren finally broke it. "If you don't mind my asking, Mistress. Why *did* you visit the girl?"

She looked surprised by his question. "She's a historian, boy. Do you think my kind grows on trees?"

He nodded. "You evaluated her?"

Her grin was slow and filled with respect. "Well done, young man. I can see why you earned your wings at such a young age."

I glanced at Gren. Young? He looked to be in his mid to late thirties. At least ten years younger than me. I'd hoped his youth was part of his magic. The last thing I wanted was to embrace the cougar life at my age. It wasn't dignified. I fought a grin. Did I care if it was dignified? Really care? What would I do if he wasn't just magically young, but actually the age he looked?

"And the answer to my question?" Gren prompted.

The crone laughed, scooping the pretty piebald off the floor and nuzzling the dog's silky throat. "She earned high marks. The girl is very bright. Very intuitive. She's much like her mother was."

The room stilled, the silence filled with barbs.

It was a moment before the old witch seemed to notice. When she did, she stopped fussing over her dog and turned to us. "You weren't aware that her mother was a historian?"

"From what Wanda told me, I assumed her mother was a witch. But we didn't really know. We only knew she was taken away the night Wanda was cursed," I said. "And Wanda was told the curse was a penalty for her mother's crime."

"That is true, as far as it goes." The ancient witch gave me a speculative look. "Are you aware of what the girl's mother did to earn the wrath of a demon?"

I shook my head, my throat suddenly tight.

"You won't like it. Are you sure you want to hear?"

Nope. I wasn't sure. Not even a little. I found my gaze sliding to Gren, a question in the glance.

He stared back, unable or unwilling to advise me. At that moment, I missed Ferral more than ever. He would have responded with a cold, condescending retort that would have made me angry enough to weather any horrors the crone sent my way.

Instead, I found myself facing those terrors with a bleeding wound for a heart. "Tell me."

The crone's expressive eyes held mine as she opened her mouth and ripped that wound into a bleeding mess. "She bedded a demon, bore him a child, and then sliced his throat as he slept."

18

THE PURSUIT OF KNOWLEDGE
LANGUISHING THERE

"A demon?" I mumbled incoherently. "How is that...?" I suddenly found myself unable to complete a thought or a sentence. "Wanda is..." I stared blankly at the crone, my brain fried to cinders.

"You're telling us the girl has a demon heritage?" Gren asked, his expression a clear reflection of his own shock.

"That's what I'm telling you," the crone said smugly.

"Does she..." I swallowed hard. "Does she know she's part demon?"

"Half," the crone said. Apparently, she was unwilling to allow me even the slightest obfuscation to soothe my nerves.

"Half demon," I mumbled.

"I do not know if she is aware," the crone said.

"She looks so human," Mavis said, her face white with shock.

The crone nodded. "Her father comes from a long line of earthbound demons. They're basically humans with demonic energies."

"Like a lost one?"

"No. Earthbound demons have always lived on the earthly plane. Their genetics are completely different from devils or demons who come from the demonic realm. The speculation is that they origi-nated from the royal demons, who have always called the earth their home."

"Are they...?" Bev frowned. "Is she...?"

"Evil?" the crone finished almost gleefully. "Most of them are like humans with minimal magical powers, except that they embody the worst of humankind's traits. They tend to be cold and calcu-lating, selfish to an extreme, thoughtless, and gener-ally unkind. But they're wicked smart and almost always successful. I'm going to speculate that Wanda's father had power and money. Willow prob-ably overlooked a lot of his flaws in their early time together. By the time she had the child, she likely couldn't overlook them anymore."

"Why did she attack him?" Bev asked.

The crone shrugged. "He might have threatened the child. It wouldn't be beyond the realm of possibility."

"Why would a demon want a human woman if

not for offspring?" Bev asked.

"Willow must have fulfilled some need. Maybe he was having her hex his business adversaries. Maybe she gave him access somewhere he couldn't go on his own. I can guarantee that, whatever it was, it was helpful only to him."

I stared blankly into space, thinking about my interactions with the teen. Had I seen any evidence of cruelty in her thoughts or actions? Had she seemed demonic in any way?

Realizing that the crone was watching me closely, I lifted my brows in silent question.

She settled the dog back to the floor, and the three dachshunds tumbled across the room together, happily falling back into play. The crone narrowed her intense gaze on me. "Madam Lares, does this news change your mind about looking for the girl?"

Her words speared ice through my chest. I jolted under their effects. "No! Of course not."

She stared at me. "Do not respond so quickly. That was a response fed by your human soul. It is what you believed you *should* say. Unfortunately, that does not make it the truth."

I wanted to bristle at her insinuation. I wasn't so cold that I'd allow the teen to suffer and possibly die because she'd had poor luck with her parents.

Was I?

But...demon.

A warm hand found my shoulder. I looked up

into Gren's face, his expressive eyes giving me the support I needed to face my true feelings. I sighed, nodding. "I won't lie. The demon thing has thrown me for a loop. But I've spent a lot of time with Wanda. I believe I know her heart. She's a typical teen who's just looking for her place in the world. If anyone has a reason to hate...to lash out...it's a young girl who was abandoned by her parents, her life ruined by a curse."

But Wanda had done everything she could to help when I'd needed her. She'd settled into our lives...our hearts...as if she'd always been there. She loved my dog.

And he loved her.

I shook my head. "Wanda is like my own child. I know in my heart that she's good. And, even if she wasn't, I'd want to save her. I owe her that much and so much more."

The crone nodded. "Excellent. Then we must begin with the mother."

I sat up, feeling renewed hope that we were actually going to get real information which would help us find Wanda. "Good. Do you know where she is?"

"I do not."

I sagged in my chair as hope crashed around me.

"But I know where you should start looking."

"Okay," I said. "Where?"

"With the girl's father, of course."

Confused silence thrummed through the room.

We all stared at her as if she'd lost her mind. Of course she had.

"You just said Wanda's mother killed him."

The crone flipped a dismissive hand. "Well, she tried, didn't she? But demons are much harder to kill than you'd suppose."

I didn't know if that was good news or bad. "He survived?" I asked. "Is he the one who cursed Wanda?"

"Have you not been paying attention, girl?" The crone's voice rang through the room, slamming against the walls and roaring back to rattle my brain. I ducked my head with a grimace, rubbing my temples again as she reignited my headache. "I told you that earthbound demons look like humans," she continued. "You described a creature with crimson eyes and black lips. Does that sound like the description I gave you?"

"Maybe it was one of the father's servants?" Mavis suggested.

The crone was suddenly lost behind a blinding flash of light. I blinked and the ancient healer reappeared. She was wearing a different dachshund tee shirt and it said, "I don't people. I wiener."

I slid my gaze up to her face and found her grinning. "You like?"

"I do." The woman's mood swings were exhausting. But I couldn't fault her fashion sense.

She sighed. "The man you're looking for lives a

few miles from Rome. His property is vast and, like yours, borders on the Mystical Wood. You cannot get to him from the front gates. His people will simply make you leave."

"He doesn't people either?" Bev asked, grinning.

The crone barked out a laugh. "He does not."

"So, how do we get to him?" Gren asked. "By air?"

"No. He has winged guardians as well. The best way to enter is through the Mystical Wood. However, he's magicked the path near his home to confuse and distract, so you'll need a special guide to get you there."

"Special guide?" I asked. "Where do I find a guide?"

"You will not," the crone said. "The guide will find you."

She stood and whistled for her dogs. The little girls tore around a bookshelf and ran to her, tongues lolling. "You must leave within the hour while the light still bathes the bottom of the sea. Once the light starts to lift, my pets will come out to play. You will not enjoy their games."

"Yeah," I agreed. "Been there, didn't get a tee-shirt."

The crone's eyes sparkled with mirth. "It *was* very entertaining, though. I particularly enjoyed the ripping off of limbs. I fully expected the princess to start beating the Puss with it."

Aside from how very wrong it was to call such a monstrous creature Puss, her words reminded me of our missing party members. "What about the lost ones? Can Layla's men leave? Are they in shape for travel?"

"They will be fine. My healing powers are like none other." She gave Gren a wink, and he flushed. "However, the other one may need to stay with me for a bit. He's healing much more slowly."

The room went silent and still.

The other one?

My pulse spiked into the red zone. "You have Ferral here? He's okay?"

She grimaced. "That one will never be okay. He is a turd. But his body is strong and virile. He is an acceptable male."

The glint in her eye made me cringe.

Behind me, Bev said, "Ew."

I felt the same. However, I wasn't stupid. If the crone was going to put the moves on the advocate, I really wanted it on video that I could use to blackmail him with. "Can I see him before we go?"

"If you really want to. However, I have no idea why you would. Did I mention he's a turd?"

"You did." I laughed, surprising even myself with my giddiness. Ferral was alive! "And, you are right. Even on his best days, he's a horse's backside. But he's a member of my council, and I'd like to see him before we leave."

"Very well." She sighed, clearly put out by my sentimentality. "Come with me. But he's been particularly foul since the spike in the gut incident. You'd better gird your loins, Lares."

Ferral was lying in a bed much like the one in the room I'd been given. Somehow, despite his snootiness and old world ways, even he didn't look right swathed in crimson velvet.

The advocate scowled in my direction as I stepped through the door, his silver gaze narrowing. "How nice of you to visit, Madam Lares. I trust you didn't harm yourself rushing to see me?"

I rolled my eyes. "I actually just found out you were here, advocate." I allowed a smile to form. Despite his obviously foul mood, I was very happy to see him. "I thought you were dead." My voice broke on the last word, and I quickly cleared my throat.

Ferral's scowl deepened. "Please tell me you haven't forgotten the most basic of our lessons? You have a connection to each member of your council. Did you forget to tap into it?" He sounded so disgusted with me that I almost smiled. No matter how things changed, some things always stayed the same. "I did tap into it. You weren't there."

He stared at me, something softening slightly in his coolly handsome face. "That's not possible."

I shrugged, moving across the room and lowering myself to the edge of his bed. "And yet it happened." I allowed emotion to show in my gaze. "I'm glad you're okay."

He looked away, his hands clasped on top of the covers, the knuckles white. He was upset or... emotional. The thought bloomed warm in my chest. The advocate fought to hide his emotions, but he apparently still had them. A fact I would have never guessed if I hadn't seen his struggle with my own eyes.

"Tell me how you're doing."

He opened his mouth, a sly light moving through the silver gaze. I put a hand up to stop him. "Honestly. Don't be snippy. I really want to know."

He closed his mouth and sighed. "Honestly, I feel like a hound's backside."

The metaphor surprised a laugh out of me. "You *are* a hound's backside. And its front side. And its middle."

His lips twitched. "Point taken."

"Is the crone taking care of your injuries? Can you leave with us?"

"Yes. And...no." He hesitated a moment and then pulled the covers back to show me a massive wrap around his flat belly. "Unfortunately, I took a leviathan spike in the belly. I was all but dead when the crone's people found me. I'm lucky to still be on this side of the veil."

I swallowed hard. I couldn't see the actual wound, thank the goddess, but his entire torso was swollen and purple from the injury. He had to be in incredible pain. I placed a hand on his arm, giving it a squeeze. "Do what you need to heal. I'll miss your judgmental eyebrows on my team until you come home."

Amazingly, he laughed. For once, a glint of humor even reached his eyes. "It will be my pleasure to continue judging you from afar." He speared me with that cool silver gaze. "Tell me where we are on the search for the girl."

I filled him in on what the crone told us. When I finished, we sat quietly for a long moment. He finally nodded. "The father is a good place to start. You might also ask the Reverend to find Willow in the deathly veil and question her. It's possible her ghost can help find the girl."

"You think Willow's dead?"

"I do. They don't need the mother if they have the child. I'm certain they expect the child to be more malleable than her mother."

Okay, that alarmed me. I'd been assuming Wanda's hex was simply a punishment. It never occurred to me that someone might be grooming her for something. "Why would someone want to keep Wanda in limbo? What would they want with her?"

"She is a powerful magical historian. Perhaps the

most powerful of our age." He paled to the color of chalk. "Do not tell the crone that."

I mimed a zipping motion over my lips.

"The girl's demonic heritage only increases her power. She holds both human and demonic magical history within her DNA. In the wrong hands, the girl will one day be very dangerous."

"One day? She's not there yet?"

He shook his head. "She is young. Historians don't reach their apex until their mid-twenties. By locking her into the curse, her tormentor has ensured they keep her in limbo until she reaches the age of usefulness."

The cold cruelty of that possibility turned me to ice. I shuddered violently, realizing the inhumanity of our foe. "What's your best guess on who we're dealing with?"

"Probably the same as yours. It's someone with uncommon cruelty in their hearts. Someone with large aspirations and zero humanity." He grabbed my hand, surprising himself as much as me if the look on his face was any indication. A feverish heat pulsed through my skin where we touched. "Whoever it is, they think they're in control, Aggy. When you threaten that sense of control, they'll panic and that will be very dangerous. Do you understand?"

"Yes." Unfortunately, I understood all too well.

19

ALAS A FRIEND HATH COME
TO CALL

As we trudged out of the passage back onto the rock wall, a strident caw filled the air, and my head snapped up. "Ray?"

My gaze scoured the rugged cliffside that contained the maze, and then the trees. I didn't see the raven. Knowing he'd show up when he was ready, I scooped Monty up and slid into the water. A second caw sounded as we started back to shore.

I stumbled wearily onto the sand a moment later. My lack of sleep and the chaos of our journey were taking a toll on me. Monty wriggled with excitement, so I put him down. "I'd give almost anything to have even half his energy right now," I told Mavis.

"Ditto," mom agreed. She looked tired too. Dark circles underscored her pretty gray eyes.

Sand geysered up in an area twenty feet away from us, and Niele landed in a graceful crouch. He lifted his gaze and gave me a smile. "Madam Lares. I trust you had a good visit with the crone?"

I'd never been so happy to see the gnome, stick and berries and all. "It went about as well as could be expected. How was your little project?"

He straightened, squaring his shoulders. "Amazing fun. I'd like to come back again soon. There's still a bit of fine tuning I'd like to do to the coral beds."

I nodded. "Of course. For now, though, are you ready to go home? We've got a lead on Wanda."

His smile died as he remembered why we'd come in the first place. "Of course." He examined his sandy feet for a moment, then said, "I'm sorry I wasn't more help with...everything."

He'd apparently heard about the leviathan. "No worries. The good will you created with the crone was probably all that kept her from feeding us to the monsters herself."

He nodded, his brows lowering in a concerned expression. "She was very pleased with my work."

"Caw!"

My head jerked up at the sound. Shock sent me stumbling backward, slamming to my butt in the sun-warmed sand. I'd expected to see Ray perched high in the rocks or atop one of the delicate little palm trees several yards away from the water's edge.

I never expected what stood in front of me.

The white horse tossed her silky mane and snorted, the raven dancing over her wide back.

Bev gave me a hand up from the sand, never taking her eyes from the horse. "Was that there a minute ago?"

I brushed sand off my butt. "I'm pretty sure it wasn't."

"Why does that horse look familiar?" Mavis murmured for our ears only.

Gren heard her anyway. "She was at the Hell-mouth battle," he said, giving me a look filled with concern. "She came out of the Hellmouth with a demon on her back."

It had been a very handsome, white-haired demon whose considerable charm lasted only as long as it took me to kill him.

Bev and Mavis flung up their hands and began weaving a spell.

I stepped in front of them. "She's not an enemy," I told them, hoping it wasn't a lie.

When they continued to look worried, I glanced at Gren. "Tell them, please?"

"I don't believe the creature is of the dark. I'm fairly certain she was a victim of the demon control-ling her."

My family relaxed slightly at his words. If I hadn't been so full of questions about the horse's sudden appearance, I'd have gotten my feelings hurt that they'd believed him and not me.

I was suddenly relieved that Layla and her guards had elected to stay behind with Ferral so the crone could continue healing the lost ones.

"What do you suppose it's doing here?" I asked Gren. "Do you think she followed us from home?"

He was staring fixedly at the beautiful equine, and she was staring back at him, her bright green gaze snapping with defiance.

I reached out and touched his arm. "Gren?"

He seemed to shake himself out of his thoughts, turning a sharp brown gaze my way. "She's here for a specific reason," he said. "Her kind doesn't appear to just anyone." His gaze held mine, speculation tightening his features. "She did seem to bond with you at the Hellmouth," he said.

I considered telling him about seeing the horse on my property but decided against it. If the horse had wanted her presence known, she'd have shown herself to him too. I started toward the mare, speaking in low tones so as not to startle her. I extended a hand, palm up, to show her I meant her no harm. "Hello, gorgeous."

The horse knickered softly, nuzzling my palm and then licking it.

I laughed. "She licked me."

Monty barked his distrust of the white horse, and she pinned her ears at him. But, when I picked him up, the White Mare gave him a wet snuffle.

Monty yelped and fought to get free.

I laughed. "There's my big, brave hero."

He drooped slightly, looking embarrassed.

The mare tossed her head and danced with impatience, nudging me with her velvety nose.

"She's right. We need to go," Gren said.

"We need to wait for our guide," I told him before the light bulb flared to life above my head. "Ah. Oh!" Excitement injected me with a shot of adrenaline. "You're our guide, aren't you, gorgeous?"

The horse knickered and stamped an anxious hoof.

"Okay then," I said. "Let's get going."

We turned toward the maze.

"Wait!" a voice called.

I spun on my heel, seeing Layla coming out of the ocean, her gaze riveted on the horse. Her hands were clenched into fists at her sides, her expression murderous.

I moved to stand in front of the horse. "You will not hurt this animal," I told the princess.

"Step aside, Aggy. That mare is dangerous. She can bring demons across worlds. She needs to die."

S creaming with outrage, the mare rose up onto her hind legs and pawed the air. Her hooves had barely touched the sand again before she was galloping toward Layla.

The princess suddenly held two deadly-looking curved blades in her hands, the carvings in the blood-red blades clearly demonic. Her jaw tight, she took a stance, the blades swirling around her fingers before settling into place in her palms. The mare stopped just out of range and spun. She leaped off the ground, her back hooves flashing out in a blur of motion.

Layla flew backward, splashing back into the water.

The mare turned and pawed the air again, trumpeting her rage.

Layla was up and out of the water with inhuman speed, her hands flashing in circular strikes that severed strands of the mare's thick mane, sending them drifting to the sand.

The mare's head whipped forward, her teeth snapping with each strike, and blood ran from an assortment of wounds on Layla's arms and shoulders.

Agile and fast, Layla struck back, managing to score several hits even as the mare drew more of her blood.

The White Mare leaped into the air, her hooves flashing in deadly strikes as she flew over Layla's striking blades. One hoof landed, then another, every blow sending Layla reeling, her eyes rolling as if she was fighting to stay conscious. Each attack was accompanied by a flash of light that seemed to disorient Layla even more.

Finally, one huge hoof caught Layla in the temple and she went down under a shimmering white glow of power, her body still.

I hurried over as the mare galloped along the water's edge, clearly trying to work off the last of her rage.

Dropping to my knees, I pulled the strange knives off the princess's fingers and handed them to Gren. A red-hot anger tangled with my worry about Layla's too pale state. She was so still lying there. She barely breathed. She'd started a battle with a creature who'd done nothing to harm any of us. She'd probably gotten what she deserved. But I didn't want her to die because of it. "We need the crone to heal her."

Gren shook his head. "She'll be fine. Look."

The color was returning to Layla's cheeks, and she was starting to stir. Even the deep wound on her head was healing.

When I gave Gren a surprised glance, he nodded toward the horse. "The White Mare knows the princess is your ally. She sent magic along with her strikes. Layla will recover quickly. But you need to keep her from trying again to harm the mare."

"It looks to me like there's more danger of Layla being harmed."

He nodded in agreement. "We need them both, Aggy."

I sighed. "Can you take the others and leave me with her?" I nodded at Layla. "I'll talk sense into her before we join you in the maze."

He stared at me a moment and then went to speak to the mare. A moment later, the horse trotted past, throwing a final whinny of reproach over her glossy shoulder. Layla groaned, and her eyes snapped open. She started to sit up, but I stopped her with a hand on her chest. "Stay right there." I glanced around, surprised to find Mavis and Bev sitting astride the mare. With a final glance our way, the horse spun on her hooves and took off running. She didn't go into the maze.

I started to object.

"She can pass directly through the veil," Gren said. That was the first I realized he'd stayed behind. "She will return for you shortly."

Layla shoved my hand off her chest. "Why are you helping the beast?"

"The crone gave her to us as a guide," I told Layla. "I'm pretty sure you didn't intend to offend the crone?" I lifted my brows for emphasis.

"That would be a very bad idea," Gren added to season the stew.

Layla climbed slowly to her feet. "If the beast is under the crone's protection, I'll leave it be." She gave me a look. "For now."

"Good," I stood too, brushing sand off my butt and legs. Monty bounced around Layla's feet, tongue lolling.

"The little hero wants to go home," Layla told me, unable to suppress a grin.

"So do I. And he *is* going home. But, I'm afraid we're not staying there for long." I frowned. "Why did you follow us out? I thought you'd planned to stay with your men."

She shook her head. "They will escort the hound back to Rome. I need to come with you to find the girl."

"Why?" Gren asked, his expression curious.

"Because I know the demon Bathos."

"Who's Bathos?" I asked.

"The girl's father. He will lie to you. He will also lie to me. But I will know when he is lying."

Gren and I exchanged a look. He gave me the slightest of nods, confirming that he thought it was a good idea to bring Layla.

"Okay. But only if you promise not to try to hurt the mare."

Inclining her chin, Layla said, "You have my word as your ally."

I nodded, looking at Niele. "You're staying with me?"

"Yes." He threw Layla a glance. "The protector and I will stay close."

Layla rolled her eyes at his inference that I needed to be protected from her.

Monty barked as if to assure me he'd stay close too. I petted his sleek head. "Then let's start walking. It appears we've lost our ride."

20

THE COMING JOURNEY
UNPLEASANT FOR ALL

After much argument, I convinced Mavis and
Bev to stay back with Monty. Mavis was still
weak from her injuries, and Bev had a day job which
she'd already neglected too much in helping me. I
appreciated her help but didn't want to cost her a job
she loved.

Besides, I didn't expect the next leg of our
journey to be anything more than an information-
gathering exercise.

I know what you're thinking. That had been the
plan with the crone too. And look how that had
turned out.

I shook off the thought and waved goodbye to
Bev, Mavis, and Monty. My dog, at least, was enthusiastic for a new adventure. Especially one that
included a ride in Bev's sporty red convertible.

Gren, Layla, Niele, and I scarfed down some food

and I took a hot shower while waiting for Luke and Trish to arrive.

After my shower, I took a side trip to the grave-yard and called to the Rev.

Reverend Dodson eased into view. With the sun still bathing the consecrated burial ground, the ghost was a wispy figure. "Hello, Madam Lares. Did you have a pleasant trip?"

I snorted out a laugh. "It was definitely exciting."

The Rev clasped his hands in front of him. "That's good. Can I help you with something?"

"Yes. As you know, we're trying to find Wanda. The advocate suggested you might be able to locate her mother in the deathly veil? We're hoping she can help us find her daughter."

"Willow." He nodded. "I know of her. I'll see what I can find."

Sadness for Wanda swept over me. Her mother was really dead. I'd been holding out hope it wasn't true. I thanked Reverend Dodson for his help, and joined the others, who were waiting at the edge of the woods, where the White Mare also waited.

An hour later we stood at the edge of a different part of the woods, looking out over acres of manicured green grass, perfectly sculpted shrubbery, and a crystal clear pond that sported massive black and white swans, gliding serenely across its surface.

Like a floating chessboard.

I looked at Niele. "Get as close as you can without being noticed."

He nodded and leaped into the air, diving into the earth and disappearing beneath its surface. The perfect grass mounded for several yards and then flattened out as Niele plunged deeper into the earth.

Ray lifted off my shoulder with a soft "Caw!" and took off toward the mansion in the distance. "He'll be my eyes in the sky," I told the group. Sitting astride the White Mare, I smoothed a hand over her damp neck beneath the heavy mane. She knickered softly at my caress, her green gaze sparking brightly for a moment before returning to normal.

Layla walked up behind us, and the mare's nostrils flared wide. She gave an alarmed snort and spun to face the princess.

Layla rolled her eyes. "Chillax, horse. I'm not going to make dog food out of you. At least not today." She gave the mare a sly smile. "I promised Aggy."

"You will never hurt this horse," I told the princess. "Or our alliance is over, and you and I will be enemies."

Layla flipped a dismissive hand and lifted her gaze to mine. "The woods are too quiet. There are no pixies. No wildlife or flutterflies. Nothing except an icy wickedness that's making me kind of twitchy."

I smiled at her description. But the smile didn't last long. She wasn't wrong. I'd been feeling kind of twitchy myself. "What does that mean?"

Gren responded before Layla could. "It means the demon Bathos has vile friends."

"Curse, swear," I murmured, feeling the mare shifting nervously beneath me.

"What are we doing?" Luke asked.

He looked agitated, his gaze constantly skimming the area around us.

The wolf was twitchy too.

"I need to wait for Ray and Niele's reports. Then we can figure out what to do next."

We didn't have to wait long.

The world went crooked on its axis as Ray looped me into what he was seeing. A green, brown, and multi-hued panorama drifted before my eyes, the horizon tilting one way and then the other as wooziness nearly knocked me off the mare.

Warm hands found my thighs and held me in place. "Thanks," I told Gren, fighting my way through vertigo to accept the view of a massive white stone home built around a sizeable courtyard. Large pots overflowing with flowers of all imaginable colors adorned a small pool whose surface glittered silver beneath the sunlight. The grounds were dotted with a decorative assortment of flower and fruit-bearing trees.

People scurried back and forth through the centrally-located courtyard, clearly using it as a pass-through to get from one part of the mansion to another.

The furnishings of the outdoor area looked luxurious and expensive, probably better quality than anything I had *inside* my own home.

The horizon tipped again, and we plummeted from the sky at a stomach-clenching speed. For a single heartbeat, I thought Ray had been attacked and he was falling. But then his flight pattern evened out, and he landed on a window sill at the front of the house.

Like the rest of the mansion, the glass was spotless, giving back a reflection of the raven as he strutted and pecked and pressed closer to see inside.

It took my eyes a moment to adjust to the scene.

But then I saw him.

He leaned against an enormous fireplace, a blazing fire dancing within. The oversized hearth was no doubt meant for a room four times larger than the one where Bathos stood, but he appeared perfectly comfortable, even as the dancing flames bathed him in uninterrupted heat.

His coal-black hair was smooth and glossy, with just a touch of silver at the temples that made him look very distinguished. He was a handsome man.

Tall and agile as he moved away from the fire and lowered himself gracefully into a chair. He shot pristine white cuffs and lifted a perfect black brow at the figure sitting across from him.

I couldn't see much of his visitor. The graying brown hair hung a few inches above a set of narrow shoulders, leading me to think it was a woman. But that wasn't necessarily true. In the magical community, many men wore their hair longer, and not every man had the broad shoulders I admired so much in Gren.

The chair hid everything else about the figure, and he...she...didn't speak with his or her hands or turn his or her head, robbing me of those additional details that might have helped me identify the person.

I refocused on Bathos, finding him looking just as calm as before. His expression was relaxed, and his body loose. Until he lifted his black eyes toward the window and spotted Ray.

Bathos' dark eyes widened at the discovery and he stood.

"Ray, get out of there!" I screamed.

The world tilted and whirled, and I tilted with it, vertigo pulling me right off the horse.

Gren managed to catch me before I hit the ground, and held me upright as the world continued to sway.

Wrenching his perspective brutally away, Ray

took off with a strident call. As my vision cleared, I looked across the grass to see his sleek black wings pounding the air in an attempt to escape as two enormous birds came at him from opposite directions.

I turned to Gren. "Help him."

Gren inclined his head and took off running. With a single leap he was airborne, the width of his charcoal-colored wings pulling the breath from my lungs as they thrummed against the air.

But he would be too late.

The two predator birds dove at Ray, one striking him with its beak and, as he tumbled toward the ground, the other slashing at him with its claws.

I screamed his name as he fell...too fast...too far from the ground to survive the impact, and took off running.

Hoofbeats thundered up behind me. The mare's hooves tore up the ground as she caught up with me, slowed to match my speed, and whinnied.

I turned and grabbed her mane, leaping off the ground and onto her back without missing a stride. Then we were off, running so fast the world was a blur around me.

Gren dove toward the falling raven, his wings plastered flat along his muscular legs to reduce wind resistance.

I watched the small spec of black begin to stir as he plunged, wings lifting to fight the downward spiral. But he was tangled and weak. And he wasn't going to be able to save himself.

Panic made me helpless.

Instinct made me act.

A simple word formed in my mind, my intent built into the instinctive command, "*Slow!*"

The word slammed into reality, its power like fire against my skin. A soft boom met its arrival, and it grabbed hold of the world, braking the action around me, slowing it until I could catch up.

And suddenly we were there, beneath Ray as he fell. I stretched out my arms, and the bird fell into them, his wings akimbo and his neck extended in an unnatural way as he fought to regain his equilibrium. I thought, at first, that he hadn't yet realized he was safe. But then I heard the strident call of an enormous hawk and looked up in time to see the monster-sized bird diving toward my face.

The mare screamed, threw on the brakes, and sent Ray and me flying as she rose off the ground, hooves flashing in a violent strike against the hawk.

I curled myself around Ray and we slammed into the thick grass. We skidded a few feet and came to a stop near the edge of the pretty pool. Above our heads, the second hawk screamed its rage as Gren barreled into it, wrapping his wings around the bird and crushing it against his body.

The nearest hawk fluttered away, one wing not

quite working properly, and disappeared around the house.

The white mare stamped her hooves in the grass and threw back her head, screaming her victory. She trotted over and gently nuzzled me, snorfling hot breath into my hair.

I groaned, sitting up and shoving hair off my face. "Well, that was unplanned."

Ray ruffled his feathers and shuddered from head to toe. He stretched his wings experimentally before taking off with an enraged cry.

Gren landed a few feet away, a bloody blade in each hand and a hard look in his dark brown eyes. Trish buzzed by in her warrior form, and Luke bounded up to us as the black wolf. He lifted his muzzle and flared his nostrils, coating the air with a feral growl as he stared toward something behind me.

I turned to see what they were all looking at and found the demon Bathos lounging against a pillar of the home's long, elegant porch. My pulse quickened at the sight. Power pulsed off him in waves that brought gooseflesh up on my arms and painted my spine with ice.

"Visitors," the demon said, his deep voice echoing with a strange bass growl. "How nice. Shall I kill you before tea? Or after?"

I pushed to my feet, ignoring Gren's offered hand because I didn't want to appear even a little bit weak in front of the demon. "That depends. Will there be cookies?"

His laugh had the ring of real pleasure, even with the echoing growl. "I believe that can be arranged."

Nodding, I forced my feet to move forward. "Then let's have tea first. I can always kill you later. After I have a full belly."

He indicated a seating area alongside the pool. "Please, Madam Lares, sit." He eyed my council and the White Mare. I didn't like the look in his black gaze when he looked at the horse.

"I'd heard amazing things about our new guardian," he said, sitting down next to me as my council spread out around the pool, far enough away to give the illusion of privacy, but close enough to intervene should Bathos decide to be naughty. "But I had no idea you'd acquired the White Mare. Impressive."

"She's a friend," I told him. "I don't own her."

The horse's eyes gleamed with angry green fire as she stared the demon down.

"Really?" He looked delighted. "Then you won't mind if I take her for my own."

It wasn't a question. I was pretty sure the demon never asked anyone for anything. He had an air about him of a spoiled prince who was used to getting anything he wanted.

It would please me very much to ruin that streak for him. "Actually, I'd mind that very much. If you try to harm or trap her, you and I will have a problem."

He laughed again, shaking his head as if I were a difficult child.

Two servants came out of the mansion, both dressed in crisp black shirts and pleated black slacks. The woman settled a large tray filled with cakes, small pies, and cookies onto the table between us. The man set his tray down on a larger table behind us and poured.

A moment later, he handed me a perfectly brewed cup of tea that smelled like jasmine. I thanked him. He nodded and melted silently to the background to await any further requests.

I tasted the tea, finding it sweetened just the way I liked it...with just a touch of raw honey. "Mm," I said. "Delicious."

"I am pleased to hear it. Now, Madam Lares, to what do I owe the honor of this visit?"

He has a dungeon, Niele said in my mind. *There is a human in it*.

I tensed at the news, my gaze no doubt showing my displeasure.

He noticed. "Is there a problem?"

"Yes." I put the cup down and stood. Gren was at my side in a heartbeat. Trish buzzed closer and Luke lowered his head, eyeing the two servants with a snarl that sent them scuttling inside. "I must insist you release the human you're holding in your dungeon."

Bathos' dark brows lifted in quick surprise, but he rapidly smoothed out his expression as he stood too. "And if I refuse?"

"Then we will take the prisoner from you." When he started to smile, I added, "And you and I will be at war."

He stared at me for a long moment, the unsettling eyes narrowing just slightly. He didn't want to release his prisoner. He didn't like it even more that I was telling him what to do. But he also didn't seem to like the idea of being on my bad side.

I filed that away to be examined later.

Bathos sighed, picking at an invisible piece of lint on his sleeve. "You may take her. I've proven my point. But in return, you must do something for me."

I bit back my instinctive desire to tell him I didn't owe him anything. "What could I possibly do for you, Bathos?"

His smile was tight. The name thing always curdled demons' whey. There was power in names. And my using his irritated.

"I'm afraid I find myself in kind of a pickle," the demon said to me.

I felt my brows peaking in surprise. "Oh?"

"Yes." He clasped his hands behind his back and began to pace. Watching him, I realized he was genuinely upset.

Intrigued, I waited for him to tell me what he wanted.

Layla came up next to me, throwing me a look I couldn't read. When Bathos saw her, a small smile curved his lips. "Princess. I'm surprised to see you here."

"I don't know why, demon Bathos. Like you, I recognize that the key to thriving in this world is to work with the guardian."

He inclined his head and finally stopped his pacing. Standing an uncomfortable distance of two feet away, Bathos lowered what appeared to be a sincere look on me. His black eyes filled with as much sincerity as they could manage. "Something of mine is missing. Something very precious." He stepped closer, and I fought the urge to step back. "Madam Lares, I need your help. My daughter has been taken. And I fear that she's in great danger."

21

AN UNWORTHY PLEA FROM ONE
MOST FOUL

I fought to keep my expression neutral. I must have been successful because Bathos became agitated as if he feared I'd refuse him. Glancing at Layla, I found her staring at the demon with a contemplative look.

"Layla?" I urged.

She finally turned and gave me a little nod.

Behind Bathos, a commotion erupted, and the glass doors into the house flew open. Covered in dirt and grass, Niele marched out, his homely face tight with anger. He stopped just outside the door and reached through, taking the arm of a frail woman dressed in torn, filthy clothes. Her gray hair was plastered to a pinched and weary face. Dirt smeared the exposed flesh of her face and arms and she was limping, her shoes covered in muck.

I started forward when I saw her. "Dell?"

"Madam Lares..." Bathos began.

I jerked to a stop and grabbed his pristine shirt, shoving my face close to his. "You imprisoned a member of the coven in your dungeon?" My voice throbbed with power, the sudden uncontrollable rage tightening the muscles of my jaw and neck. I wanted to send a wave of unrestrained power into the demon and watch him fly away. I wanted to show him who he was dealing with.

A warm hand found my arm. I all but snarled at Gren.

His expression remained calm, though I could see the anger pulsing in the depths of his molten dark chocolate gaze. "Don't act rashly, Aggy," he warned softly. "You'll start something none of us wants to finish." He gave a quick, minute jerk of his head toward Bathos, and I swung my gaze back to the demon, seeing the pulsing aura of his magic, black and oily, rising around him like a fog.

It took me another second to regain my calm. Finally, I realized Gren was right. If Ferral were there, he'd have told me the same thing. I forced my fingers to loosen on Bathos's shirt and stepped back. "Explain yourself."

He inclined his head. His smile was cold, his eyes swirling with the colors of flame. "The witch knows something about my daughter's abduction. I was... questioning her."

I skimmed a glance over the purpling bruises

nearly hidden by the dirt, and the ragged cut on Dell's cheek, just beneath her eye. "Are you unable to question someone without beating them?"

He squared his shoulders, lifting his chin. "Only when they don't lie." He ground out the last word, turning a wrath-filled scowl in Dell's direction.

To her credit, she stood tall and glared back at him. "I didn't lie to you, demon. I was at your daughter's home." She slid me a look. "At the Lares' request. We were *trying* to find her."

Curse, curse, swear, swear! Had I inadvertently gotten Dell beaten?

"She's telling you the truth," I told Bathos. "Wanda came to me in a vision. She was scared. She asked me for help. We did a tracking spell to find her."

Bathos' eyes widened, he stepped forward, his fingers curling as if to grab my arm.

Gren's hand snaked out and gripped Bathos' wrist before he could touch me. "Stand. Down. Demon," he ground out.

Bathos was a small man. Probably not more than five feet eight inches tall. Gren stood nearly six inches taller than Bathos and probably outweighed him by fifty pounds. But the demon held my protector's stare for a long moment, no doubt assessing how they stacked up magically. Apparently, he decided it would be more difficult to find out than the situation warranted. After all, we appeared to be on the same side of things. Both of us searching for Wanda.

If the demon could be trusted. Which was a huge "If."

Bathos jerked his arm from Gren's grip and paced away as if he didn't trust himself to stand close to me.

I knew the feeling. "Tell me what you know about Wanda's abduction."

"Not much," he said, swiping a hand through the midnight silk of his hair. "I've been magically monitoring her." His head jerked up at my outraged gasp. "Purely for security reasons. My spell only keeps track of who enters and leaves the apartment. And..." He grimaced slightly. "Her moods."

"Her moods?" I asked, not believing what I was hearing.

"Yes." He sighed, dropping gracefully into a poolside chair. "I feared for her mental state after her mother was taken. After..." He took a deep breath. "The spell she was under was sometimes hard on her."

"Ya think?" Layla asked, earning a sharp look from the demon.

"It wasn't generally bad, you know. The hex," he said. "It kept her safe. While that pastor was there she had a friend who kept her from dwelling too much on the loss of her mother." He sighed. "But then he died, and she was...lonely."

"You knew what was going on, and you left her in that apartment? Alone" I ground out. "You left that hex on her? If you truly loved her as you're pretending to, you'd have gotten her out of there. You'd have removed the hex."

"And then what?" he asked, his gaze turning fiery again. "Bring her here?" He lifted his arms to indicate the massive property. "I'm sure you know what goes on here, Lares. It's no fit place for a child."

"Here's a radical thought," I yelled back. "You could have cleaned up your act. For Wanda. For your *daughter*."

Surprisingly, he looked sad. "I can't. You wouldn't understand. But I have certain obligations here. I report to others. Those who are more powerful than you can imagine. What I do here is relatively harmless in the grand scheme. But if I tried to step away..." He shook his head. "You don't want to know the consequences."

"Surely you knew about your daughter's magic," Gren said softly. "You had to know those who cursed her would come for her, eventually."

"No." He shook his head again. "She was safe. I was closely monitoring her. Seeing to her needs. Food, clothing, anything she needed. And then she found you, and she was happy again." His expression softened as he looked at me. "I thought it could be the best of both worlds. She would be safe, and she would have someone who cared for her." He dropped his head into his hands. "This should never have happened."

"You don't know who took her?" I asked.

"No." He threw a glare at Dell. "The coven had something to do with it."

"I told you we know nothing about it," Dell said. "You need to look closer to home. The Lares believes there might be a demon involved."

Bathos' gaze snapped to me. "What do you know?"

"I only know what Wanda told me," I said evasively. "Tell me what you know about the curse? How did you find out about it? What did Willow have to do with it?"

He jolted slightly at the mention of Wanda's mother. Real pain crossed his handsome features, catching me off guard.

Was everything he was telling me true? Had he truly been in love with Willow? Did he really love his daughter?

"Willow came to me a few months before she disappeared. She was scared. She wanted me to take her and the girl in. Let them live here. I'm ashamed to say I didn't even listen to her concerns. She said something about a dark force trying to make use of her magic. I discounted it as hysteria. Willow was prone to random bouts of drama based on nothing except her unending need for attention."

"Apparently, you should have listened to her," I

said. I didn't even bother to try to hide my disgust at his cool disregard of the woman and child he professed to care about.

"Apparently." Bathos fell into thought for a moment. Then went on. "For the girl's sake, I put the monitoring ward on their apartment so that I'd know if anyone who didn't belong tried to get inside." He glared at Dell again. "The night Willow was taken, a witch entered the apartment."

My brows peaked. "You're sure of that?"

"I am. Witches have a very specific magic signature."

"None of the covens would have taken the girl," Dell said, her expression becoming even more pinched than normal. "We have members on the Lares' council. Do you really think we'd be that stupid?"

Her words gave me pause. Would they have been stupid to steal Wanda out from under my nose? Or would they have believed they'd be the last people I'd look at because of Bev, Mavis, and Trish?

I glanced at Trish. She popped from her warrior fairy form back to human. "If the coven was involved, Aggy, I can promise you that Bev, Mavis, and I knew nothing about it."

"Is there a way to test the remnants of witch magic in the apartment to determine which witch was there?" I asked.

Before Trish could respond, Dell interrupted.

"Even if that were possible, which it isn't..." She threw a glare at Trish. "—you wouldn't trace the magic to us. I'm telling you, we didn't do it."

I ignored Dell and kept my gaze pointedly on Trish. She didn't flinch from the question in my gaze. "Madam Lares, if my coven is involved, I will personally take them down. I believe with my whole heart that they are not."

Nodding, I decided to talk to Mavis, Bev, and Trish when Dell wasn't around.

I turned to Bathos. "Why would a demon be involved in hexing and abducting Wanda?"

He frowned. "The girl's magic isn't particularly useful to demons. We try to keep ourselves and our business separate from the rest of the magical world. Other magical races tend to judge our practices poorly."

"You don't say?" Luke asked, his voice dripping with disdain.

I hadn't even noticed him shifting back.

Bathos didn't give the shifter the respect of a glance or response. "The only reason a demon would get involved is if it were compelled to do so."

"What about the promise of money? Power?"

He shook his head. "Money holds no sway with our kind. We take what we need either through force or magic."

Angry color rose into my face at his admission.

Seeing it, he shrugged. "I'm being honest with

you, Lares." He narrowed his gaze. "Why do you believe demonkind was involved?"

"We found a demonic signature at Wanda's home," Trish said.

Bathos sighed. "That would be from me. I...go there when Wanda is out to bring food and other things." He gave me what looked for all the world like an apologetic look. "You'll find my signature in your belfry too, Madam Lares. I..." He frowned. "I sometimes go there because Wanda leaves residual magic when she visits. It calms me."

Goddess! Did the demon really love his daughter?

"So, what kind of compelling are you talking about?" Luke asked, bringing us back to the possibility of demonic influence in Wanda's disappearance.

"I'm talking about force. Magical force."

Gren and I shared a look. His expression was grim. I knew exactly how he felt. As much as I disliked creatures from the demonic plane, I disliked the idea of someone from Rome making use of their dark powers even more. "Could a witch compel a demon?" I asked, just to make sure we were on the same page.

He inclined his head. "It's extremely difficult. Unless you are lucky enough to have one thing."

Bathos frowned, and I knew exactly what thing he was referring to. "The demon's genuine, full name."

"Yes."

"Who were you talking to in there?" Gren suddenly asked.

Bathos looked surprised. "I'm sorry?"

Gren pointed to the house. "The person you were speaking to when we arrived. Who was it?"

Bathos shook his head. "It's not someone you need to concern yourself with."

"We'll decide if that's true," Gren said.

I glanced at my protector, wondering what he was thinking.

"Just a business associate," Bathos said after a brief pause. "None of your concern."

22

THE VILLAIN'S COMPLAINT A TAINTED HOWL

"I'm pretty sure we should be very concerned about who Bathos was talking to," Gren said as we headed back toward the wood.

I agreed. *Ray? Can you sit on the house? Let me see when anybody comes or goes.*

The sound of fluttering feathers filled my mind, followed by a strident caw as the raven headed away from the building and settled into a tree across the street, where he'd hopefully be safe from the oversized hawk things.

"Ray will watch the house," I told the group. "If Bathos gets a visit from someone in the coven, I'll know it."

Dell had elected to find her own way home. She'd left us with a sniff and a flick of her wrist, mumbling about going back home to Chicago where things made better sense.

I walked alongside the White Mare, my hand on her neck just because the contact felt right.

I glanced at Layla. "What's your impression of Bathos? Do you think he was telling us the truth?"

She didn't hesitate. "Yes. On most of it. The part about his visitor was suspect. I think he was lying about that having nothing to do with Wanda."

We stepped beneath the trees, the familiar snap of magic against my skin a reminder that, despite all the thoughts tumbling through my mind, I needed to stay sharp as we passed through the Mystical Wood.

"What's next?" Luke asked.

Hey mama, ho mama, answer your dang phone, mama...

I sighed.

Trish and Layla laughed.

Hey mama, ho mama, answer your dang phone, mama...

I hit the answer button. "That one has a nice ring to it," I told Mavis. "Get it? Ring?"

Mavis giggled happily. "I liked it. Hey, I'm going over to Willy's for a bit. Will Monty be okay at my house alone?"

"You can just drop him off at my house if you don't mind. We're on our way back."

"Sure. How'd it go? What's the demon daddy like?"

I thought about how best to respond and finally settled on, "Better looking than I expected."

"Really?" Her question was laden with innuendo. "Do tell."

I rolled my eyes and caught Gren staring at me. My cheeks heated. "Not a chance," I told Mavis. "Are you coming over later?"

"You mean like, in time to cook dinner?" Her voice held a teasing note.

"Not at all, smarty pants. I was going to order Chinese takeout."

"Of course, you were." She laughed. "I'll be there. I have a new chili and cornbread recipe I've been wanting to try. I'll see you later."

"Love you," I said before she hung up.

"Love you back."

We trudged on in silence, everyone seemingly lost in thought.

I glanced at Niele, surprised to see him topside with us. His homely face was folded into a deep frown. The usually good-natured gnome didn't look at all happy.

"What's wrong?" I asked him.

He jolted slightly, settling a startled look on me. "What?"

"Why do you look like somebody just kicked your kitten?"

"My k..." He grimaced. "Kittens are not my

favorite, but I would definitely not allow one to be kicked, Madam Lares."

"Just Aggy, please."

"Your wish is my command, Madam Lares Just Aggy Please." A ghost of a smile tilted the outside edges of his wide mouth.

I fought a smile. The name thing was a private joke between us. He hadn't done it for a while and I'd missed joking around with him. Things had been way too crazy and dangerous since I'd entered everybody's lives. There'd been little time for fun. "Why do you look so unhappy?" I asked the gnome.

"Something about that dungeon bothered me," he said. "Well. Everything about that dungeon bothered me. But one thing stood out over the rest."

"What one thing?"

He stared at his feet for a long moment, seemingly trying to find a way to voice his concern. Finally, he said. "Death, Aggy. The place was saturated with the stench of violent death."

I thought about what he'd said until we stepped back onto my lawn, happy to have the cold, malevolent feel of the forest behind me. The stain of dark magic from the woods near Bathos' place stayed with me all the way to the edge of my property, never releasing me from its icy grip.

Something besides the obvious was bothering me about Niele's statements regarding Bathos' dungeon. Something niggled just beyond my mental reach.

"Niele?"

He turned to me, his expression still tight.

"Tell me again about the dungeon."

"Aggy!" I glanced at the house to find Bev running toward us, her steps fast and her movements frantic.

I increased my pace. "What's wrong? Is it Mavis?"

She shook her head. "Mom just called. She went to see Willy..."

I nodded. "I know. She told me."

Bev gulped air, her chest rising and falling. She was breathing too hard for the short run. Unlike me, my sister was in great shape. She visited the gym regularly. The paleness in her cheeks told me the panting was emotionally triggered.

I grabbed her hands. "Tell me."

"Willy's beside herself. She said the boys..."

"The twins?" I asked, clarifying.

"Yes. They're gone."

"What do you mean, gone?" Gren questioned, moving up alongside me.

Bev shook her head. "She said she went down to their room to check on them because, in her words, they hadn't whined at her about anything for a while. They weren't in their room. They're not in the house. They're just gone."

"Maybe they went out for something?" I offered.

"No. Willy said they never did stuff like that for themselves. Especially when they were sick. Besides, their car was still in the driveway."

I scrubbed a hand over my face. The timing was terrible. I was already stressing about finding Wanda. My gaze snapped up to Bev's. "Could this be related to Wanda's disappearance?" I asked. "Did the kids know each other?"

"Not as far as I know. I hate to do this to you," Bev said. "I know you're worried about Wanda, but..."

Whatever Bev said was lost beneath the rich, ringing tones of the bell in my belfry.

A summons.

Willy's boys were in trouble.

I turned around and looked at the mare. She tossed her head, trotting over and stopping just long enough for me to grasp her mane and launch myself onto her back. She spun as Gren screamed my name, and we took off, galloping toward the woods.

The thing about a true summons was that, along with the awareness that one of my people was in trouble, it usually came with an instinctive knowledge for where I needed to go. That guidance didn't always work, as it hadn't for Wanda, probably because the curse affected her location and confused the magic. But it had told me where I could find Wilhelmina's twins.

I only hoped I'd be in time.

We dove beneath the verdant umbrella of the Mystical Woods, and the mare increased her speed. Galloping past massive trees through impossibly narrow spaces, the White Mare dug in and ran even faster whenever the trees gave way to small pockets of open ground.

Magic bit at my skin, its touch and texture changing as we passed from one visibly amorphous sovereignty to the next. Large shapes skulked in the shadows, watching us gallop past. But nothing stopped us. Even if they could catch the mare, I suspected the fact that she was under the crone's protection was well known in the magical world.

Which also made me wonder how she'd been caught by the demons and ridden through the Hellmouth. A question for another day.

The magic changed as we entered Bathos' dominion. I shuddered violently as the cold malevolence danced across my skin, leaving behind an almost crippling sense of despair. The mare seemed unaffected. She was nearly flying as we headed for the edge of the wood. Her sides heaved. Her nostrils flared, her green eyes flickered in the darkness.

We were ten feet away from the edge of the wood when two massive demons stepped in front of us, long, deadly-looking spears clutched in their claw-like hands.

The mare reacted instantly, but it almost wasn't fast enough. Dropping her haunches and skidding to a stop, she managed to stop with only inches to spare. Her sweat-foamed chest was dangerously close to the deadly tips of the spears.

I was flung off her back with the abrupt stop. A crystal clarity filled my mind as I flew over the demons' horned heads. Lifting one hand, I called for my staff. The weapon hit my palm just before I reached for the ground and tucked, rolling and coming to my feet behind the guards.

I snapped my arm, extending the weapon to its full length.

I couldn't send a stream of killing magic toward the two guards without risking the mare, so I lunged forward and slammed the staff into the side of the first demon's head. He staggered away under the force, even as I spun, utilizing my dancelike warm-up exercises defensively as I dodged and wove to avoid the demon's spear.

I stabbed the orb of my staff into the second demon's chest, shooting a thick bolt of energy through the bony torso.

The first demon came at me again and I spun, dipping low to avoid his slashing spear. The weapon mostly missed me, carving a ribbon of flesh from my side rather than impaling me through the heart.

Still, the pain nearly brought me to my knees.

The second demon flew past me on a scream, slamming into a tree trunk and sliding bonelessly toward the ground.

The mare had taken her own pound of flesh. Bless the goddess.

Gasping from the fiery pain in my side, I struck out with my staff, infusing it with as much power as I could grab, and slammed it into the demon's spear as he prepared to attack again.

The spear shattered in his hands. A thousand wooden projectiles pierced his mottled red flesh and lanced his face. He howled in pain as a particularly large shard found the tender flesh of his eye.

Panting with pain and effort, I whacked the orb of my staff into the creature's chest, sending the demon to the ground, where the mare promptly stomped on its head.

I grabbed a handful of silky mane and leaped onto the white mare's back again, and we were off, heading for the enormous house, as a blood-curdling screech tore the air.

Ray! I reached for the raven with my mind. *Ray, where are you?* Too late, I realized he'd never reported in about the comings and goings at Bathos' mansion.

Something must have happened to him. *Ray*!

A horrifying picture filled my mind. A small pile of mangled black feathers lay on the grass, unmoving. The raven's talons were outstretched, curved and stiff, a mottled brown feather speared onto one claw.

No, no, no, no! *Ray!!*

Tears burned my eyes and slid down my cheeks. Rage followed quickly in their path. I embraced the rage because it would get me through the coming encounter. The slashing pain of loss would bring me to my knees.

Aggy! Where are you? Gren asked, sounding much calmer than he should.

Approaching the mansion. Ray's... I swallowed between heaving breaths. *He's down.*

I'll check on him, Madam Lares, Niele promised.

I nodded, unable to speak.

Luke and Trish are on their way, Gren said. *And... you should know that the coven is coming.*

Curse, curse, swear, swear!

I wanted to demand that they keep Willy away. But I suspected that, if they were my kids, nobody would be able to talk me out of joining the fight. *We'll deal with it,* I told my protector.

The mare leaped over a hedge maze and kept going, her hooves hitting the concrete around the pool and clattering toward the door Bathos had come through earlier.

I sent energy through my staff and the door flew off its hinges, flying into the house in a shower of spiky bits and shattering glass.

I ducked low on the mare's neck as we galloped through the door and kept going. The sound of the horse's oversized hooves on the marble tile was almost musical. Some instinct deep inside my brain told me to just hold on for the ride as the horse galloped down a long, tiled hallway, not looking left or right and never slowing as several men with rifles suddenly appeared.

I fired magic as fast as I could, the attacks more calamity than finesse. But they did the job. Gunman flew in all directions, and only one of them climbed back to his feet. He didn't stay up for long. The mare slammed into him, knocking him over like a wobbly bowling pin on an uneven alley floor.

The horse hit the end of the hall and barely slowed as her hooves clattered against the floor in a fast but surprisingly graceful turn into an enormous kitchen. She galloped straight across the room, scattering screaming cooks dressed in stained aprons with dripping spoons clutched in their hands.

The mare headed straight toward a wooden door on the back wall.

I blasted the door out of the wall, ducking as splinters flew. A wave of cold, musty air wafted from the darkened space beyond the door, along with the nauseating stench of death and fear.

I had a beat to realize there was a steep flight of stairs descending into the inky darkness. My pulse roared in my ears as fear enveloped me.

"Wait!" I screamed, both hands wrapping the beautiful white mane in a death grip. To my sheer, breathless horror, I might as well have been talking to my dog for all that the horse listened to me.

The White Mare's hooves left the shiny kitchen floor, and she leaped through the shattered doorway, into the slimy darkness beyond.

23

A SURPRISING PARTNER IN THE FIGHT

Underneath the roaring of blood through my ears, I heard a sound like a rug snapping in the air. The horse jerked slightly and then rose into the clammy atmosphere as the largest set of pristine white wings I'd ever seen caressed the air on either side of us.

I realized I was all but laying on the mare's muscular neck and forced myself to sit up and look around, my breath sawing through my lungs in wheezing gasps.

We were flying!

I dropped my head to the mare's neck and groaned. "You could have warned me."

The horse knickered, and it sounded a lot like laughter.

I glanced around and was shocked to see that we were in some kind of underground cavern. The place was enormous, with several wide arches cut into its walls. Each opening sported a burning lantern that illuminated the first few feet of the passage.

The mare's wings stilled and we drifted downward, her hooves touching the dirt floor with barely a jolt or sound. With another soft snap, her wings disappeared and I scanned the area for movement, tasting the air with my magic. "Bathos has to be here somewhere," I whispered to the horse. She inclined her head with a snort.

Aggy?

Tension I hadn't known I was feeling softened at the sound of his voice. *Go to the kitchen,* I told Gren. *Past the traumatized cooks and through the door that's been blasted away. Stairs lead down into the dungeon. They're steep. You can fly, though. The ceiling's really high.*

On our way.

I explored a few of the passages as we waited, listening carefully at the mouth of each one for the sound of voices or activity. A moment later, I heard several sets of footsteps moving quietly down the steep wooden stairs.

I was glad to see Niele with them. As they approached, I hurried up to him. "Ray?"

The gnome's homely face gentled. "He was stunned but will be fine. I sent him home."

Relief allowed me to finally draw a breath. I

nodded. "Where were the prisoners being kept down here?"

He nodded toward the largest archway. "Through there."

With a thought, I called my staff to me. Snapping my arm to expand it to its full length, I nodded at my people. "Lead the way," I told the gnome.

He took off with an alacrity that told me better than words how he was feeling. He was out for blood. And I had a feeling he was going to get it.

Trish popped into her warrior form and buzzed after Niele. Luke followed, still in human form.

I turned to the mare. She knickered softly, tossing her head to make the silky white mane ripple like waves on a beach. "Thank you for getting me here."

The horse bobbed her head and spun around, flinging herself into the air and disappearing with a pop of displaced air.

I stared after her, eyes wide with wonder.

"Are you ready, beautiful Aggy?" Gren asked. His touch was like a brand on my arm.

"What?" I blinked a few times. "Oh. Yeah. Let's go."

The passageway led to a smaller cavern, and I quickly realized that the stench permeating the larger cavern had likely come from there. Prison cages made of iron bars that glowed with suppression magic lined both sides of the long cavern. They were all empty. Though a few of them showed signs of having recently been occupied.

Niele nodded toward another archway at the end of the cavern. We headed that way.

As we stepped into the much narrower passage, a sense of déjà vu swamped me.

Ahead of me stretched a long hallway roiling with the shadow-filled fog. I sensed the walls on either side rather than seeing them. The floor beneath me was only real because I felt its rough surface against the soles of my feet.

The shadows pressed closer. Nearly close enough for me to form them into recognizable shapes. But they never lingered long enough for that.

A rhythmic chanting sound eased through the mist, the individual words lost beneath the drone of voices.

My movement brought me closer to the chanting. Then closer still. Until I was standing in an archway, the mist cold and wet against my skin. The chanters were there, in a large circle, arms outstretched and faces obscured by dark robes.

Heat bathed my back, moving around to my side

as Gren pressed closer, lowering his head to speak softly into my ear. "Aggy, are you all right?"

I snapped out of my vision, feeling as foggy-headed as I had the first time I'd experienced it. "I..." Clearing my throat, I nodded, pushed the vision from my thoughts, and turned to him. "I think Wanda was here."

"Was?" he asked, flashing a worried gaze forward, where my people were already closing in on the end of the passage. "You don't think she's still here?"

I frowned. "I'm not sure. It's just like my vision. Minus the mist." I frowned. Where was the fog? Did the fact that it was missing mean anything?

Ahead of us, Luke jerked to a stop, lifting his head and scenting the air. In a flash of heat and light, his form dropped and lengthened, becoming the black wolf. He scented the air in that form and the hairs along his back lifted. A low growl sounded deep in his throat.

Trish buzzed back to Gren and me. "There's something going on in that small cavern ahead. I hear..."

"Chanting," I finished for her. "The boys are there."

She nodded, not questioning my assertion. Her gaze swept past me, widening.

As I turned to meet whatever was coming, I

yanked power into my staff, and the orb flared to life, illuminating the passage in pale, golden light.

The light bathed two massive devils and their petite princess, whose pretty face was tight with rage.

Layla strode toward me, her slender form outfitted in my leather battle gear and her small hands clutching matching demon blades. She stopped in front of me, flicking her guards a glance. "Check it out," she said in a harsh whisper.

To my shock, Matthew and Glenn skimmed me a look before moving. I inclined my head. "I'm glad you're both okay."

They didn't respond. Moving past us, they headed toward the distant chanting.

"They'll be able to blend into whatever's happening," Layla said, all business.

"Can you feel the type of magic being used?" I asked.

"Yes. There is at least one demon." She flicked Trish a look. "And witches."

I felt my eyes go wide. Had the coven gotten to the cavern before us? Then I remembered that the twins were technically witches, if very unskilled. "Willy's boys are here," I told Layla.

She frowned.

The shadows behind Layla shifted, and I again yanked power into my staff. Gren was suddenly holding his blades, his expression tight.

A large, gray hound moved out of the shadows, its movements lithe and silent.

Relief swept through me, and I grinned at Ferral. *It's nice of you to join us,* I teased. *Better late than never.*

The hound chuffed in a doggy laugh. *I couldn't let you do this without me,* the advocate said. *You'd likely bungle it and get yourself hurt.*

I glanced at Gren. He still held the blades, his expression dire.

I nudged him with an elbow. "It's just Ferral," I said.

"I am aware," my protector ground out through gritted teeth.

The hound chuffed again.

I shook my head. "Let's save the hostility for our enemies, okay?"

"I am," Gren said before finally relaxing. "But, it's getting harder to tell who they are."

Not having any idea what that was all about, I decided to ignore it. I turned on my heel and headed toward the end of the passage, my ears tuned for the familiar sound of chanting.

There was no sign of Matthew or Glenn, but Layla stayed close, her knuckles white around her matching blades.

I was wondering if we should move in or wait to hear back from Layla's men when a husky, pain-filled scream took the decision away from me.

Layla took off running, disappearing into the chamber ahead.

Trish shrank to the size of a butterfly and shot toward the ceiling, buzzing through the passage before my eyes even had time to register the change.

When I looked back to the archway, I caught the last few inches of Luke's tail disappearing around it.

Niele was already gone, and I realized I hadn't seen him leave, making me wonder how long he'd been in that chamber without us.

Gren clung to my side, his muscles taut with anticipation. A soft warmth pressed against my other side as Ferral took his spot.

We took off running too, moving effortlessly as a strangely cohesive unit.

I noticed two things the moment we burst through the archway into the prison chamber.

First, there was a shift in the air. Instantly it went from cool and clammy to heavy and filled with the stench of magic.

Then I felt the fear. My chest tightened, my heart pounding hard against the cage of my ribs. Sweat trickled down my temple and coated my palms, making it hard to hold onto my staff. I concentrated on moving one foot in front of the other, but it was like trudging through cooling tar, each slight movement turning my muscles weak with exhaustion.

Pressed against me, Ferral's silky gray body had a

slight tremor, his muscles tight and his hackles spiking along his back.

Gren's jaw was so rigid I thought he might crack some teeth, and he was too close, nearly tripping me with his feet. He kept glancing my way as if trying to reassure himself that I was still there.

It had to be fear magic. We'd been in tenser situations before and had never reacted so strongly.

Witch magic.

Curse, swear, curse!

A deep voice begged for mercy out of view. The words occasionally broke on a high note as fear and obvious youth gave the young man's begging a heart-rending edge.

It had to be one of the twins.

"Please, don't hurt him anymore. We'll do whatever you want, man."

Another short, sharp scream told me the begging hadn't had the intended effect.

The twin who'd begged was crying, deep, ragged sobs that nearly broke my heart in half. "Please, please, please. Hurt me instead. Leave him alone."

Gren touched my arm and we moved to the right, sliding along a jutting wall of rock that trickled with black, sulfureous water from the magic infusing the space.

I stopped at the corner and I peered around it, nearly gasping at the sight laid out before me. A dark-haired young man hung from rings embedded into the rock wall, tears tracking from his dark eyes and his clothes torn and filthy. His gaze was locked onto a hooded figure standing in the center of the space. He was shaking his head, sobbing wetly.

On the floor next to a bubbling cauldron was a second teen, the mirror image of the first. Blood ran from a dozen shallow cuts on the second twin's face, neck, and arms, painting his ragged tee-shirt a deep crimson.

Bile rose into my throat, and rage brought my magic flooding forward.

Matthew and Glenn were laid out on the rock floor. They were completely limp, only the slight rise and fall of their chests telling me they were still alive.

Luke lay a few feet away from the two lost ones. Layla was draped over him, knives still clutched in her hands. Her eyes were open, staring sightlessly toward the hooded figure.

Trish was nowhere to be seen.

I started forward, but Gren grabbed my wrist, stopping me.

I looked at him, a question written in my expression.

He stared at the scene before us, concern on his face.

It's a trap! Trish screamed in my head. *Get out, Aggy. Run!*

24

AN AWFUL VERDICT, A STUNNING PLIGHT

The hooded creature in the center of the room spun around, magic flaring from fingers that protruded, long and straight, from beneath the sleeves of the robe. Black energy speared the rock that was mere inches from my head, sending a thousand tiny shards into the air to pummel my exposed flesh.

I ducked with a yelp, diving behind the wall as the next attack cut toward us through the cavern.

From high above, pale green magic sliced downward, hitting the robed creature in the throat and drawing blood. But the hooded creature never even flinched. Instead, it turned its shadowed face up to where Trish hovered just below the ceiling and sent a fresh wave of magic in her direction.

"No!" I screamed, drawing a look from Trish. Her

tiny, pale face was lost behind a wave of deadly power.

I started forward, fearing what I'd find when the sulfurous residue cleared. The oily black energy hit some kind of barrier and exploded outward, slamming into the walls and sending rock dust raining down on us.

The ground exploded upward behind the hooded villain and Niele was suddenly there. He clamped his hands around the robed figure and threw him at the fiery cauldron. Without a sound, the villain slammed into the hot metal of the cauldron and slid bonelessly toward the ground. Hot liquid spilled over the rim and painted his robe with fire.

In the blink of an eye, Niele was bending over the limp form with a blade, his homely features twisted into a rage-filled snarl.

Despite the knife at his throat and the flames dancing over his robe, the figure didn't cry out. He didn't move. In fact, I realized, he hadn't made a sound since we'd entered the smaller cavern. He'd barely tried to defend himself.

I screamed, "*Apagar!*"

The fire lifted away from the crumpled figure. It danced on the air for a beat and then folded in on itself and was extinguished with a soft hiss.

Niele rose and stepped away as I hurried over to the pile of scorched fabric on the ground. I carefully peeled back the hood. Bathos' face looked up at me, eyes fixed and blank.

I moved to Luke, finding him unconscious but still alive. It was the same with the others.

Gren and Ferral woke them with the equivalent of a magic slap on the cheek.

Footsteps pounded down the passageway toward us. Willy ran into the cavern, her gaze unerringly finding her two boys. "Oh my goddess!" Her eyes filled with tears and she ran to the teen who was crumpled on the ground. He'd used the distraction of our arrival to move away from the cauldron and was huddled against the wall in a small niche. Willy sobbed when she saw the bleeding wounds covering his body.

"Mom," the twin said, his eyes filled with tears.

Willy pulled the boy into her arms, her gaze sliding up to her other son. "Bev, can you help Derick?"

Bev ran past me, magic already forming at her fingertips.

Light flared on Willy's fingers, and she sent magic into her son's wounds, healing them one by one.

"Is the demon dead?" Dell asked.

I turned to find the older witch, looking very tired and frailer than she'd been earlier in the day. I shook my head. "No. He's in some kind of stasis."

Trish buzzed down from the ceiling and popped

into full size. "He'll stay that way until I release him," she said, frowning.

I glanced at Mavis. "I wish you hadn't come."

"There was no holding Willy back once she heard you had a bead on the boys." She glanced around, looking unhappy. "Poor things. Any idea why Bathos took them?"

"Not a clue. We'll get him locked safely away and question him."

"Wanda's not here?" Bev asked, joining us.

I fought tears and disappointment. "No."

"One thing is certain. There has to be a link between the boys' abduction and the historian's," Mavis said.

I realized she was right. And to find that link, we were going to have to get past a frantic mother bear, so we could question her cubs.

"**A**bsolutely not!" Willy yelled.

We were in Bathos' kitchen, sitting around an oak table that was big enough for twelve people. The boys cradled cups of hot coffee between their hands and seemed to have regained most of their color.

"Willy…" Bev began.

The witch held up a hand, palm out. "Stop right

there. My boys have suffered enough. I'm taking them home and warding my entire house."

I couldn't really blame her. But I had to try to get her to see reason. "I understand..."

"Do you?" she asked with fire in her eyes. "Do you have kids?"

I sighed. "No. You're right. I can't understand how you're feeling right now. I just meant I understand why you don't want us to ask them questions. But I promise we won't hurt them in any way. I'm just trying to save Wanda."

Willy shook her head, motioning to her sons. "Come on, boys. We're going home."

The boys shared a look that seemed to contain a lot of unspoken information. Finally, Derick, the twin who'd been manacled to the wall, looked at Willy. "It's okay, mom. If someone else is in trouble, we want to help."

Tears filled Willy's eyes, but she turned away, stalking across the room. She stood with her arms crossed over her chest, a glower firmly fixed on her face.

I gave Derick a smile. "Thank you. Would you like to tell us how you came to be here?"

The boys shared a look. Finally, Derick said, "We were sleeping in our room. There was a flash of light..." He frowned.

"We don't know what happened next, his twin

finished. "We just woke up here, in one of those cells down there."

I nodded, letting that sink in. The boys had clearly been targeted with some kind of sleeping spell. Probably the same one that hit my council down in the cavern. "My...ward, Wanda, is missing. We thought the demon had her here. Did you by any chance see her?" I described Wanda to the boys, and they shared another look.

The second twin, David, nodded. "That sounds like the girl who was down a few cells from us when we woke up. She was curled up on the cot and didn't talk to us. We heard her crying for a while. And then somebody came and took her away."

I suddenly found it hard to breathe. "She was crying?"

The boys nodded.

"Could you tell if she was hurt?"

They frowned. "No. Sorry. It's kind of dark down there."

"The demon did seem kind of fond of her," David added. "He was talking real soft to her before that monster-thing took her out of there."

"Monster thing?" Layla asked.

The boys glanced toward Glenn, who stood quietly by the door.

"Yeah, you know, like those guys."

Layla skimmed me a look, a defiant light in her eyes. "My people had nothing to do with this."

I held up a hand to stop her from working up a head of steam. I might be an idiot, but I really didn't believe Layla's lost ones were involved in taking Wanda. "She was carried out? Did she struggle?"

Derick frowned thoughtfully. "You know, now that you ask, she *was* kind of limp when he carried her out. Like she was unconscious."

"Do you have any idea why she was here?" I asked.

"The demon told us she was going to give him power," Derick said. "He said that about us too."

David shook his head. "I don't know what he thought we were going to do. We suck at magic, right, mom?"

Willy winced but nodded. "They refuse to practice. They'd rather play sports and ogle girls."

Both teens rolled their eyes. "Hormones, mom. We've had this conversation. If we didn't obsess about girls, the guys would think there was something wrong with us."

Gren cleared his throat, looking away. I could almost feel his smile in my mind.

"Um," I went on, fighting a grin myself. "So, the demon didn't tell you what he was going to do to you? What specifically he wanted from you?"

"Okay, that's enough," Willy said, marching over and scouring me with a glare. "The boys have already told you they don't know anything. Now, I want to get them home."

I nodded, giving her what I hoped was an understanding smile. "Thank you for letting us talk to them, Willy. I'm glad they're okay."

Her glare softened and she pursed her lips, finally nodding. "Come on, boys. I think we'll stop for ice cream on the way home."

"Cool!" they said in unison.

Watching them leave, I sighed, dropping into a chair. Niele placed a steaming cup of coffee in front of me. "Thanks." I studiously avoided looking at the gnome. Sometime during our spelunking in the caverns down below, he'd lost his mossy shorts. "Did you go digging?" I asked as I carefully averted my gaze. I really should have been getting used to seeing his stick and berries waving around. It had been a couple of months since he'd first arrived in my kitchen as naked as the goddess made him.

"There was a strange vibration beneath the floor down there. I was checking it out."

"Did you find anything?" Gren asked. He stood behind my chair, hands resting on the back. Even with a smudge of dirt on his bristly cheek, he was perfect. Self-consciously, I hid my dirty hands in my lap.

Niele nodded. "Someone has done foul magic down there recently."

"What do you mean by foul?" I asked.

His gaze was intense when he looked down at me. "Death magic."

Bev and Mavis clomped up the steps from the caverns. They looked even more unkempt than I did, with dirt on their faces and hands and in their hair.

"Coffee!" they declared at the same time. Like Willy's twins, they seemed to be on the same wavelength. Niele took his stick and berries across the room to get them some.

Mavis flopped into a chair, shoving graying blonde hair off her filthy face.

"What were you two doing down there?"

Niele handed each of them a mug.

"Snooping," Bev responded. "Thanks, gnome. Did you lose your drawers?"

He looked down at himself as if he hadn't noticed. "I left them downstairs. I'll go get them."

I mouthed, "Thank you," to Bev and she grinned. She was amused by my squeamishness.

"Somebody did blood magic down there," Mavis said, wrinkling her nose. "The ground around the caldron is mushy with blood."

"Recently?" I asked, grimacing.

"In the last few days," I'd guess. Bev sipped her coffee and closed her eyes, moaning with pleasure. When she'd swallowed, she said, "We need to ask the demon what he's been up to."

"Among other things," I muttered.

"You won't get any answers," a deep voice said from the door.

We turned to find Ferral striding toward us,

looking cranky. If he ever lost the permanent scowl, he'd be a really good-looking guy.

Probably no danger of that.

Trish, who'd been quietly frowning since we'd come back into the house, got Ferral a cup of coffee, handing it to him.

"Thanks," he said, nodding in lieu of a smile.

"Why won't we get any answers," I asked the advocate.

"Because somebody's put him under a zombie curse."

"What does that mean?" I asked. "Does he eat brains? Is he shambling around grunting?"

"You watch too much television." Ferral looked down his long, perfect nose at me. "Put simply, it means he's under someone else's control."

"Is he dead?" Mavis asked, suddenly interested.

"Not quite," Layla said, striding into the room. "But he will be soon if nobody heals him. He's got sludge for blood, and it's worsening quickly."

"You left him alone?" I asked, starting to rise.

Layla put a hand on my shoulder, gently easing me back down. "Matthew is guarding him. He's not going anywhere."

"Tell us about this spell," I told her.

"We don't know much about this particular curse," Ferral said. "It's an ancient spell. I wasn't aware anyone even knew how to perform it anymore." He glanced at me, opened his mouth, and then closed it again, seeming to think better of telling me whatever he was thinking.

"What?" I encouraged. "Tell me what you were going to say."

His eyes found mine and held, like silver lasers cutting a path all the way to my soul. "The spell was banned in the eighteen hundreds and lost to history. It's one of a dozen deadly curses that sorcerers once used to control people, forcing them to do their will. The ancient church hunted down and killed all who knew the spells and destroyed all evidence of them."

I nodded. "Okay. So how did this one turn up now?"

I wouldn't have thought it possible, but the intensity of his look deepened. "There's only one place the spells might still live."

I stared back at him for a moment, trying to figure out what he was telling me. Then it hit me. Some of the pieces fell into place. The source of the magic. The reason for everything that had happened.

I shook my head, but Ferral's gaze held mine in a relentless grip. "That's why they took her," I muttered, horrified. "They needed a historian."

25

INTO THE DEMON'S FETID NEST

The good news was that I was pretty sure I knew what had happened to Wanda and why. But I still lacked the most important information. I didn't know where she was.

"Willow must have refused to help them," I told my council later, at home. "Wanda's punishment was both a holding pattern for her and leverage to get Willow to help."

They'd likely told Willow that if she did what they wanted, they'd stop torturing Wanda. They'd let her daughter live a normal life. Apparently, given the way things turned out, Willow hadn't capitulated. Respect for the woman I'd never known blossomed alongside a painful knot of worry for her daughter.

The soft, warm weight of my dog draped over my feet beneath the table soothed some of the agitation in my soul. His happy twitching, along with the soft yips of a dream pursuit which I assumed featured his favorite lop-eared gray squirrel, made me smile. But there was too much stress...too much worry...to be completely soothed. The continually tightening knot of worry buried beneath my ribs was relentless, bordering on real pain. And the regrets...the self-recriminations...If only I'd paid closer attention to Wanda's problem. If only I'd dug a little deeper with her. If only...

"The death magic," I said, interrupting the quiet flow of conversation around me. I knew I should have been paying attention to what my council was discussing, but I couldn't find my way out of my own thoughts. I was caught in a whirlwind of speculation and doubt, and I couldn't shake the feeling that I was on the cusp of knowing it all. If only I could grasp that last little piece. I looked up and found everyone focused on me. "Willow was sacrificed to call a demon. I'd bet everything I have on that."

Gren grimaced. "If that's true, we'll have our hands full with this demon. Only the most powerful demons require a death sacrifice in the summons."

"But, why?" Niele asked, quite reasonably. "After what happened with the Hellmouth, why would anyone in Rome even consider bringing a powerful demon into our dominion?"

"Power, most likely," Mavis offered.

Trish frowned. "There's something else. I've been

thinking about what happened in that dungeon. The sleep trap...the kids being tortured...it all seemed designed to hold our attention."

"It *was* strange," Ferral agreed. "Almost..."

"Too easy?" Trish said, nodding. "Exactly."

"You're saying, you think that was a distraction." I shook my head, mentally berating myself. "You're right it was way too easy. I'm so stupid. I should have seen it."

"Don't beat yourself up, Aggy," Bev said. "This is a convoluted mess. Nobody else would have been able to see through it any better. This plan was formulated a long time ago. Somebody's been planning it for a while."

Nodding, Luke said. "Willow was taken what... three years ago? Bev's right. This has been in the works since that time. Nobody noticed. Even the crone didn't seem too concerned about Willow's disappearance and Wanda's hex." He shook his head.

He was right, and I couldn't understand why the crone hadn't done something. It wasn't like historians were plentiful. "I need to understand the motivation for everything," I told them. "I understand at a high level, but I have no details. The solution is in the details. Why hex Wanda? Why take Willow? And why keep them both alive all this time?"

"We know they wanted the twelve forbidden spells of control," Mavis said.

"Right. I think we can assume Willow either didn't cooperate, or she didn't cooperate as fully as they wanted," Gren said.

"It's clear someone gave them the zombie curse," Ferral said. "We can assume it was Willow."

"But they wanted all the spells," Luke added. "Since they couldn't get her mother to cooperate, they probably hoped to scare Wanda into giving the rest to them," Luke said, giving me a slight nod. "They were counting on Wanda being timid and unsure of herself. Given her age, that would be a good assumption."

"But they don't know our girl," I said, smiling at Luke.

"No. They don't," he agreed.

"Maybe it's simpler than that," Ferral said with a frown. "Perhaps the goal was to simply possess the girl, allowing the demon to extract her magic."

My pulse shot skyward at the thought. I could not allow that to happen. Then I realized it might have already happened, and the knot in my belly twisted painfully. All the blood left my face in a dizzying wash.

Seeing my panic, Gren reached out and squeezed my shoulder. "The girl isn't helpless against such things," he told me. "Because of the importance of their magic, historians have safeguards built into their power. It would take a long time and a lot of spell-casting for a witch to get through that barrier."

"And even more time for the practitioner to sever the internal impediments protecting the girl's historical knowledge," Ferral agreed. "The young historian should be safe enough for now. But every day we delay puts her at greater risk."

"I think you're missing an important point," Layla said, straightening away from the counter where she'd been leaning. "To summon a demon, you need to have something to offer it. Something it wants. What a demon from this plane wants is to go back to the demonic plane. No witch has the power to grant that. So, I believe that what you're looking for is someone who's capable of summoning a demon from the demonic realm."

I grimaced, remembering what demonic influence had done to the people of Rome during the Hellmouth incident. I never wanted to see that again. "You're telling us the demons on the demonic plane want to come here, and those that are here want to go there?"

"That pretty much sums it up," Layla agreed.

"The brimstone is always more sulfuric on the other side." Luke nodded. "Demons are more like humans than they know."

"I'm assuming that summoning a demon isn't a common skill?" Trish asked.

"Very rare," Layla agreed. "If it wasn't, you'd have

Hellmouths like the one we battled last month popping up all the time."

"So, we're looking for someone who practices death magic to summon demons," Mavis said, frowning.

"Not just anyone," Layla clarified. "A witch."

Trish, Mavis, and Bev shared a look. Their expressions were grim. "We need to hit the library at Willy's," Bev finally said. "Every living witch should be listed in the registry. That's where we'll find those who are suspected of performing dark magic and summoning demons."

"Suspected?" Gren asked. "That could be a long list."

Mavis shook her head. "What we're talking about is a very specific inclination. There won't be many witches that fit the parameters. The registry contains a lot of information. Witches are assessed along a numbered range, which takes into account age and when they were discovered to have magic, the number of years studying their craft, proficiency with that craft, and any non-traditional proclivities either suspected or observed. Just like with any group, though we're dispersed across the country and number in the tens of thousands, it's still a very small world. It's hard to practice the dark arts without someone knowing or finding out."

"Historians aren't usually included," Bev warned, looking sheepish. She was, no doubt, remembering that she'd assured me she'd find information on Wanda for me. "Which is why we couldn't find Willow or Wanda in the registry when we looked a few days ago."

Mavis nodded. "Technically, they're considered witches, but their historian magic is so rare they've been given a designation all their own."

"Does this book include fae practitioners?" I asked, giving Trish an apologetic glance.

She inclined her head to let me know she understood that I had to ask.

"No," Bev admitted. "But there are only a handful of them around the country. Most fairies don't like our magic."

Trish made a sour face. "Bev is being kind. It isn't the magic the fae dislike. My people are infamous snobs. But there are a few of us who understand we have a natural kinship with earth-witches." She stood from where she'd been sitting on the floor near the mudroom door. Pulling out her phone, she said. "I'll call the queen and see if I can get a list of those of us who've worked in the past or are currently working with the witches."

"Thanks, Trish."

As she left the room, she was already talking to someone.

"There's something else you need to be aware of," Layla said, her expression tight.

We all looked at her, but she avoided our gazes.

Instead, she watched Monty twitch and yip. "I'm afraid your young historian is in terrible danger. Even worse than what you think."

The knot in my chest twisted tighter. "Go on."

"I told you they would have needed to promise a powerful demon something they wanted to get them here."

I nodded.

She frowned. "Demons and devils are a predatory group. On the demonic plane, it's survival of the fittest. Nobody thinks twice about eating somebody else."

We all made faces of disgust.

She finally looked up, her gaze hard and cold. "I know how horrible the outcome of that mindset can be. It's the biggest reason I want to stay here."

Not for the first time, I wondered about Layla's story. Had someone she'd loved been killed? Had she fought back? Was that why she'd been banished?

Her next words seemed to confirm my thoughts. "Believe me when I say that the elite in that realm would do anything to gain control of the earthly plane. If they could find a way to turn this world's magic practitioners into mindless robots who would do their bidding..."

"They'd have a whole new hunting ground," Ferral murmured, his silver gaze darkening to steel.

"How does Wanda fit into all that?" I asked. I thought I knew but wanted to make sure I was right.

"To them, she is a source of vast knowledge. That is all. She'd be kept alive for that knowledge, but her life would be one of pain, loneliness, and deprivation. And if they ever managed to extract all the control hexes from her mind, she'd be of no use to them anymore."

"Bathos said Wanda's magic wasn't particularly useful to demons." Luke argued.

"He lied," Layla said.

We sat in silence for several moments. Then I nodded, blinking away the tears that wanted to fall. "That just means we can't fail. We have no choice but to rescue Wanda before it comes to that."

"One more thing," Layla said. "The witches who called this demon will not get what they want from Wanda. The demon will kill all but the most powerful witch before the girl breaks. They might already be dead. It will keep the last witch alive in case something goes wrong. But even she will be slaughtered once the demon has its claws into Wanda." I winced and she sent me an apologetic look. "Sorry. Just a figure of speech."

"How will the demon get home again?" I asked.

"It won't. At least not immediately. It will begin preparing for when they have the control hexes. Then more demons will come."

Curse, curse, swear, swear!

I rubbed my eyes, suddenly exhausted. "It looks like it's going to be a long night." I glanced at the coffee machine. "I need coffee. Does anybody else want some?"

Bev shook her head, reaching for a large bottle of cabernet. "You need to catch a few hours of sleep. If you face off with this witch as tired as you are, you'll make mistakes and endanger everybody."

I narrowed my gaze on her, not missing her ploy. If she'd told me I'd endanger myself, I would have shrugged it off. But, by reminding me that my mistakes would harm everyone, she forced me into a corner. "Is this just an excuse to drink wine?"

Bev laughed, tugging the cork from the bottle. "Who needs an excuse?"

"I agree," Trish said. "I'll get the glasses."

"Do you ladies really think it's a good idea to get drunk before pursuing a blood-magic witch?" Ferral asked, always the party pooper.

"One glass," Mavis said, giving him a quelling look. "Just to destress a bit." She scanned me a quick look, sending Ferral a silent message that I needed destressing.

I didn't mind. Deep down, I knew they were right. I was too wound up to rest, and if I didn't rest, I was going to make mistakes.

I pushed out of my chair, feeling every minute of my forty-five years. "I'll make PB&C sandwiches."

"I'll help," Gren offered.

"Woof!" added Monty helpfully.

I wasn't sure how it had happened, but somehow I'd managed to fall asleep. My dreams were frantic, terrifying, and much like climbing an endless set of stairs that led to death and chaos. I knew I needed to get to the top, but everything inside me rebelled at the idea.

Caw!

The sound made me whip around, an icy wind scouring my face and peeling sand and dirt off the ground to lash my bare ankles.

Something pulsed high above my head. Something dark and ominous. Something that made me want to run.

But I couldn't run. I couldn't scream. I could barely move.

My limbs felt heavy. I was so tired. It was as if my veins held sludge instead of blood.

I was under a spell. The kind of spell that was so horrible, it had been banished hundreds of years earlier.

Caw!

The echo of hooves clacking against the concrete found its way to me beneath the sound of the wind. I thought of the white mare, wondering if she had come back to help.

Please goddess, she'd come back to help.

Caw!

Why was Ray yelling at me? Come to think of it, where was the raven? I hadn't seen him since...

Caw!

My head snapped around as the amorphous shape above my head twisted and shrank, becoming...

Ray clacked his beak, flying around me in tight, frantic circles.

"What's wrong?" I asked the raven. "Tell me?"

His beak opened as he writhed and twisted again.

And then he was gone. But something else had taken his place.

The bat was larger than usual. Nearly as big as Ray. Its eyes glowed yellow in the dusky light, exuding a magical pulse that splashed in cool drops against my face.

Bathilda fluttered in erratic dips and lunges across the air in front of me, never straying far. Always keeping me in sight.

I struggled forward, not even sure what I was pursuing, but knowing I had to pursue it.

Squeak!

The bat sounded scared. I spun around, trying to find her. Instead, I saw...

Come to me, Agnes Bethany Lenore. You and I have unfinished business.

The creature was wreathed in shadow, its bloody gaze flaring from the shadows like burning embers in a dying fire.

Woof!

My gaze jerked downward. Monty's hackles were up,

his tiny body vibrating on a growl. He snarled and lunged at the shadowy creature, his teeth snapping together as the glooms reached for him.

"No!" I grabbed for my dog...

...and found myself sitting up in bed, my heart racing and my entire body covered in sweat.

A warm, wet tongue scoured my elbow.

My hands still shaking from the dream, I pulled Monty into my lap, hugging him close. "It's okay, buddy. It was just a nightmare."

Just a nightmare. Was there anything more terrifying than a nightmare? The mind in an unhinged state, unencumbered by reality or rational thought.

I shuddered.

Glancing at the clock, I realized it was nearly midnight. We would need to leave soon. Dropping a kiss on the top of Monty's soft head, I shoved the covers back and headed for a quick, very hot shower.

26

A DEADLIER VISIT THAN THE REST

"**A**re you sure she'll be awake?" I asked.

Bev nodded. "She's a night owl. She's just getting started about now."

Well dang. There was my last excuse, gone.

Curse, swear!

Bev knocked on the door and I glanced upward to the large, winged form flying through a moonlight-drenched sky high above us. Gren had insisted on checking out the entire neighborhood to make sure there were no nasties lurking around.

Trish had gone to speak to the fae queen face to face. Apparently, her request had brought up a whole *thing* —Trish's word—that the fae needed to discuss. I was left worrying that I'd gotten her into trouble. Sighing, I added that to the list of things I needed to address...later.

Luke and Ferral were nearby in their doggy

forms, also sniffing for trouble. Since I didn't expect to have to deal with any demons in Willy's home, I'd told Layla to stay at my house. Instead, she'd gone to check on Bathos, who'd been locked into one of the special cells at her compound.

I was hoping she'd decide to return to that compound after the current crisis was resolved. Not knowing her reasons for leaving in the first place, I had no idea why she'd rather stay with me than her own people.

The door opened, and Willy gawked out at us, looking surprised. She was wearing sweatpants with one torn knee and a matching sweatshirt covered in paint speckles. Since the paint appeared dry, I figured the damage was likely from a past project.

Her fiery hair curled out from under a baseball cap, which she was wearing backward on her head. There was a smudge of dirt on one pale, freckled cheek.

The witch self-consciously brushed her hands down her thighs. "Sorry I'm such a mess. I wasn't expecting company, and that basement won't clean itself." She laughed, but there was no humor in the sound.

"We'd like to look through the registry, Willy," Mavis told the other witch. "If you don't mind."

Willy flashed a worried glance behind her and started to shake her head.

I stepped forward. "Please, Willy. We've pledged

to keep the boys out of this, and we'll keep our promise if that's possible. But we have a lead on Wanda, and we need to follow it up."

Willy sighed, directing her response to Bev and Mavis. "Okay. You can look at the book. But I won't let you talk to the boys." She looked at me. "And the Lares cannot view the library."

"Don't be stupid, Willy," Mavis said. "That rule was always unreasonable. Right now, with one of our own at risk, it's downright suicidal."

Willy stared at me for a long moment, a range of emotions running through her expression, and then nodded. "Okay, but I'm not changing my mind about the boys. No more questions. They've been through enough."

I inclined my head. There was no point arguing with her since I didn't intend to bother Derick and David anyway.

Willy stepped back, leaving the door open. When I started to move forward, Bev put out a hand, giving me a quelling look, and stepped in ahead of me. My entire council was in uber-protective mode. It was kind of sweet, in an annoying way. I sighed and followed her inside.

The house was small, sporting aged furniture and even older flooring. The carpet under my feet was a worn shag in an ugly tannish-gold color. The carpet was etched with clear wear patterns leading from the linoleum square in front of the door to both the kitchen, and a hallway that presumably led to the back of the house.

The living room smelled faintly of dirty socks, probably the unfortunate byproduct of living with a couple of teen boys. The couch was covered in an ugly caramel, tan, and green fabric, dotted with piles of unfolded laundry. The empty basket was overturned on the floor, a glass of something that looked like flat cola sitting on its stained bottom surface.

Willy saw the direction of my gaze and flushed with embarrassment. "I told them to fold the laundry. That was three days ago." She sighed, shaking her head.

"Boys," I said as if I had experience. "Amiright?" I walked over to a wall filled with photos of Willy's family. The pictures represented much of the boys' lives, from when they were infants to their current age. In the first half of their lives, a dark-haired man with dull brown eyes was also in the pictures. But there was no sign of the man I assumed was their father in the more recent pictures. "Handsome boys. They have fire in their eyes in nearly every picture."

Willy snorted out a laugh. "You have no idea. The registry is in my guest room. It's kind of cluttered in there," she warned.

We followed her down the hall to a closed door near the end. Willy pushed the door open and stepped back. "Can I get you ladies some coffee?"

"No thanks," I told her with a smile. "It would just keep me up all night."

Mavis and Bev declined too and Willy left, mumbling something about checking on the boys.

It took Bev and Mavis fifteen minutes to find the right book on the long wall of shelves. The bookshelves were the only furniture in the room that appeared to be less than twenty years old. The queen-sized bed took up most of the space, the headboard some kind of dark wood that was covered in scratches and scars. Apparently, having boys was even harder on a house than having a naughty dachshund.

I tried to help locate the book at first, but I just kept getting in the way, so I shoved some shoe boxes, winter coats, an umbrella, a box of handmade cards, and a dozen other things carefully back from the edge of the bed and gingerly sat down. I took a moment to admire the quilt covering the bed, wishing I was talented enough to make quilts. The stitchwork was fine and straight, and the pattern was pretty, with lots of flowers and butterflies. Quilts like that would probably sell really well in my candle shop when it opened.

I got lost in considering that idea for a few moments and made a mental note to ask Willy who'd made the quilt for her.

"Aha!" Mavis finally exclaimed, holding up a

green, leather-bound book with gold embossing on the cover that simply said, Registry.

We looked around for a place where we could all view the registry, finally deciding to take it to the kitchen table. The light would be better there, and we could put it on the table, where we could all gather around to look at it.

There was no sign of Willy as we headed toward the brightly-lit kitchen. I listened to the too-quiet house for a moment, the silence discomfiting. Lost in contemplation of the sound-proofing quality of older homes versus newer ones...a side-effect of rehabbing an old building myself...I went to join Mavis and Bev at the kitchen table.

They were staring down at the book, frowning. "What's wrong?"

Bev glanced up. "There are ten thousand names in this thing. We're not sure where or how to start."

My stomach sank. They were right. We'd stupidly thought we'd just waltz in, peek at the registry to find our culprit, and waltz back out again. Sighing, I rubbed a hand over my face. "How are they arranged in the book?" I asked.

"By geographic location," Mavis said.

"Logically, the practitioner is likely to be from around here or know someone who is."

That statement deepened their frowns even further. "I just don't believe it's someone from the Rome coven," Mavis told me unhappily.

"I agree," Bev said, looking equally miserable. "But Aggy's right. Wanda and Willow lived here. Bathos lives here. The connection is here in Rome."

"Let's just read up on all the witches in Rome and the surrounding areas. Once we weed them out, we'll figure out where to go from there."

They nodded and started reading. There wasn't much for me to do since I didn't really understand the code-like shorthand the book was written in, so I went back to looking at the photos on the wall.

A half-hour later, I realized I hadn't heard a sound from Willy and the boys. Was it possible for teenaged boys to be that quiet? Even my limited experience with Wanda had taught me that loud music was a key element of being a teen.

I didn't hear anything. Not a single note.

I went into the hallway and pressed my ear against the closed door that Bev had told me led to the basement.

Silence.

I went back and forth over whether I dared go down and check on them. I'd just about decided I had no choice, given the current situation, when Bev and Mavis came out of the kitchen.

Without a word, Bev handed me the book. I quickly skimmed the writeup for the witch on the page, my heart sinking. Lifting my gaze back to Bev and Mavis, I realized how badly the upcoming conversation was going to hurt them. "Do you want me to speak to her alone?"

Bev shook her head. "She knows us better. There has to be a good reason for what she did."

I doubted that, but I'd been wrong before. Many times. Many, many times.

"I was just debating going down there anyway. It's been really quiet."

"You're right," Mavis agreed, skimming the basement door a glance. "It *is* quiet, isn't it?"

I tugged on the door and it didn't budge. "It's locked," I told them.

Mavis gently pushed me aside and settled a hand over the tarnished brass knob, closing her eyes. She spoke a few words, too softly for me to hear, and the knob turned in her hand. "There ya go, honey."

I stared at her, wide-eyed. "Mom, is there something you want to tell me about your former life as a thief?"

She snorted. "Nope. There's nothing I *want* to tell you."

No denial. Alrighty then.

I pulled the door open and stopped, my pulse spiking into heart attack range. I couldn't even see the stairs or the room at the bottom. An all-too-familiar mist rolled out of the stairwell and slid over my skin, smelling of brimstone and death.

Déjà vu smacked me right between the eyes as I looked into the fog from my nightmares. If I'd had any doubts at all that I was in the right place, that fog put the kibosh on them.

I glanced at my family. "It looks like we're about to take on the big bad. Are you up for it?"

Bev blew air through her lips and Mavis rolled her eyes. "Aggy, honey, I was born ready," Mavis said.

Bev nodded. "I was ready *before* I was born." She blinked, frowning. "That was weird, wasn't it?"

I shook my head, fear starting to throb beneath my ribs.

Bev glanced down at the Registry and set it on the floor. "I guess we don't need this anymore. Our questions have been answered."

Unfortunately, they had.

I sent out a call for the others. *Guys, it looks like we've stepped into the middle of this mess. We're going to need your help. We'll be in the basement.*

Then, taking a deep breath, I stepped onto the first stair, wishing I had the White Mare and her wings to help me navigate the fog.

Easing down to the next step, I braced against the railing on one side and the wall on the other. The mist was even thicker than in my visions. I couldn't see twelve inches in front of my face.

"Don't freak out," Mavis whispered behind me. She clutched the waistband of my jeans. "It's just me."

I was glad for the reminder that I wasn't alone in the soup. As in the dream, the sound of my heart-

beats seemed louder in the fog. Too fast...too frantic...too vigorous against my ribs.

None of us spoke. As terrifying as the mist was,
there was a certain comfort in feeling that it hid us
as well as it hid the others. As long as we didn't
bump into the demon, my hope was we could get
into place and form a plan before we were
discovered.

I'd been counting steps as we descended. The
typical number of steps in a basement stairwell was
just one of a thousand generally useless pieces of
information lodged in my brain.

At that moment, I was glad for the knowledge.
My foot hit step number thirteen, and I knew there
were probably no more than three steps remaining.

My foot sank into a softer surface. Carpet. I
pulled a relieved breath into my lungs, realizing that
I hadn't taken a good breath since stepping into the
mist.

When all three of us were on solid ground, I
turned and whispered. "I don't know the layout."

Mavis moved her hands from my back to my
arm, whispering a response. "I'll guide us to the
main room. That's where we usually have our
meetings."

I nodded, realizing too late she couldn't see it.

Bev's hand found my waistband, and we began to
shuffle forward, Mavis in front, me in the middle,
and Bev taking up the rear. As I had in my night-

mare, I reached my arms out and touched the walls on either side, more to give me a sense of orientation than anything else. My fingertips burned at the touch, and I snatched them away. Rubbing them together, I felt the cold greasiness I remembered from before.

Mavis turned to the right and we followed, the soft carpet disappearing as we stepped onto naked, gritty concrete with a slippery feel.

Mavis jerked to a stop. I slammed into her and Bev slammed into me.

Feeling like Moe in the Three Stooges, I was glad nobody could see our little clown act.

The mist surrounding us was utterly silent. Eerily quiet. The lack of sound was more unnerving than any type of identifiable noise would be. I knew there was something in that mist. I could feel its presence like a low-level thrum riding the haze. And the complete lack of sound told me that it was stalking us.

But, when the deep silence continued for several more minutes and nothing happened, I started to wonder if I'd been wrong. Was it possible the house was empty? I shook off that idea immediately. It was more likely the mist was swallowing sound. Which meant we could be inches away from the monster and not even realize it.

My heartbeat thumped within my ribs. A prickle of unease danced along my spine, and icy sweat dripped from my temples. I looked into the fog and suddenly felt...something. Tugging Mavis gently backward, I reached a hand back to Bev, giving her arm a squeeze.

The mist swirled and thinned, and Mavis screamed as a face from my nightmares appeared, mere inches away.

27

AT LAST, THE LARES FINDS HER STRIDE

The hooded figure seemed to rise out of the mist, its gaze blazing through the fog. Eyes the color of old blood glowed from beneath its hood, the skin around the eyes yellow and thin, the veins clearly showing underneath. The rest of the face was obscured by shadow and the body was much smaller than I would have expected, given the power rolling off it in waves.

The musty stench of death magics combined with the smell of brimstone as the creature's robes shifted around it. The thing's gaze was locked on me, ignoring Mavis and Bev, who were dragging me backward as if we could outrun it.

I reached for my magic, bracing for the bite of its power on my fingertips. With a terrible sense of déjà vu, it failed. The magic didn't come.

The monster flung out a clawed, misshapen

hand and a black wave of magic slammed into me, sending all three of us flying to smash against the wall near the door.

The impact knocked the air out of me and I shoved to my feet, wheezing as I turned to make sure Mavis and Bev were okay.

Mavis flapped a hand at me, telling me to go. Then she and Bev started weaving magic.

I turned back, putting myself between them and the hooded figure.

I blinked. It was gone.

Panic ripped through me. I looked frantically around and yelped, stumbling backward as the thing reappeared in front of me. A clawed hand reached toward my throat.

"I knew you'd come, Agnus Bethany Lenore," It said. The voice was thick and wet, its teeth jagged and yellow inside torn lips. But beneath the telltale bass echo when it spoke, something about the voice was familiar.

Sharp claws clamped onto my shoulder. The torn lips curved, showing way too many teeth.

Power rolled off the thing in stomach clenching, blood chilling waves.

Terror clawed the breath from my lungs, leaving me wheezing in a desperate attempt to quell the panic. At that moment, I knew I was a fake. I was no guardian. I was a forty-five-year-old woman who fretted about the new crepey-ness of her skin and the deepening of some laugh lines around my hazel eyes. Lately, I'd been obsessing that my straight black hair was thinning a little. And that the silver tips I'd once been so proud of too closely matched the roots trying to gain dominance on the other end of each strand.

I wasn't special. I was just a woman...just a...

I blinked. Wait a curse, swear minute. *Just a woman*? Had I lost my farking mind? Some of the most formidable people I knew were women. I could be self-conscious. I could even feel inadequate to the task. But I had no right to downgrade an entire sex because I was feeling scared.

I gave myself a mental head-smack. I could do this. I'd leaped into a Hellmouth with a lost princess, for goddess sake. I'd fought the big nasties in that Hellmouth and come out of it alive.

I'd beaten back not one but three sea monsters and, with the help of my friends and council, managed to come out of the water breathing and with all my limbs intact.

I was woman, hear me...

Squeak!

"Squeak?" I mumbled. *Curse*! I was hearing things.

"Squeak!" the mist said again. I twitched in surprise as a small, black creature fluttered out of the fog, yellow eyes burning the mist away as it headed directly for the nasty hooded monster tightening its claws painfully around my shoulder.

The monster's gaze swung to Bathilda and widened. It actually took a couple of steps back as if it was considering making a run for it.

A golden glow emanated from the bat, and I blinked as I realized Batty had grown several inches. "Squeak!" The sound came out as a roar, not a chirp, and suddenly the hallway was clogged with an enormous bat. Bathilda's wings spread as wide as the passage, and her fangs were as big around as my pinkie fingers.

Mavis grabbed my shirt and tugged. "Come on!"

We started to run, the blustery haze that had filled the room dissipating around us.

A roar vibrated through the room, so thunderous it shook dust from the beams above our heads. I tried to turn around to make sure Bathilda was okay, but Bev nearly wrenched my arm from its socket, pulling me along.

"Wait," I called out. "I have to..."

The floor ahead of us exploded upward and an enraged howl filled the room. We shrieked and whipped around, running back the other way. We hit the steps, and I shoved Mavis and Bev in front of me. "Go. Get upstairs and find the others."

"Oh no," Mavis said. "We're not leaving you here alone."

I threw out my hand, and the staff smacked into

it. "I'm not alone. I have my sometimes loyal bat and my kind of trusty staff."

Bev snorted. "I dare you to use that sentence the next time we go to a bar."

"Whatever! Go!"

A long, pain-filled squeal spurred me to action. *Batty*!

I dove into the remaining wisps of mist, heading for the big, unfinished section of the basement where we'd run up against the hooded monster.

As I ran through the arched doorway into the room, I yanked magic forward and sent it into my staff. Slamming to a stop, I looked for the beast.

It was gone.

Bathilda was gone.

"Aggy?"

I whipped around.

Willy stood in the doorway, frowning. "What are you doing in my basement?" The twins stood behind her, looking tall and awkward.

Unsure who I was supposed to fight, I pointed my staff at Willy. "We know, Willy. We know you're behind the demon and Wanda's disappearance. I just need to know where she is."

Magic roiled and spat from the orb at the end of my staff. Willy didn't even seem to notice.

She was calm. Strangely so. My gaze slid to the boys. They looked a little dazed, lost in their own worlds. "That's unfortunate," Willy said in an unemotional voice. She lifted her hands and started to weave a spell.

I looked into the witch's blank gaze and horror pierced my confusion. That was when it hit me... "You're under the zombie curse too. All three of you."

"Aggy?" Bev called from the hallway. "What can we do?"

Curse, swear, curse! Would those two ever listen to me? Thank goddess they hadn't listened. I looked at Bev. "Can you deal with Willy? She's under the curse."

Looking sadder than I'd ever seen her, my sister nodded and pulled energy into her hands.

Willy didn't respond. I hadn't expected her to. The knowledge finally clarified what I'd been fighting to understand. "She's not the one who summoned the demon," I said to no one in particular.

Slow clapping erupted behind me, and I whipped around with a soft cry. Energy spurted from my staff and slammed into the unfinished fire-place across the room, obliterating the top corner.

Oops!

The overhead bulbs suddenly flashed on, dusting the room with weak light. The hooded figure reached up and folded the hood back on her robe.

I made a small sound of shock.

"It's a shame you had to stick your nose into this,

Aggy. I hate the idea of killing a guardian. But I suppose it will be for the best. My friends will have a much harder time culling the humans with you around."

Dell's eyes glowed with pleasure at her words.

"That's not going to happen, Dell," I told the witch. I glanced around the shadowy room, looking for Bathilda.

I fervently wished there were more than a couple of bare bulbs hanging from the unfinished ceiling for lighting. The size of the room and the lack of finished surfaces swallowed what little light the yellowed bulbs managed to cast.

Aware that Mavis and Bev were weaving magic behind me, I decided that keeping the witch talking was the best course of action. "So there is no demon after all," I told her.

She laughed. "There is, my dear. You're looking at her."

I narrowed my gaze. She didn't look anything like she had the last time I'd seen her. She looked bad...like a walking corpse. Her eyes were no longer crimson, but her skin was sallow and deep purple arcs underscored them. "You're possessed?" I could see the demon from the fog beneath the thin veneer of what she used to be.

She flipped a hand. "Possession is only good for the possessor. I am a host, but I have all the power."

"I didn't know that was possible," I said, fighting the urge to look over my shoulder.

"Just another handy little spell I took from dear Willow. It's really too bad she wouldn't give me everything. She gave me only the two ancient, forbidden spells." The witch grimaced. "All to protect that stupid little girl."

Still furtively looking for Batty, I bit back an enraged response. "Wanda? Your deal with Willow was to spell Wanda instead of taking her?"

"It's too bad Willow was so poor at making bargains. Bargaining with a demon is a tricky business." The nasty lips curved into a terrifying smile. "Sometimes, the payment is swift and lethal."

My eyes finally fell on a small dark area in a shadowed corner. Was that Batty's crumpled body?

Rage rose and the magic boiled through my veins, burning me from the inside with its ferocity. I swung the staff toward Dell and sent a dense wave of magic over her, not bothering to try to contain the power to keep her alive. At the moment, I had three witches and one demon witch against me. The only way I'd survive would be to alter the odds in my favor.

Oily black energy shot up between my magic and Dell. She stood with her hands outstretched, palms out, and easily walled off my attack with her own power.

I tried to amp it up, to blast through her magic,

but hard hands ripped the staff from my grip and sent it flying toward the possessed witch.

I fought the twins' grip but had no chance against their strength. Even if they hadn't been under a curse, they'd have been too strong for me to shake off without using magic. Unfortunately, if I used magic, they might not survive. I didn't think I could live with myself if I killed two innocent teens.

Still...

The concrete behind the boys blasted upward, and they released me, stumbling backward without so much as a change in expression. Niele leaped from the hole in the floor, blades slashing toward the two boys.

I yelled, "No!" and yanked energy forward as I spoke a single word. "Sleep!" Putting as much magic as I could into the command, I held my breath as the two boys wobbled on the spot, like badly hit bowling pins, and then slowly crumpled to the ground.

I looked at Niele. "Take them someplace safe."

He nodded and scooped the two boys up as if they weighed nothing, flinging one over each broad shoulder.

Fire erupted in a perfect circle around me, the deadly magic flames rising above my head and giving off enough heat to singe my hair. I gasped, fighting panic as I reached for my magic.

It wasn't there!

Like the mist, the flames seemed to be nulling my magic.

Dell sauntered over and stood just beyond the flames' reach. She looked like the thing in the mist again. Her eyes burned crimson, yellow skin stretched over fragile bones and I could see her veins beneath the papery flesh. "Agnes Bethany Lenore," the thing that was both witch and demon intoned in a husky, echoing voice. "It is good you have come. We have much to discuss."

"No!" Like a bad case of multiple personality disorder, Dell screamed at herself, her body twisting and morphing as if someone had hold of both ends and was wringing her out.

"There will be no discussion," Dell roared, her voice pulsing through the room and ricocheting back on us with a painful reverberation. I winced and covered my ears, accidentally moving too close to the fire and getting singed. "The Lares dies!" Dell screamed.

She morphed again, her features twisting with agony. "We will take the girl and the Lares," the demon screamed through Dell's lips.

Dell stepped through the flame, those terrible eyes fixed unrelentingly on me.

I cringed back with a cry, unable to get more than a few inches away

"I have learned much from your historian," the creature inside Dell said, its foul breath bathing my cringing face. "She cares for you. Were you aware?"

I glared at the monster, refusing to give it anything. "I've come to take her home."

The demon's laughter abraded my flesh. I fought back a shudder of revulsion. "I wish to keep *you* for a pet, Madam Lares. I like the taste of your magic." The demon leaned closer, Dell's nostrils flaring wetly. "I enjoy the smell of all that power."

Clenching my fists, I tried to stay calm. If the thing meant to hurt me, it would likely already have done it. And as long as it was paying attention to me, it was leaving the others alone. "Your body-buddy has nulled my power. You're probably smelling my body wash. It smells like roses."

"You will not disobey me!!" Dell roared into the room again. I gritted my teeth against the slicing pain of her power and watched in fascination as her body began to writhe and twist.

Her eyes widening in terror, Dell fell to the ground screaming, her limbs thrashing wildly. Blood ran from her eyes and nose.

Then the screaming stopped.

The thing inhabiting her body rose off the ground, its limbs twisted and broken, joints bent the wrong way. It didn't seem to notice.

My fire prison winked out when Dell stopped screaming, leaving me standing way too close to whatever was inhabiting her body. I stumbled backward, raising my staff. Without another thought, I hit the demon with my magic, enough to cause it to stumble backward a few steps.

But it laughed at my efforts.

I doubled down, remembering the vast amount of magic it had taken to kill the last powerful demon I'd encountered.

Footsteps pounded into the room. Gren was suddenly there, his wings snapping into place as two short swords appeared in his hands. I fell to my knees as I forced even more energy through the staff. Gren threw the first of his blades toward the demon, hitting it in the center of Dell's throat. The second blade found a fiery crimson eye.

The monster screamed its rage, flinging a clawed hand toward Gren and sending him crashing across the room. Niele blasted up from the floor directly behind the demon and stabbed a strange-looking blade into its back, quickly diving beneath the floor again.

Aggy, he screamed in my mind. *Get out of there!*

Energy still lashing from my staff, I felt my muscles weaken, my vision blurring as I sent energy in weakening waves toward the demon.

I wasn't running anywhere.

Bev and Mavis screamed, "Die!" in unison and sent a curse in an icy blue shimmer that wrapped around Dell's body and pulled tight, locking her arms against her torso.

The demon inside Dell struggled and raged, lumbering toward me with its hideous mouth spread wide. One clawed hand had worked its way free and a thunderous roar reverberated off the concrete walls.

With a last, harmless spurt, my energy died away and I crashed to the floor.

Wings pounded the air above me.

Gren dropped to cover my wrung-out form with his body.

My eyes fought to close, exhaustion pulling all the strength from my muscles. But, before I could give in to it, I saw something that forced my eyes wide again.

Bathilda, as big as a pterodactyl dinosaur and just as ugly, dropped down between Dell and me with her wings spread. I didn't even have time to register what she was doing, before a massive explosion ripped through the spot where the demon had been.

The explosion sent a concussive blast through the underground space, reverberating against the walls and floor with the force of a volcano exploding into the air. The concrete beneath my feet shuddered and split, wide fissures bleeding outward from the spot where the cauldron had once been. It was no longer there. Beneath the spot, a hole yawned, the fractures in the concrete like crooked spokes in a gigantic wheel.

Slowly, the world stopped shivering and went still again, until only the sound of concrete falling away from the damaged walls remained. The air was thick with smoke and dust. It was hard to see anything beyond what was right in front of me.

I shuddered as a wave of blustery cold slid through me, my energy so depleted I couldn't even warm myself anymore. Gren's arms slid beneath me and pulled me off the floor, carrying me out the door and up the stairs.

"Bathilda?" I murmured, the words emerging in a husky croak.

"Don't worry about anything, lovely Aggy," Gren said, his lips close enough to touch my ear. "Just heal. I need you to heal."

The tainted atmosphere of the basement disappeared, replaced with the sounds of fire and the smothering stench of fire.

Outside the air was cool, with only a hint of smoke, and sirens sounded in the distance. Flashing lights flew toward us from the other side of town.

Gren laid me carefully on the grass of Willy's yard.

The sirens came closer. Smoke thickened on the air, a sharp sense of déjà vu making me think I was back in that mist-drenched basement.

Something important niggled. Something that had me trying to sit up...to dive back into that smoky house. "I have to..."

Gren lifted me off the ground, pulling me back against his chest, and wrapped his arms around my body, his legs framing mine. Delicious warmth infused me from his nearness.

Someone handed me coffee. "Drink," Niele said.

"She needs calories!" someone else said. Mavis, I think. Their voices sounded far away and hollow, like cartoon characters on an old black and white TV.

Smoke billowed from the house, and the niggle burst into a memory. "The twins?"

"They're okay," Bev said, handing me an enormous cookie. I took the cookie and just held it. "Willy?"

"She's with the boys." Mavis pointed to an ambulance and I saw Willy and her family sitting on the grass with EMTs hovering around them.

But there was something else. Fear, worry, and sadness still nagged my subconscious.

A cry went up and everyone turned as a tall, raven-haired woman strode from the house. She wore black leathers much like my own battle leathers, and her sleek hair was pulled back in a long braid, the loose strands in the front painted silver in the moonlight. She was carrying something in her arms.

No. *Someone.*

Ferral walked alongside the woman, his square jaw set and rigid with pique. He kept throwing glowers at the woman, but she didn't seem to notice.

Very slowly, my mind fought to recognize the object in her arms.

The straight black bob and too skinny form. The ambulance lights sparking off the large silver ring piercing a delicate nose.

"Wanda!" I climbed to my feet and started running.

"Wait, Aggy!" Gren called, but I ignored him.

The raven-haired woman carefully placed Wanda on the ground. I slid to my knees without stopping, skidding across the grass, and ran my hands over the teen's too-skinny form, checking her for injuries.

"She is unharmed, Aggy Lares of Rome," a soft voice spoke.

My gaze jerked to the woman and I found her staring at me, her expression serene. Her lips never moved when she said, "She will need a mother's love in the coming months."

"But, I'm not her mother," I said. "I've never been a mother."

Ferral's eyes went wide when I responded to words I was pretty sure no one else had heard.

"You have already proven yourself up to the task, Aggy. The child loves you. You love her. That will be all the knowledge you need."

I looked down at Wanda, gasping as her eyes

fluttered open. "Aggy?" Before I could answer, she jolted upright and threw herself at me. "I knew you'd come for me. I knew it!"

At that moment, the independent, standoffish teen was just a scared kid who'd been praying someone would love her enough to bring her home.

I hugged her back and said the only thing I could. "Of course I came for you. I'll always come for you."

Wanda's answer was a shuddering sigh and the tightening of her arms around my neck.

I glanced up at the woman, wanting to thank her for bringing Wanda back to me, but she was no longer there.

She'd disappeared like a phantom into the night.

28

THE LOSS OF DOUBT, A MOTHER'S PRIDE

"Who was she?" I asked Ferral again, getting the same blank stare back from him.

"Madam Lares, I don't know to whom you're referring. I believe you sustained some damage to your head during the extraction."

I clenched my fists, fighting the desire to throat punch him...but just barely. "You walked out with her. She was carrying Wanda."

"I carried the girl out. Do you really believe I would allow some perfect stranger to grab her and carry her out?"

I wouldn't have believed it. If I hadn't seen it with my own eyes. "But..."

He held up a hand. "Please stop." The advocate's generally harsh expression softened. He placed a hand on my arm. "Get some rest. You're exhausted. We'll talk about this later."

Speechless, I watched him walk out of the house, leaving behind Bev, Mavis, Trish, and me.

And Wanda. But she was asleep in my room. I'd gone in there no less than five times to check on her in the hour since we'd returned home.

I was having trouble convincing myself that we really had her back.

"Aggy," Mavis called. "Come eat. You need your strength."

If calories translated to strength, then I was pretty sure I had the strength of at least three people coursing through my fat and sugar-laden system after eating the giant frosted cookie at Willy's house. But a glass of wine to send me off to sleep wouldn't be amiss.

I shook my head when Mavis tried to give me a sandwich, but I happily stole her wine. An action that earned me a narrow-eyed glower until she turned away to get herself another glass.

I sipped, closing my eyes with pleasure as the liquid warmed its way down my insides and heated a nice spot in my belly.

"It was perfect," Bev was telling Trish. "As usual, you're a genius."

Trish slapped her coven sister a high five.

"What are we talking about?" I asked.

"You don't remember what happened to the Dell demon?"

I sighed. "I was almost comatose at that point.

Besides, all I could see was the giant backside of Super Bathilda when I peeked through Gren's wings."

"Trish made a death trap, and Niele stabbed it into the demon. When that thing blew, it was better than the Fourth of July. Red, white, and goo everywhere."

"Ah!" That explained the explosion. "I owe that bat big time," I told the ladies. "She could have been seriously hurt."

"That was nothing compared to what she did for the kid," Trish said.

I widened my eyes in question. "What do you mean?"

"The bat was guarding Wanda while we battled the Dell demon," Mavis said. "They apparently had that poor child stuffed into a closet in the boys' room. Bathilda managed to chase the Dell demon off several times before we got there."

"Are you telling me that stupid bat knew where Wanda was the whole time?"

They exchanged looks, probably worried they'd just set off the crazy lady. "Not the whole time," Bev said, frowning.

"Aggy, honey, you need to understand. Magical creatures don't do things the way the rest of us do. They have agendas that we have no hope of understanding. Let's just be happy the bat protected Wanda until we could get to her."

I harrumphed. My wine was starting to do its job. "Willy and the boys will be okay?"

Bev nodded. "They're weak and severely dehydrated. I think they've been under that spell for a few days. Dell was an evil genius."

"How did she get the zombie curse if Willow didn't spill the beans?" Mavis asked.

"If we can believe Dell," I said, rubbing my tired eyes, "As we suspected, Willow gave her a couple of the ancient spells in return for hexing Wanda instead of killing her. I'm sure Willow was playing for time to figure a way out of the mess she was in."

"Or she hoped the girl's father would save her," Trish offered, grimacing.

I shook my head. "I'll never understand some people's need to control other people."

"Me neither, honey," Mavis agreed.

"How is Bathos?" I asked. "Has anybody heard from Layla?"

They all shook their heads. We stood in silence for a moment, trying to figure out if we wanted Bathos to survive or not. At least that was what I was thinking. "One thing's been bothering me," I finally said. "Does anybody think Wanda was ever really in Bathos' dungeon?"

"The boys likely lied about that," Trish said. "I'm betting she's been at Willy's the whole time." She narrowed her gaze on me. "How'd you know Dell would be at Willy's? I thought she'd gone back to Chicago."

I grimaced. "Yeah, about that..." I glanced at Bev.

She sighed. "We thought Willy was the culprit. She'd invited Dell to Rome for no apparent reason. Since Dell had a reputation for dabbling in demon magic, we assumed Willy had asked her here to entice or force her to call a demon."

"Why would Willy do that?" Trish asked. "That doesn't seem like her at all."

I shrugged. "Several things. First and foremost was the fact that she was the one who invited Dell to come to Rome. Plus, she'd been acting strangely. Not wanting us to talk to the boys." I frowned. "And, to be honest, seeing Dell as Bathos' prisoner fooled me completely."

"I'm guessing that *was* her that Ray saw talking to Bathos at his house," Trish said. "She must have put herself into a cell after Bathos spotted Ray watching them, so she'd have cover for being there."

"Well, it worked," I said. "I was fooled."

"But, why was she there?" Mavis asked, frowning.

Bev shrugged. "That seems obvious."

Mavis gave her a look. "Humor me."

Her lips twitching with a restrained smile, Bev said, "She needed Bathos to play the bad guy to throw us off her trail. Thus the carefully orchestrated scene in the dungeon with the twins."

"And she probably hoped he'd be useful talking Wanda into giving Dell what she wanted."

"We should have put two and two together after Layla told us the demon would kill most of the summoning witches," Bev said, looking unhappy. "I'm guessing the freak magic accident that supposedly killed Dell's coven sisters wasn't an accident."

"Blood magic always comes back to bite you in the posterior," Mavis said, nodding.

I yawned widely, and Mavis's motherly instincts took over. "Let's go, ladies. Aggy's exhausted." She gave me a hug and a peck on the cheek. "You did good tonight, honey. I'll come over in the morning and make you a big breakfast."

"I love you," I told her, tears burning my eyes.

"I love you more," she said, hugging me again.

I locked up behind them and headed to my room. Stopping in the doorway, I stared at Wanda. She was curled around Monty, her chest rising and falling in deep, rhythmic breaths that told me she was fast asleep. Monty looked up at me, and I held my finger in front of my mouth. "Go back to sleep, buddy," I whispered.

I'd already decided I would sleep on the couch. I didn't want to disturb Wanda by climbing in and jostling the bed. I'd have to speak with Trish about where we could add a second bedroom for Wanda. The idea made me both happy and stressed. I really needed to call my dad and find out about Lares funds.

My gaze lifted to the bat hanging from the light above the bed. I narrowed my gaze. "You have some s'plainin' to do, bat."

The yellow eyes flared brighter in the darkness and then closed again. Yeah, Batty was going to try to ignore me. We'd see how that worked out for her.

I softly closed the door and went to get a pillow and blanket from the hall closet. After throwing them on the couch, I was drawn away, some instinct telling me to go up to the belfry before turning in.

I carried my wine glass up with me, an inch of ruby liquid still sitting at the bottom for me to sip and savor. As I topped the steps, I glanced around for Wanda by habit, and then smiled as I remembered she was safe downstairs. It would take me a while to get past the instinctive worry I always felt when I thought of her. We'd have challenges in the future. I was sure of that. But they'd be the normal trials of dealing with personality differences and midlife versus teenage mood swings. I could deal with those. After all, I'd been her age once. Surely I could put myself in her shoes when it was called for.

I thought about the words of the leather-clad woman who'd carried Wanda out of the burning house. Whoever she was...she hadn't questioned that Wanda would stay with me. She hadn't seemed at all worried about what kind of mother I'd be.

That was okay because I was worried enough for all of us. Then I remembered Mavis and relaxed. She was the world's best mother. She'd even mothered me, a child without parents, for much of my life. In fact, I'd been close to Wanda's age when Mavis had taken me into her home and her heart. Mavis would help me navigate the tricky waters of parenting a teen.

The thought made me relax a little more.

I sipped my wine and looked out over the yard. The graveyard was empty. No Reverend Dodson walked among the tombstones. I made a mental note to check on him in the morning. I hadn't seen or heard from him since I'd sent him after Willow in the afterlife. I had no idea what type of trouble a ghost could get up to. But with my luck, he was stuck in a ghostly realm somewhere, unable to escape.

"I surely hope a foray into the deathly plane isn't necessary to save you," I murmured into the darkness. "I'm really not a fan of ghosts. Present company excluded, of course." I smiled as I imagined the Rev's reaction to that statement.

The night shifted near the tree line at the back of my property. My gaze slid toward the movement, and my pulse quickened as the White Mare stepped out of the trees. She tossed her head, whinnying softly and doing an agile little dance as I laughed.

Thank you for your help, I said in my mind. I

didn't know if she could hear me, but something told me that she could.

She tossed her head, knickered softly, and spun around, galloping back into the Mystical Wood.

The sound of wings fluttering in the air had me turning. Ray dropped down to the sill in front of me, looking slightly ruffled but physically all right. "Hey, buddy. You look better than the last time I saw you."

The raven lifted his wings, dancing sideways and clacking his beak. "Pee!" he called into the night, the sound shocking against the stillness.

I nodded, feeling my lips quirk. "Yep. I about peed myself too. Let's try not to fight prehistoric predator birds again, huh?"

Ray's feathers rippled as he bobbed his head in agreement.

Gren's arrival was softer than air. My only warning was the quiet snap of his wings folding away after he landed. I turned to find my protector striding my way, a question on his impossibly hand-some face. "How's the child?"

I nodded, pulling air into my lungs and slowly releasing it on a sigh. "She's sleeping. Poor thing's probably exhausted. Monty and Batty are keeping an eye on her."

Gren nodded, his expression softening. Looking down at me with eyes that had warmed to melted chocolate, he touched the side of my face with a heated fingertip. "And you? Are you good?"

I closed my eyes, my body leaning into his without conscious thought. Warmth infused me wherever our bodies touched, and something that felt like home sifted through my awareness. "I'm...a lot of things. Tired. Relieved. Happy. Terrified." I laughed softly at the last. "I've never been a mother. I don't know if I'm going to suck at it."

He pulled me against his chest, wrapping his arms around me and dropping his chin to the top of my head. I listened to the strong beat of his heart, and the last of my tension melted away. "I've seen you with the girl. You're going to be an amazing mother."

"I have no idea what I'm doing."

"Then you have good instincts because you're good with her." He put a fingertip under my chin and tipped my head up, pulling away just enough to look into my eyes. "She loves you. You care for her. There's no better foundation upon which to start a relationship."

My breath caught in my chest and I stared up at him, unable to shake the feeling he wasn't just talking about my relationship with Wanda.

Finally, I nodded, nuzzling back against his chest. "I guess, as long as I have peanut butter, grape jelly, and chips in the house, we should be good."

"Don't forget the squishy white bread," Gren said with a smile in his voice.

"And the squishy white bread," I agreed. "As long

as I feed her and keep her safe, that's a good start. Right?"

His lips touched the top of my head, and the spot warmed and tingled under the magic of the contact. "She's going to adore you. You've already given her a dog and a bat to love."

I pulled back, looking up into his laughing brown eyes. "Every girl needs her own bat."

"Without a doubt," he agreed. He lowered his head and settled his heated lips onto mine. The kiss was sweet and gentle, and full of emotions that made me shiver with delighted anticipation. It didn't last nearly long enough, but I was too tired to be disappointed. When Gren and I took our relationship to the next level...if we did...I wanted to be fully conscious for the experience.

We stood in contented silence for several moments. My eyes grew heavy. My body turned languid, and I found myself yawning. I thought about asking him if he'd seen the leather-clad woman at Willy's whom Ferral kept denying was there, but decided against it. My cranky advocate already thought I was fruit loops. I didn't want Gren to worry about my sanity too.

So I sighed and just enjoyed the moment. If the night turned to charcoal and I drifted away in the arms of Morpheus, it was all right. Because I knew my protector would see me safely inside.

And my world was richer than I'd ever thought it could be.

The End

DON'T MISS OUT

Stay up on all Sam's news by joining her newsletter, and get a copy of a fun mystery just for signing up!

SIGN UP FOR SAM'S NEWSLETTER!
https://samcheever.com/newsletter/

Kudos for Sally Booth

First Place in the Saratoga Romance Writers of America "2016 Great Beginnings Contest"

~*~

Second Place in a Tampa Romance Writers Contest in Romantic Suspense.

Samantha's head crashed against the wall.

"Oomph." Stars exploded before her eyes. A wild thumping echoed in her ear, the one buried against a hard-muscular chest. Arms of steel wrapped her in a vise grip. She could feel every flex of his steely muscles, every heavy breath filling his lungs. A hint of citrus invaded her senses.

Detective O'Reilly had her pinned to the wall.

Samantha felt safe for the first time in weeks.

"You okay?" Nick whispered in her ear.

His warm breath against her face made those butterflies flutter again. "Just dazed a little." She shook her head in a desperate effort to tear her thoughts away from how this man made her feel. "Did I hear a gunshot or was that my skull cracking?"

"Right the first time."

A chill crawled up her spine. "No. N-Not again."

"You're safe now." He moved his head back away from her and studied her face. "You sure you're okay?"

"Yes, thanks to you."

"That's why I'm here," he growled. "I need to check things out. Don't move."

Samantha nodded. That she could do.

Detective O'Reilly stepped back, taking his warmth with him. Samantha wanted to yank him back, to feel secure in his arms once again. Not wanting to be a wimp, she managed a strong, "Be careful."

"Always." Nick moved the curtain, checking the outside before heading for the door. "Be right back. Stay put."

ALSO BY SAM CHEEVER

If you enjoyed **Which Witchery Is That?** you might also enjoy these other fun series by Sam. To find out more, visit the **BOOKS** page at www.samcheever.com:

Mature Magic Paranormal Women's Fiction
(for more fun adventures with Aggy and Monty!)
Enchanting Inquiries Paranormal Cozy Mysteries
Yesterday's Paranormal Mysteries
Reluctant Familiar Paranormal Mysteries
Country Cousin Mysteries
Silver Hills Cozy Mysteries
Gainfully Employed Mysteries
Honeybun Heat Series

ABOUT THE AUTHOR

USA Today and Wall Street Journal Bestselling Author Sam Cheever writes mystery and suspense, creating stories that draw you in and keep you eagerly turning pages. Known for writing great characters, snappy dialogue, and unique and exhilarating stories, Sam is the award-winning author of 100+ books.

To learn more about Sam and her work, visit her at one of her online hotspots:
www.samcheever.com
samcheever@samcheever.com